BETWEEN THE WINDOWS
OF THE SEA

RAY WOOD

To Linda,

Everyday's an adventure

Ray

ZP

ZP

Copyright © 2022 by Ray Wood

Published by Zamoge Press, December 2022

Paperback ISBN: 978-0-473-66441-1

Formatted by www.AntPress.org

CONTENTS

PROLOGUE

The black water came over the side of the ship and flowed across the deck, streaming around the sea boots of the four men standing in the near darkness. Their faces were weakly illuminated by a single bulb behind them, mounted over the hatch into the ship. The enclosure where they stood offered some shelter, but the gale-force wind swirled around the ship and bursts of rain blew through the opening in the side of the hull and into their faces. The men felt the heave of the deck and they could dimly see the waves as their white crests surged past the ship.

The men stood in a rough circle. At their feet lay a body, its wet-weather gear gleaming in the faint light. One of the men held a short gaff by his side, a metre of hardwood handle with a large hook at one end.

The tallest man rubbed a hand across his face and beard. 'Well fuck.'

The man to his right, shorter and bulky in his layers of clothes, shook his head. 'Jesus Christ, Phil. What the fuck?'

The man with the gaff looked at the others. His features were a pale blur but they could hear the tension in his voice. 'I didn't mean to hit him that hard. I didn't know what to do.'

Even in the near darkness, the posture and manner of the fourth man exuded an air of authority. He wore no hat and his short, greying hair glistened with rain. His dark eyes were hidden in shadow but his lips were pressed together. 'Nothing we can do now. Get some chain from the locker and put him over the side. Phil, we'll deal with you later.'

'Aye, skipper,' said the shorter man, but before anyone could act, the ship rolled hard to starboard and the men reached for support as sea water flooded on board and flowed around their knees. They watched in silence as the water lifted the body as gently as a pallbearer and carried it over the side, not even nudging the rail as it passed through.

No one said anything for a long moment. Then the skipper said, 'Won't need the chain. Hope the bastard gets eaten by a fucking shark.' He shook his head in anger. 'Right. Put that gaff away and get back to work.'

PART I

ALASKA AND NEW ZEALAND

CHAPTER 1

I heard about my brother's death before dawn on the 14th of January. We'd just pulled a full pot of snow crabs and dumped them on the stainless steel table to sort out the females and the bycatch of non-quota species. The air temperature was near freezing but felt colder with the 25-knot wind blowing from the northeast. The waves were running three to five metres and the boat was pitching badly when we slowed to pull the pots. Spray was flying everywhere and, despite my waterproof outer layer, an icy rivulet ran down my back. I shivered despite my thermal underlayers, but that was one reason why the job paid so well. Halogen lights attached to the rigging above us provided harsh illumination on the back deck. The lights overlapped and there were almost no shadows.

I'd come to the Bering Sea for the winter snow crab season to earn enough to knock a big chunk off my mortgage back in New Zealand. We'd had a good season so far and I was glad to be there. The boat wasn't big, about forty metres in length, but she was sound and Mark, the skipper, looked after her well. The food was good and the other four members of the crew worked hard and were easy to get along with.

I was pitching crabs into the chute that led to the hold when Mark appeared at my side and grabbed my arm. He leaned into my ear and shouted over the noise of the boat and the sea, 'Adam, come with me.' He waved towards the bridge at the bow and moved forward, automatically adjusting his stride to the roll of the vessel.

I started to ask what was up, but he was gone before I could say anything. Rodrigo, standing across the table from me, had seen Mark speak to me. He just nodded when I gestured to him and followed Mark forward.

Mark waited for me at the steel hatch into the boat's interior. He swung it open and paused for a second until the top of a roll before stepping inside. I followed quickly and shut the hatch behind me. The clank of the closing hatch punctuated the transition from the cacophony outside to the relatively quiet, regular drone inside the vessel. We stripped off our waterproof clothes and hung them on pegs by the hatch. I asked Mark what was going on but he just said we'd talk in his cabin. He led the way along the passageway, which had initially been painted white before years at sea had turned it beige. Handrails along each side provided support when rolling or pitching made the boat lively. It was very lively that night and we both instinctively used the rails as we went for'ard and up the stairs to Mark's cabin.

At the door, Mark gestured for me to enter and then followed. He didn't bother to close the door; the crew were either on deck or on the bridge. The room was small but efficient. A bed was behind the door, with sheets and blankets pulled tight even in this rough weather. A desk against the opposite wall was secured to the floor with cleats. To the left of the desk was a door into a small room with a toilet and shower. The cabin was on the wing of the deckhouse and portholes gave views for'ard, aft and to starboard.

I turned and looked at him quizzically. 'What's going on, Mark?'

He sighed and said, 'Sit down, Adam. We just got a message over the radio. It's for you.'

I sat on his bunk but couldn't think of anything to say. We'd been at sea for almost two weeks, and the only communications we'd had were related to our catch. There were never any personal messages. As far as I knew no one would want to communicate with me anyway. My parents were dead, I wasn't married and was between girlfriends, and my brother hardly communicated even when we were in the same city.

Mark met my gaze and said, 'Adam, it's your brother. They think he's dead.'

It felt as though the icy rivulet of water that had flowed down my back had spread in a flash to my chest. My lungs and throat contracted and I couldn't breathe. I lowered my head, put my hands over my ears and concentrated on breathing. In. Out. In. Out.

Mark reached for me and asked anxiously, 'Adam, hey, Adam. Are you okay? Do you need something? Some water?'

I reached out blindly and gently brushed his hand away and shook my head. In a few seconds, I felt the icy clamp relax and my breathing began to ease. I sat back up and looked at Mark. I shook my head again, trying to make sense of what he'd said. 'No,' I said, 'you're wrong. You've got to be wrong.'

Mark shrugged. 'Sorry, Adam. I don't know what to say.'

I felt dizzy, disoriented. 'That's crazy. Theo's on one of those big longliners. In the Ross Sea. Modern ship. Safe as houses. How can he be dead?'

'I don't know any details. All the report said was he's missing, presumed drowned.' Mark pulled a crumpled sheet of paper from his shirt pocket and handed it to me. 'They say he was last seen before midnight a day ago. He didn't show up for breakfast and they couldn't find him. The crew searched the ship but found nothing. No sign of your brother. No sign of anything wrong. They notified Maritime Safety and spent six hours searching but they didn't find him, or his body.'

I held the paper and read the terse description of my brother's death. Two short paragraphs, far too brief a summary of his life.

Mark said, 'We've planned another couple of days fishing, but we can head for port now if you want. We can be in Dutch Harbor in a day and a half.'

I looked again at the paper and shook my head. 'No, keep fishing. The position they report for the accident is hundreds of kilometres from New Zealand. It will be days before they get to port.' I looked at

Mark and added, 'And it doesn't matter, anyway. Theo's not going to be there. There's no reason to rush back. Nothing will happen until I arrive, whenever that is.'

'Okay,' he said, 'but take some time off. We have two more pots here and then a transit to the next site. Have some coffee. Have a sleep. Think about your brother, not crabs.'

'Thanks, Mark,' I said absently. I nodded and got up, not really conscious of my actions. I went into the corridor and headed for the galley on the deck below. The galley was spotless, but the faint odour of fried food was part of the essence of the vessel. Coffee was always ready and hot, the pot in a gimballed holder so it wouldn't spill. I poured some into a heavy white china mug and wedged myself in a corner on a padded bench behind one of the tables. I sat without moving, without conscious thought, for a long time – long enough for the coffee to grow cold.

Finally, I thought about Theo. We'd always been close. Not in the sense that we exchanged letters or phone calls or anything like that, but in the sense that we knew that if anything ever happened, the other would be there. Always. No questions. No conditions.

He was a couple of years younger than me but that never seemed to make any difference when we were growing up. Anything I got to do he got to do as well. He was bloody smart and could be wickedly funny, but he was reserved and didn't often show that side.

Our parents were environmentalists before the word had been invented. We grew up reading and talking about the ocean and all things marine. I studied biology at Otago University and did an honours project in the marine science department. Some mates' families were in the fishing industry and I got summer work through them, first in the factory and eventually as a hand on an inshore trawler. Theo followed in my footsteps, doing better academically than I did and getting a Master's degree in marine science. We spent most of our free time together, usually fishing or diving.

When I graduated I saw that the government was looking for fishery observers. I tracked down an observer and had a chat with him. From his description of what he did, I thought the job sounded cool, and it offered the opportunity to work around the world. I applied, was accepted and never looked back. I enjoyed being at sea and loved contributing to the science that underlies the fishery management system. When he graduated Theo also became a fishery observer; he was probably better at that than I was too.

Between trips, Theo and I would try to get together and talk about what we'd seen and done. Like any job, some of the trips and crew were hard going. We'd been at the receiving end of all sorts of petty grief. Some of the fishermen thought we were working against them rather than with them – a threat to their jobs. They didn't realise that it was observers like us who make sure the fishing quotas are set so the fisheries are sustainable and they get to keep their jobs.

A fishery observer does not have normal hours, and long periods at sea were offset by long periods ashore. After a while, I started using that time off to take the occasional fishing job. If the fishing was good then the pay was better, and it helped my credibility as an observer if the fishing crews knew I'd done the hard yards on the ships.

The last time I saw Theo was just before his last trip. I was heading for Alaska at about the same time he sailed and we had a few beers together before we left. I'd never seen him quite so excited – he had scored a position as an observer on a longliner, fishing for toothfish in the Ross Sea. All he could talk about was icebergs, polynyas, ice blink, penguins and albatross. You'd think he was heading off on the *Calypso* – Jacques Cousteau's famous ship – instead of a fishing vessel. There was a hint of melancholy, though, when he mentioned Emma, the woman he'd been living with for the last few months. Unlike his other girlfriends, Emma sounded like someone he would genuinely miss while he was at sea.

And now he was gone. Gone for good. I finished my coffee, put on my wet-weather gear and went back to work. I decided there was nothing I could do, and it was pointless to dwell on Theo's death. Thinking about it only made his loss worse. The guys on the boat were good blokes, but they weren't my close friends. I had no one to talk to, no one to get drunk with, no one to grieve with. His death made me realise that, regardless of how similar our lives were, Theo and I shared few friends. Even when I got back to New Zealand there would be hardly anyone who would grieve alongside me.

I made it through the next few days. The hard, routine work helped me forget for a while that Theo was dead and helped me fall asleep at night. The crew knew, of course. Knowledge of Theo's death put a pall over the trip, even though none of the crew had ever met him. If Theo had died on land I might not have shared it with them, but I had to tell them that my brother had disappeared from a ship in the Ross Sea. Because they'd all thought about it. We've all thought about it. Thought about what could never be talked about: what it would mean to go over the side in freezing waters.

So we were all relieved when we saw the snow-covered peaks of Unalaska appear through the morning sea mist, glowing softly like ripe peaches in the weak light. We steamed southwest into the large bay on the north side of the island until it felt as though the hills would close around us, and then we turned northwest into the harbour. We made fast to the wharf just outside the large fish-processing plant.

The ship's agent was waiting for us. He was a big man, bigger since he'd stopped going to sea without cutting back on the calories. He had a broad, open face and seemed oblivious to the cold, wearing a light jacket and no hat. After the usual formalities Mark called me over. 'Adam, this is Toby Winter. Toby says he's got a ticket for you on the next flight to Anchorage. You connect there for a flight to San Fran and then on to New Zealand. Sound good?'

I shook Toby's hand. 'Sounds good to me.' I turned to Mark and said, 'Thanks, mate. I'm sorry I'm leaving the boat.'

Mark shook my hand, hard, and gave a half-hearted smile as he said, 'Just go, Adam. Our production will go up 50 per cent once you're off. Toby's got us a new guy. Samoan. Big. Outwork you seven days a week.'

Usually it's not hard to leave a boat. I look forward to going to sea because it's what I love to do. But it doesn't matter how good or bad the crew were, how good or bad the weather was, how good or bad the catch was: when the time comes to leave I go without looking back. It is always just a job, always temporary. And I always look forward to catching up with family and friends back on shore.

This time was different. I had no regrets about leaving the boat, but I wasn't looking forward to what would be waiting for me in New Zealand. I walked away from Mark, but there was no spring in my step as I contemplated the trip home.

Nothing's far away in Dutch Harbor. The airport's only a couple of kilometres from the harbour, but I wouldn't want to walk it with a duffel bag in the middle of winter. No one else was leaving the boat, so it was just Toby and me in his GMC ute. It was a big 4WD unit with knobbly tyres, a winch on the front and floodlights on the roof. Colourwise it was dark green and rust in about equal proportions.

The cloud and mist were coming and going, cloaking and revealing the snow-capped hills around the airport like a meteorological dance of the seven veils. The plane was there, but because of the weather, I wasn't sure it would leave on time. In addition to my plane, there were a couple of C-130s on the apron, one in Coast Guard colours.

In the end, I was lucky and only had time for a cup of coffee before my flight was called. I was flying on a Ravn Alaska De Havilland Dash 8, a plane that looked as old and tired as I felt. I told myself sometimes old is good, old is reliable. I was asleep before takeoff.

CHAPTER 2

Tyler Moss loved birds. He watched birds, he listened to birds, he dreamed about birds. Tyler lay on his back and wasn't sure he ever wanted to see a bird again. He listened to the rain beating on the tent and didn't think he'd ever been this uncomfortable in his life. The tent was pitched on the only unoccupied spot on the island. The ground was rocky and lumpy and sloped towards his feet. He could smell the slurry of guano and seal crap that flowed a few centimetres from his sleeping bag. Just about every square metre on the island was occupied by birds' nests. There were no nesting materials on the island so the thousands of birds fashioned small mounds of bird and seal droppings into nests. As a result, the entire island smelled like shit.

It was late in the season and there were a few vacant nests, the result of accidental deaths of birds, inexperienced young breeders, or predation. Tyler and Mira, his field assistant, had managed to scratch out a spot among the occupied nests just big enough for the tent. The guy ropes intruded into the adjacent nests but that couldn't be helped. There was no soil and there was nothing between Tyler and the granite of the island except his thin inflatable mattress. He rolled onto his side and groaned as his hip bones pressed into the unyielding rock.

Mira Savelle lay beside him. She was so far down in her sleeping bag that only her nose was visible. They'd been stuck in the tent for almost twenty-four hours while a storm raged outside. Not for the first time Tyler thought it's not called the Roaring Forties for nothing. He wanted to make a joke about it but nothing funny came to mind.

There are no good places to land on the Bounty Islands. The double handful of small islands and rocks lies almost seven hundred kilometres southeast of New Zealand, and getting onto the islands is always a challenge. Tyler and Mira had come ashore the previous day on a rigid-hulled inflatable zodiac from the *Storm Petrel*, the small sailing boat that had brought them from Dunedin. From previous visits they knew where to look for landing spots on Proclamation Island, the primary site for their research, but the conditions for getting onto the island varied with the tide, wind and state of the sea. Every step of the journey to the island was hazardous: boarding the zodiac from the boat, both vessels surging up and down in the waves; getting off the moving zodiac onto a small, rocky platform; and then reversing the process to return to the boat.

Conditions had been good when they arrived at the landing site the previous morning. A light southerly swell and a bit of surface chop were about as good as it ever got. Nigel Pierce, the skipper of the *Storm Petrel*, eased the zodiac up to the rocks, judging the swell carefully so the craft wouldn't be damaged by the contact. Tyler was poised in the bow, one foot on the hull tube, balancing the pack on his back with the vessel's motion. His heart was beating fast as he watched the gap of water narrow. No matter how many times he did this it always made him nervous. With the zodiac right there a fall into the water would be more embarrassing than life-threatening, but that didn't matter. The brain's response to risk isn't always rational.

The zodiac kissed the rocks and he lunged forward, arms outstretched to balance himself on the small rock platform. Unfortunately, his lunge became a lurch and he landed awkwardly on all fours, grazing his hands on the rough surface. He scrambled to his feet and dropped his pack, moving it as far from the water as he could. He turned and stepped towards the edge of the platform, watching the zodiac edge back towards him. Mira stood in the front, her strong right hand holding the handles of one of their dry bags. The other bag lay behind her on the floor of the zodiac.

They didn't need much gear for their scientific observations, but planning for the expedition included preparation for every eventuality they could think of, including being stranded on the island. So every day they brought everything they would need if they couldn't return to the *Storm Petrel* – tent, sleeping bags, food, cooker – even though unloading and loading the extra bags from the zodiac were a complete pain in the ass.

The transfer of the dry bags went smoothly and then it was Mira's turn to come ashore. Once again the zodiac nudged the rock platform and she stepped effortlessly across. Tyler ruefully thought she moved like a gazelle, and he like a water buffalo. They waved to Nigel and watched him spin the zodiac around and open the throttle to return to the *Storm Petrel*.

They hauled their bags to a safe spot above the landing platform and made the final preparations for their scientific work. They separated the gear they'd need for the day from the camping gear and food inside the bags, and in less than fifteen minutes they were ready to set off to the area where they planned to start work.

They intended to follow the same routine as they'd done on their previous visits to the island: spend the day working with the birds and then return to the *Storm Petrel* in the evening. Tyler had a research grant to study the Salvin's albatross, a medium-sized bird in the mollymawk group. Very little was known about them, and he and Mira had come to the Bounty Islands to gather data on this season's breeding success, part of a project to determine whether the population was stable or not. It was mid-January, and at that time of year they would count chicks and leg-band birds so they could be identified in subsequent surveys.

Tyler's grant proposal had been funded because the Bounty Islands are a particularly important breeding site for penguins, albatross and the world's rarest cormorant. Their remote location in the Southern Ocean has contributed to the development of a distinctive variety of animals and plants that live on them and in the sea around them. The islands have World Heritage status in recognition of their environmental and conservation significance, and access to them is tightly controlled by the Department of Conservation. Tyler had been granted permission to land on the islands, but there were strict protocols about what could be taken onto them to minimise the chance that plant or animal pests such as mice or rats might be introduced.

Tyler and Mira were an efficient team: he held the birds while she leg-banded them. Holding an albatross in his arms, Tyler never ceased to marvel at the diversity of nature, how a creature the size of a border collie could evolve to weigh so little. It was their light weight and broad wingspan that allowed them to glide effortlessly a few metres, sometimes centimetres, above the waves.

The pair made good progress during the morning and only disturbed one chick enough that it projectile-vomited stomach oil, smelling strongly of partially digested squid, onto Tyler's overtrousers. The mess and smell were unpleasant, but they were part of the job and didn't particularly bother him. He was sorry, though, that the bird had lost the meal its parents had worked so hard to catch.

Tyler and Mira were so absorbed in their work they didn't notice the change in the weather until they stopped for lunch. When Tyler finally paused and looked up he realised that the predicted spell of calm seas and light winds had unexpectedly come to an end. A blanket of light grey clouds covered the sky, and the wind had shifted and increased in speed. Tyler looked anxiously to the south and swore. The swell had increased dramatically, and he could see the white spray thrown upward when the waves smashed onto the rocky shore of the nearby islands. Black clouds on the horizon were the harbingers of rain.

'Mira,' he called out. 'Come on! We have to check the landing site.'

Mira looked up from her notebook and then around at the sky and ocean. She instantly understood Tyler's concern and started throwing her gear into her pack. Together they made their way as quickly as they could through the maze of nests and down to the landing site. They arrived at the small bluff overlooking the landing platform and looked in dismay as the waves broke across it, smashing into the rocks just below their feet. As Tyler's experience that morning had demonstrated, getting on and off the zodiac offered heart-stopping moments even when the seas were calm. When it was rough like this it would be suicidal.

'Shit,' Tyler swore resignedly. He opened his pack and pulled out the radio. Mira watched him anxiously as he began broadcasting. '*Storm Petrel, Storm Petrel*, this is shore party. Do you read us, over?'

He released the transmit button and listened to the crackle of static. It was only a few seconds before they heard Nigel's reply, 'Shore party, shore party, this is *Storm Petrel*. What is your situation, over?'

'We are at the landing point. Waves estimated almost two metres breaking across the platform. It is now impossible to leave the island at this location, over.'

They listened to static for a few moments before Nigel said, 'Bugger. That's the only safe spot to land I know of when the sea's from this quarter. You'd better prepare to overnight there. Over.'

'Roger that. We've got all the gear we need. I just hoped we'd never use it. Over.'

'Roger. Monitor your radio. We'll give you an updated forecast when we receive it. Fresh cod here for dinner. What's on your menu? Over.'

Tyler smiled and responded ruefully, 'Freeze-dried something. Want to swap? I'm sure we could toss it into the zodiac for you. Over.'

They heard Nigel's laugh through the static and then, '*Storm Petrel* out.'

'Shore party out.'

The clouds thickened and lowered as Tyler wrestled with the dry bags, extracting the things they'd need to camp on the island. The wind had increased to force 5, and he and Mira struggled with the tent, trying to control its wild flapping while fixing the poles and guy ropes. It had taken quite a while to find a bare spot large enough for them to camp. The temperature had plummeted as the southerly storm strengthened, and the first cold, fat drops of rain fell as they threw their sleeping bags and cooking gear into the shelter of the tent. By the time they were both inside, the rain was a steady drumbeat on the nylon.

Tyler looked at Mira and said, 'Damn, I bet you never thought you'd spend the night here.'

Mira replied, 'No way. Part of me is worried that we can't get off, and part is excited that we're camping where almost no one else has been before.'

Listening to the rain hammering on the nylon tent Tyler observed wryly, 'Yeah, it's going to be memorable.'

They started the stove and heated their dehydrated meal. After dinner, they settled into their sleeping bags and Mira said wistfully, 'I like the way Nigel cooks cod.' She hurried on before Tyler could say anything, 'Just a comment, not a criticism. Your spaghetti is the best I've ever had. Um, in a tent. In the rain. Seriously.'

Tyler just smiled and rolled over. 'Good night, Mira.'

They woke after a restless night to a grey dawn and no abatement of the wind and rain. By midday the wind had dropped and the rain had slackened to a drizzle. Tyler extracted himself from his sleeping bag and began to put on clothes to go outside: he had a serious case of cabin fever and needed to take a pee. 'I'm going to have a look at the landing,' he said as he put on his boots and unzipped the tent.

Mira had expected as much and had begun to put on her outer clothes as well. 'I'm coming,' she said, 'I've gotta get out of this tent too.'

Together they picked their way across the island and descended to the landing site. As they neared the edge of the bluff overlooking it they both prayed that the waves had subsided and the zodiac would be able to take them off the island.

So they were delighted when they looked down on the landing platform and saw that the waves, though still larger than when they landed, were no longer breaking across it. If they were careful then it would be possible for them to board the zodiac. However, Tyler's good mood didn't last long – it was shattered when he looked down at the base of the bluff and saw the bundle of bright yellow wet-weather gear lying there.

The hood was back and an unruly mop of dirty blond hair was all that was visible. 'Damn,' said Tyler.

Mira had been searching for the radio in her backpack and hadn't noticed anything. She looked up at Tyler and queried, 'What?'

'Damn,' Tyler repeated. 'Looks like a body.'

Mira's eyes grew large and she quickly rose to her feet and looked over the edge of the bluff. 'Holy shit,' she said, a note of alarm in her voice. 'What are we going to do?'

Tyler had already started a careful descent to the platform. 'Check him out. He may be alive.' He knew this wasn't really possible but felt he had to at least hope it was true.

Mira watched as Tyler descended and approached the body. He knelt and rolled it onto its back. The cold water had been kind but decomposition had already begun. He looked up at Mira. 'Don't come down. The poor bugger's definitely dead.'

Mira said nothing. She'd never seen a dead body before, and fervently wished she hadn't seen this one. 'What are we going to do?' she asked again, her voice a little stronger.

Tyler stood and unconsciously rubbed his hands on his trousers. He climbed slowly back up the bluff and stood beside Mira, looking down at the body. 'Damned if I know. We'll radio Nigel and tell him what we've found. He'll know what to do.'

After a brief radio exchange, Nigel said he'd bring the zodiac as quickly as he could. While they were waiting, Tyler descended back to the platform with his camera and took photos of the body from several angles and distances.

Nigel brought the zodiac in close to the landing platform and held it steady while he studied the body. 'You're sure he's dead?' Nigel called out.

'Yeah,' said Tyler. 'No doubt about that.'

Nigel fluttered the throttle on the zodiac to adjust for a set of larger waves and finally said, 'Well, we can't leave him there. I'll throw you a line. Tie it around him, under his shoulders. We'll take him out to the *Storm Petrel*. I'll need your help to get him on board. Go get your gear and bring it back here. After you've tied the rope around him we'll get you on the zodiac.'

It didn't take Tyler and Mira long to pack up their camp and return to the landing site. Nigel did the best he could to hold the zodiac steady next to the rock platform, but Tyler and Mira both got wet getting their gear and themselves into it. Once they were on board they attached the line tied to the body to the zodiac. When he was satisfied everything was secure Nigel turned the zodiac away from the island and towed the body out to the *Storm Petrel*. Nigel had decided that the body had to be stowed on the *Storm Petrel's* deck. They had no way of keeping it cold, and the thought of a decomposing body below decks was more than any of them could contemplate.

It was a struggle getting the body off the zodiac and onto the deck. It would have been impossible without the strength and calm expertise of Hare, the crewman on the *Storm Petrel*. They passed the line to Hare and he held the body while the three of them boarded the boat and secured the zodiac. It took all four of them to bring the body on deck. They were thankful for their lifelines, as they were repeatedly swept off their feet by unexpected rolls of the boat that threatened to send them over the side. Once the body was finally on deck they wrapped it in a tarpaulin, sealed it as best they could and lashed it for'ard on the port side. Stowing the rest of their gear was straightforward and they departed for New Zealand in the early afternoon.

The arrival of the body quashed the light-hearted banter that had characterised their voyage to that point. The demands of getting themselves and the body on board the boat had diverted them from thinking too deeply about who he was or how he'd died. The routine of sailing gave them ample time to reflect on those questions, but brought no answers.

When they were clear of the islands Nigel radioed news of their discovery to the Dunedin police. He included Tyler's statement describing how they'd found the body, a description of it, and their actions up to bringing it on board.

The winds were generally favourable but it still took two-and-a-half days to reach Dunedin. It was not yet dawn when they tied up at the wharf, but despite the early hour, there was a large reception party waiting for them: two police cars, an ambulance and two news crews.

The police boarded the *Storm Petrel* and took control, overseeing the transfer of the body to the ambulance. Tyler and Mira lived in Dunedin and they agreed to come to the police station the next morning to make an official statement. They ignored the questions from reporters and avoided the cameras as best they could. They watched the ambulance make its way slowly down the wharf and said farewell to Nigel and Hare before getting into a police cruiser with the officer who had offered to take them home.

Tyler and Mira were still in the car when my flight from Los Angeles touched down in Auckland.

CHAPTER 3

As always, my return to New Zealand was restorative. Even in the middle of summer the landscape viewed from the aeroplane window was impossibly green and rich. The contrast with icy water and grey skies and horizontal sleet and snow could hardly have been greater. Or more welcome.

I took a taxi to my house in Mt. Wellington, a suburb on the south side of Auckland. The house was nothing much, a small box on a small plot of land, but I'd bought it before house prices went crazy so I had only a modest mortgage. The taxi dropped me off at my gate. The picket fence needed painting, but I tried to ignore it as I stepped through the gate and walked towards the house.

Morning dew still clung to the grass. The lawns were tidy. I paid Jayden, the thirteen-year-old business tycoon next door, to mow the grass while I was away. There were bare spots where grass grubs were launching an offensive on the eastern front, and a fifth column of dandelions was infiltrating from the street, but you couldn't fault Jayden's efforts. The hydrangeas planted along the back fence by my ex-girlfriend just before she shot through were thriving, and the other shrubs scattered around the boundary had gone feral. High clouds were filtering the morning sun but I could tell it was going to be hot. I went inside.

I showered; a long shower. When I got out I looked in the mirror and saw a stranger. Eyes – tired, old eyes. Lines that hadn't been there before. Mouth – thin lips chapped from cold and wind. The beard – as feral as the shrubbery. I couldn't face dealing with it at the moment so went to the kitchen, made a cup of tea and then went into the sitting room. The light was flashing on the answering machine. After a call reminding me my car was due for a warrant of fitness, I heard 'Adam? This is Emma. I'm Theo's girlfriend, partner, maybe …' There was a long gap on the tape and then she continued, 'Look, can we talk? Theo said you were the only family he had and my family's in the South Island so …' Another gap. 'Sorry. Sorry. Just forget it. It's nothing. Bye.'

I sat on the old sofa, looked out the front window, drank tea and thought about the call. Her voice had a rich quality that even her tension couldn't hide. I'd never met Emma, but Theo had shown me her picture, something he rarely did with his girlfriends. My memory was vague but I recalled her as pretty rather than beautiful, and something else – innocent? Wholesome? Hard to describe, but definitely nice. I remember in the photo she was tall and lean, taller than Theo. And in the photo she was laughing with the uninhibited pleasure that lights up the eyes, the whole body. She was silhouetted against the sky so there was no way to tell where the photo was taken or what they were doing. But I remember thinking that I wished I'd been there; that I could share a moment of joy like that with someone.

I played the message again. I didn't think I was ready to talk about Theo, but something made me want to talk to Emma. Her number was on the caller ID and before I could over-analyse my motives I dialled.

The phone rang. It rang five times and then switched to the answerphone. 'You have reached the phone of Emma DeSilva. I can't answer right now, so leave your name and number and I'll call you back.'

I looked at my watch. Dumb. Of course she wasn't home. It was 10.30 on a Tuesday morning. She'd be at work. Whatever work was. 'Emma,' I said to her machine, 'this is Adam Stone. I just got home and got your message. I'd like to talk about Theo.' I looked at her number again. The prefix was 06, the East Coast of the North Island. I got an idea. 'Look, Emma, you live in Hawkes Bay, don't you? I know this is crazy, but I'd like to meet you. I think Theo would like me to see you. I could grab a flight and rent a car. If you wanted ...' I suddenly felt like a fool. Too presumptuous, too needy. 'Sorry. Probably a bad idea. Still jet-lagged. Emma, just give us a call. Thanks. Bye.'

The rest of the day was spent on my usual post-voyage chores: wash clothes, buy groceries, tidy the house, go for a run, check emails. I didn't feel like socialising or talking about Theo with any of my Auckland friends. I'd finished my chores and just cracked open a West Coast IPA when the phone rang.

'Hello?'

'Is Adam Stone there?'

'Speaking.' I recognised the voice immediately. 'Is that you, Emma?'

'Yes. Thanks for calling back. Sorry for the message, for bothering you. I don't ...' her voice faltered. 'I can't ...'

'Hey, it's okay. Really. I know how you feel. It's awful. Theo was a great guy. He could drive me crazy but he was a great guy.' I paused then continued, 'I know he cared about you. Cared about you a lot. I think you're the only girlfriend he ever admitted having. Well, at least since secondary school. I knew about most of his girlfriends in secondary school. Who he saw at uni was more of a mystery. You can stop my babbling any time you like.'

She laughed. It was more of a croak, certainly not the laugh I imagined from the photo, but a laugh nevertheless. 'You're as much of an idiot as he was,' she said. 'Thanks. It was terrible hearing about it. And now knowing he's dead but also knowing he'll never be found.' Her thoughts were bouncing around as much as mine were. 'He was so excited about this voyage. He'd always wanted to see the ice. He kept saying things like "even Jacques Cousteau would be jealous." You know he never ate ice cream? I never figured that out.'

'He OD'd on hokey pokey when he was about seven. We were on holiday and he got into the freezer while we were outside. Mum found him; he'd eaten about a litre. He was sick afterwards and Mum said it came out his nose. Enough to put anyone off, I reckon.'

Emma was quiet for a moment. 'I hate it that I didn't know that story; that I'll never know his stories.'

'Yeah, well, Theo wasn't big on sharing stuff. You might have known him for twenty years and still not have heard that story. He lived in the moment. He thought the past was mostly useless baggage.'

'Not like you? Your past is an open book?'

'Maybe not an open book. More of an open pamphlet.' I heard a soft laugh and sensed a change in her mood.

'Hmmm. Open to strangers? To strange women? I mean, women you haven't met?' She was teasing me, a welcome relief from the awkwardness of our initial conversation.

'Strange women, my favourite type to open up to.' I paused to gather my courage. 'Look, I'd like to meet you. Fly there and meet you. What do you think?'

'Good,' she said immediately. 'I think it's a good idea. That's why I was calling. To tell you to come. Tomorrow. If you can. There's a flight at 9.30 in the morning. I can meet you at the airport.'

My spirits lifted for the first time since I'd received the news about Theo. 'Great. What's your cell phone number? I'll text you when I have a ticket.'

She gave me her number and then said hesitantly, 'Adam, there's something …' I sensed her gathering her thoughts before she said, 'The message was so vague. And, well, people don't just fall off ships, do they? Do … do you really think it was an accident?'

I paused to consider my answer. She'd asked the question that had been in the back of my mind all the way home to New Zealand. The question I hadn't wanted to consider then. The question I wasn't sure I wanted to consider now. 'I don't know, Emma. All I know is what was in the message they sent to my boat. I guess it's something we'll have to talk about.'

I booked a ticket and the next morning I flew to Napier.

CHAPTER 4

I bought a copy of the Auckland paper at the airport. The headline at the bottom of the front page caught my eye: 'Body Found on Bounty Islands.' Still in the shop, I dropped my bag and scanned the article:

Two research scientists recovered a body while studying birds on the remote Bounty Islands. They returned to Dunedin last night. Police have taken custody of the body. The body has not yet been identified though there is speculation that it may be that of the fisheries observer washed overboard last week in the vicinity of the islands.

As the possibility that my brother's body had been found sank in, my heartbeat increased. I folded the paper and hurried to the departure gate.

While I waited for my flight I tried to read the rest of the paper and think about something else, but I couldn't. What if it was Theo? Who else could it be? And if it was him, then surely an autopsy would discover how he died.

I boarded the plane and had a window seat, but didn't notice the scenery. Thoughts of Theo and the body were swirling through my mind as we landed and disembarked. I walked into the terminal building and spotted Emma in the small crowd waiting to greet the passengers. Even though we'd never met, I recognised her immediately from the photograph. She wasn't smiling this morning though. I look enough like Theo that I wasn't surprised to see from her body language that she recognised me, too. I walked over to her, my eyes locked on hers. I stood in front of her and we just looked at each other. It was odd; I felt I already knew her. Our eyes darted over face, hair, body, always returning to the eyes.

Then I stepped forward and did something unexpected – I embraced her. I'm not a touchy sort of person and ordinarily shaking hands is pushing the boundaries of my comfort zone, but at that moment it seemed as though hugging Emma was the right thing to do. I felt her tense briefly and then relax. She moved her arms around me and we clung together, acknowledging the pain of loss and loneliness. Her brown hair was thick and fell to her shoulders and was soft in my hand. She wasn't wearing perfume, but I sensed something, perhaps her shampoo, citrus and something herbal?

I was suddenly embarrassed at this unwarranted intimacy and released her. 'Emma. Sorry. I didn't mean … I wasn't thinking …'

She stepped back and smiled. 'Adam, it's okay. It's good to see you. I'm glad you came.'

'Sorry, thanks. I was distracted.'

She cocked her head and looked at me critically. 'He was blond and you're dark, but I see the resemblance. Or I could if you shaved the beard.'

I reached up without thinking and stroked my beard. Damn, I'd meant to trim it days ago. I suddenly remembered the newspaper headline and asked, 'Did you see the paper? The story? They may have found Theo's body.'

She shook her head. 'What? Really? What do you mean, "they *may* have found Theo's body"?'

I pulled the paper from a pocket in my bag and gave it to her. 'Here. On the front page. Some scientists found a body on the Bounty Islands. Emma, it's got to be Theo. Who else could it be? It's not as if people disappear out there all the time.'

Emma read the article while the trickle of passengers and their friends and families flowed around us. She lowered the paper and looked at me. 'Adam, this is incredible. I thought he was gone. That we'd never know what happened. I can't believe it.' This time she was the one who reached out, wrapped her arms around me and held me tight, tucking her head into my shoulder. I felt her shoulders tremble as she fought back tears. Holding her I felt something inside me shift, give way, and for the first time since I'd learned of Theo's death I felt able to grieve. Tears slipped down my cheeks and disappeared into her hair.

We stepped apart and she looked at me and said briskly, 'Are you hungry? You must be hungry. Let's get some lunch.'

I picked up my bag and said, 'After you.'

Emma drove a white Toyota twin cab ute with Macintyre Forestry painted on the doors. The back seat was strewn with forms, boxes, rope and tools I didn't recognise. We discussed the discovery of the body as she drove around the hill, past the small port and into the centre of town, but we quickly realised we had lots of speculation and too few facts. She found a parking space and in minutes we were seated at a table on the sidewalk in the sunshine. I ordered a ham and cheese baguette and Emma ordered a chicken salad. We both decided to have a glass of chardonnay.

The waiter delivered the wine and we touched glasses in a toast. It was a toast of relief, not celebration. Theo may have been found, but dead, not alive. 'To Theo,' I said.

'To Theo,' Emma replied.

I toyed with my wine glass while we waited for our meals to arrive and then said, 'Theo told me a bit about you, but I confess I don't remember much. I told you on the phone that he didn't share information about his girlfriends. The fact he even mentioned you was a big deal.' The waitress delivered our meals and I took a bite of my baguette before continuing. 'How did you meet? Theo lived in Dunedin. That's a long way from Hawkes Bay.'

Emma had pushed her sunglasses up on her head and her brown eyes were clear, alert and alive. She ate some of her salad and said, 'We met during Art Deco weekend.' I looked puzzled and she explained, 'That's a celebration here in Napier every summer based around everything Art Deco. Napier was destroyed by an earthquake in 1931, and most of the buildings were rebuilt in that style.' She pointed across the road. 'You can see some typical Art Deco elements on those buildings across the street – strong geometric shapes and streamlined features.'

She ate some more salad and continued, 'There are all sorts of events, from dancing to an antique car parade. Most people really get into it and get dressed up in 1930s-style clothes. I met Theo at a fancy lunch for hundreds of people, served on a long line of tables in the public gardens by the ocean. They go the whole nine yards, with white tablecloths and silver cutlery. I was there with my boyfriend, and Theo was sitting across the table with a couple of his mates. The food was good and the wine was better, and by the end of the first course we were all laughing and talking and having a great time together.'

Emma paused, ate another mouthful of salad and looked pensive for a moment. 'I still don't know what it was, but I was immediately drawn to Theo, which was weird because I had a nice boyfriend who I liked a lot. Anyway, we had a terrific lunch, and when we stood up to leave I slipped Theo a piece of paper with my phone number on it. I remember feeling guilty as hell, as if I was already cheating on my boyfriend.'

She put down her fork and looked at me. 'You've got to understand that this was totally out of character for me. I was the classic good girl. I went to church, never back-talked my parents, never got into trouble at school – you get the picture. For me to give my phone number to someone I hardly knew was scary. Sort of good scary, if you know what I mean, but every time I thought about it I felt a little ill. After the lunch, my boyfriend took me home and I waited. That's all I remember, waiting for this strange man to call. I knew he was from Dunedin and it was impossible.'

She sipped her wine. 'I was a mess – telling myself I was a fool, that he wouldn't call, that if he did call then I should play it cool, that it was ridiculous to even think about a long-distance relationship, that it didn't matter anyway.' She chuckled wryly and added, 'Of course when he finally called and asked me if I'd like to meet in Wellington all those thoughts went out the window. All I could say was *"Yes"*. Within a week I'd ditched my boyfriend. Within a month we were talking about how we could move in together.'

She picked up her fork and played with it for a moment before putting it down again. 'It was hard. We lived at opposite ends of the country and he was away a lot. But in a way that made it easier, because when he was not on a ship somewhere then he could spend time here in the bay. We hadn't actually talked about marriage, but I'd thought about it. And I think he had, too.'

We finished lunch. I had no memory of what I'd said; only the realisation that Emma was someone special – someone whom I wanted to get to know.

We spent the afternoon being tourists. We drove to the top of the hill overlooking the town and the port. The sky was endless, the air was warm and a fresh sea breeze was kicking up whitecaps in the bay. Below us, the wharves were covered in containers and logs. Large yellow machines with massive jaws were moving the logs from their piles to be loaded onto a ship. The onshore breeze brought a faint smell of pine resin to us. To the south, the cliffs of Cape Kidnappers glowed golden in the sun, and the smudge of Mahia Peninsula was visible on the eastern horizon.

We spent an hour at one of Emma's favourite wineries, tasting the local vintage and exchanging banter with the young woman who was serving us. I bought a bottle of chardonnay and one of syrah to have with dinner.

We arrived at Emma's house at about 5 p.m. She lived in a small, two-bedroom cottage within walking distance of the town centre. It had a stucco finish and, like so many of the other buildings I'd seen, was Art Deco in style. The garden was small but much tidier than mine; a riot of flowers along the fence. She'd planted damask roses along her front porch, and their sweet scent almost stopped me in my tracks as I walked up the path to her house. The blooms were past their prime, the petals blousy, bent and misshapen by the wind, rain and time. Their blotches of colour could have been painted by a child, or by a master painter.

While we unpacked the groceries she explained she was just renting until she decided whether to settle in Hawkes Bay. 'I love it here,' she said, 'the people are nice and the weather's fantastic, but I grew up in the South Island and part of me always wants to go back.'

'Where did you grow up?' I asked.

'Methven. My father was an agricultural contractor, supporting the arable farming sector. Lots of seed-growing in the district.'

'Nice. Big machinery in the foothills of Mt. Hutt. You must be equally at home on a John Deere and skiing fresh powder.'

She laughed. 'You'd think so, but I never really got the hang of skiing. I prefer tramping.'

We were having fish for dinner, so I cracked open the chardonnay. I prepared a salad while Emma panfried tarakihi fillets. We ate at a small table on her back deck. The sun had just dropped below the horizon and the air was still warm. The sky was pale lemon along the horizon, fading to eggshell blue overhead, and Venus had just appeared in the west.

When we finished eating I raised my glass in a toast. 'Thanks, Emma. It's been a great day. The best I've had in a long time.'

She smiled and replied, 'It's good to have you here, Adam. I've enjoyed the break, too. It's fun to do touristy things with friends.' Her dark brown eyes sparkled in the last of the evening light and small laugh lines appeared at the corners of her eyes when she smiled.

As it grew dark we talked about everything – work, sports, politics, weather, travel. I was interested in her work. She provided advice on all aspects of forest development, from purchase of the property to harvesting the trees. She recounted some very humorous stories about the characters she'd worked with. In many ways they reminded me of the down-to-earth people I met on fishing vessels.

As I listened to Emma talk I realised I was becoming jealous. Jealous of Theo, my brother, a dead man. A dead man who'd dared to share his dreams with this woman. I thought of the photo of Emma and the uninhibited joy in her laughter. I thought of the way she handled sorrow and the warmth she'd shown me. I thought of my life. Of the women I'd known and the few with whom I'd had a serious relationship. I thought how sad it was that none of those relationships had been based on dreams, and laughter. And just when I felt it was impossible to feel more loss, when I was coming to terms with Theo's death, I realised there is no limit to grief. I grieved, knowing I would probably never have a relationship like the one Theo and Emma had. Fortunately, I was still able to see the irony of feeling pain for the loss of a woman I'd never met before today. But it didn't make me feel better.

We finished the bottle and finally started talking about the topic we both dreaded, but needed to discuss. I told her about growing up with Theo. How he used to annoy me, always hanging around when I wanted to be with my friends. How we'd ride our bikes, trying to outdo each other with crazy stunts, and of course our love for the ocean. She talked about sharing the outdoors with Theo, tramping and fishing in the mountains and rivers that border the bay. She talked about little things, too, like making dinner and digging the vegetable garden.

It was after ten o'clock when we surrendered to fatigue. Emma showed me to the guest bedroom, decorated in bright colours and with flowers from her garden on the dresser. She fussed a bit, making sure I had a towel and knew where the toilet was, and then said goodnight. I watched her walk back to the kitchen and longed to hug her and kiss her and drive away my feelings of loss and despair. But I knew this wasn't the right moment. Knew there might never be the right moment.

My flight back to Auckland was scheduled to leave at 9.45 a.m. Over breakfast we returned to our discussion of the body found on the Bounty Islands. 'Emma,' I said, 'we haven't talked about what to do next. I want to look at the body and see if it's Theo. And I'd like you to be there. Will you come?'

Without a moment's hesitation she said, 'Of course, Adam. I want to see him, too.'

I smiled with relief. 'Great. I have no idea where they'll take the body, or how long it will be before we can see it, or how long you might have to be away from your job.'

'No worries. Let me know where and when and I'll meet you there. It's a family company and they'll understand that I need to take some time off.'

We got to the airport in plenty of time. We had a coffee and watched the people waiting for friends and family to arrive. Finally my flight was called. We stood up and walked to the gate. 'I'll call you as soon as I hear anything,' I said.

'Call me anytime,' she replied. 'Let me know how you're doing.'

We stood awkwardly for a moment and then she leaned forward and kissed me on the corner of my mouth. She tickled me under my chin, through my beard, and winked at me as she turned and walked away. I watched her go, her scent lingering as she vanished from view. I had a goofy grin on my face all the way back to Auckland.

CHAPTER 5

The phone rang while I was sitting at the kitchen table, considering how to find out where the body would be taken. 'Mr Stone?' a voice asked.

'Yes. Who is this?'

'Mr Stone, my name is David Callaghan. I'm the CEO of Blue Ocean Seafoods. Your brother was on one of our ships when he disappeared.'

'Mr Callaghan. Yes. What can I do for you?'

'First, Mr Stone, I cannot tell you how sorry we are. Your brother's disappearance was a shock to us all. I didn't know him, but I've spoken with the skipper and several of the crew and they all tell me what a good man your brother was. Totally professional and very likeable. His disappearance is a real loss. I can't imagine how you must be feeling.'

'Thanks,' I said. His voice was smooth and he sounded sincere, but there was something about the call I didn't like, probably just because any mention of Theo's death aroused feelings of guilt and anger. I thought of several cruel, irrational responses but controlled myself. 'I miss him every day.'

'Yes, I'm sure. Actually, I'm calling to see if I can help you. I assume you've seen the newspaper report that a body was found in the Bounty Islands?'

'Yes, I read it.'

'We think it's probably your brother's body.'

'Theo,' I said.

'Pardon?'

'Theo,' I repeated, 'his name was Theo.'

'Oh. Of course. Theo. Yes. Well, as I was saying we think it's likely it's Theo's body that was found.'

'Yes?'

'Have the police notified you? Your broth–, Theo listed you as his next of kin on his employment papers. I thought you might want to go there and see if you can identify the body.'

'No, I haven't heard anything from the police, but thanks for the information. Did they say when we'll be able to see him?'

'No, not yet. But I'm sure it will be soon. They'll be anxious to get an identification.'

'Is there someone I could talk to in the Dunedin police department about this? I should coordinate directly with them.'

'I talked with a Detective Killand. He's aware of the case and should be able to advise you.' Callaghan cleared his throat and then added, 'Mr Stone, Theo meant a lot to us. We are prepared to pay your expenses when you go to Dunedin. It's the least we can do.'

I thought about his offer for a moment. I had plenty of savings and didn't need the money, but it seemed churlish to turn him down just because I didn't like his manner. 'Okay,' I said. 'Thanks. The least I can do is accept.'

'Great, that's great. My PA will be in touch. She can make the bookings for you if you like.'

'That won't be necessary. I'll give her my bank account details when she calls.'

After hanging up the phone I sat back and thought about the call. I was surprised that the CEO of the company that owned Theo's ship had bothered to get in touch with me. Perhaps the death of someone on one of their vessels really was important to him. I wasn't sure what to make of David Callaghan but he'd given me useful information.

I called the Dunedin police station and asked for Detective Killand. The voice on the line asked, 'May I say who's calling?'

'My name's Adam Stone. I'm calling about the body found at the Bounty Islands. I think it may be my brother.'

'Just a moment, please.'

I waited for about a minute before I heard the call transferred. A somewhat harsh voice asked, 'Mr Stone? Are you there? This is Detective Killand.'

'Detective. Yes, I'm here.'

'Mr Stone, we were just about to call you. We've received information that you may be able to help us.'

'You mean help you to identify the body? The body found at the Bounty Islands?'

'Uh, yes, that's right. May I ask how you knew to call us about this matter?'

'I got a call from the CEO of Blue Ocean Seafoods. Culligan? No, Callaghan, David Callaghan. He told me that you'd spoken to him about it.'

Killand was quiet for a moment and then said, 'I see. Look, I'm terribly sorry. We didn't want you to hear about it that way. We called Blue Ocean Seafoods to get information about the person they reported going overboard, including his contact details. Your details, as it turned out. We made it quite clear they weren't supposed to call you. Our protocols make it difficult for us to act swiftly. I assure you that calling you was my next task.'

'Relax, Detective, I don't give a shit who talks to me first. Getting upset is not going to bring Theo back. Just tell me when I can come to see the body. That's all I need to know.'

'Thanks for your understanding. The body will be available for identification from tomorrow morning. If you come by the station then I'll escort you to the morgue and make sure everything goes smoothly.'

'Thanks, Detective. I'll book my flight and let you know when to expect us. By the way, there will be two of us. Theo's partner will be there, too.'

'Certainly. That will be no problem.'

I called Emma and we sorted out our travel plans to Dunedin. 'Emma, from the minute I got the news of Theo's death I felt something wasn't right. But with no body, there was no way to find out what happened. Now that we may have found Theo's body I don't want to waste the opportunity. We can ask questions, and expect answers. I want to talk to the police, the fishing company, the pathologist, anyone who knows anything about what happened. I want to know how he died, and how he ended up overboard in the middle of the ocean.'

'I agree. Someone must know something. Theo isn't ...' she caught herself and paused briefly, '*wasn't* the daredevil type.'

'Good, I'll see you tomorrow. Let's hope identifying the body is the first step in a short journey to the truth.'

CHAPTER 6

I caught a direct flight from Auckland to Dunedin, but Emma had to change planes in Wellington and she arrived a few minutes after I did. I waited for her and we shared a taxi into the city. The taxi dropped us off outside Dunedin's central police station, a modern building, two storeys in front and a tower block behind. We walked through the doors and up to the desk.

A young policeman sat behind the desk and looked at us enquiringly. 'How can I help?'

'We're here to see Detective Killand,' I said.

'Just one moment.' The constable reached for a phone. 'I'll see if he's here. Your names, please? Is he expecting you?'

Emma nodded, 'Yes. It's Emma DeSilva and Adam Stone. We spoke with him yesterday on the phone and said we'd be here today.'

After a short conversation the constable hung up and said, 'Detective Killand will come to get you shortly. Just have a seat. He won't be long.'

'Thanks,' I said and moved away from the desk. Emma and I stood beside the hard plastic chairs. After sitting in the plane for two hours and in the taxi for an hour they didn't look inviting.

It was only a few minutes before the frosted door to the right of the desk opened and a man came out and walked over to us. He was medium height, stocky but fit looking, solid. He had medium-length brown hair falling over his forehead and touching the tops of his ears, and extraordinary dark blue eyes, like lapis lazuli. His mouth was wide, his lips were full and his ears lay close to his head. Other than his eyes he was ordinary. He could be a plumber or a bank manager as easily as a detective. He had a folder under his arm.

He smiled, held out his hand to Emma and said, 'Good morning. I'm Detective Killand. You must be Ms DeSilva and Mr Stone.' Emma and I shook his hand and he gestured towards the frosted door.

'Come on back where we can talk.' He led us down corridors painted pale green and opened a door marked Meeting Room 3. He held the door for us and closed it after he entered. The room was square, with a plain table and four chairs in the middle. There was a camera in the corner of the room by the door.

Killand gestured for us to sit and took a chair facing us. He put the folder on the table in front of him and folded his hands on top of it. 'Can I get you anything? Tea? Coffee? Water?'

We shook our heads and he continued, 'Before we head over to the morgue I thought I should go over what we know so far.' He paused and when we nodded he carried on. 'On the 8th of January Theo Stone, your brother, an observer on the *Polar Princess*, disappeared. A thorough search of the ship didn't find him and it was concluded he'd gone overboard. The vessel searched the area but found nothing. On the 16th of January, a body was discovered by Dr Moss, a biologist studying birds on the Bounty Islands, a hundred kilometres from where your brother disappeared. Dr Moss brought the body back to Dunedin and it is now in our morgue. The discovery of the body could be a coincidence, but it's unlikely. We would like you to look at the body and tell us whether it's your brother.'

'Sure,' I said, 'that's why we're here.'

'You're okay with that, Ms DeSilva? Any questions?'

Emma shook her head. 'No. Let's get to it.'

Detective Killand led us out the back of the station to an unmarked police car parked in the lot behind the building. He drove the short distance to Dunedin Hospital and then led us through the maze of corridors to the morgue.

In a small waiting room he said, 'Wait here a second,' and disappeared through a swinging door. We could hear muffled voices and, in a short time, he reappeared in the doorway and motioned for us to come with him.

Three large stainless steel tables dominated the next room. There was no one else in the room but, through a glass window in an interior wall, we could see a woman sitting in front of a computer in a small office. A sheet covered a body lying on the left-hand table. Killand stood by the head of the table and waited while we joined him. I'd expected more of an odour – the room was devoted to dead bodies after all – but everything was spotless and there was nothing but the usual hospital smell of strong cleaning products. 'Okay,' he said, 'I'll pull back the sheet and you can look at the face and let me know if it's your brother.'

I suddenly found I couldn't speak, so just nodded. My eyes were fastened on Killand's hand resting on the edge of the sheet, the dark hairs like wire and the hard knobs of his knuckles.

The room was silent when he pulled back the sheet and folded it neatly below the chin. The complexion was paler than it had ever been in life and the flesh had sagged during its long immersion, but there was no doubt it was Theo. His eyes were closed and someone had brushed his hair back from his forehead.

I looked at Emma. She let out a soft moan when Killand uncovered Theo's face, and although she looked stricken, she maintained her composure. I met Killand's eyes and said, 'Yes, it's Theo. It's my brother.'

Killand responded, 'I'm very sorry for your loss. Your brother's death was particularly unfortunate.'

'Unfortunate? He died on a fishing trip to the Southern Ocean and it's *unfortunate*?'

Killand frowned, 'I'm sorry. That was a poor choice of words. Of course his death was a terrible event. Believe me, we will do everything we can to find out what happened out there.' He was quiet for a few moments and then asked, 'Would you like some time alone with the body?'

I wasn't sure I needed another second with Theo's body, alone or not, his still, pale face a constant reminder that he was dead and not coming back. But I glanced at Emma and figured she might need it so I nodded and said, 'Yes, please.'

Killand went into the office and I could see him talking with the woman sitting at the desk. I looked again at Emma. Her eyes hadn't left Theo's face and I wasn't sure she was aware that Detective Killand had gone. I waited a long time, not speaking, and I thought I could see the pain slowly leave her face, the slight relaxing of her jaw and of the skin around her eyes. Finally, she looked over at me. 'I didn't think I'd miss him this much,' she said. 'I didn't know him long but what we had ...' She stopped for a second, her lips clamped tight. 'You've known him your whole life. It must be even worse for you.'

How could I explain my feelings about Theo? We were closer than most brothers but, like many blokes, never learned to express it. So now I felt sad and angry and lost and remorseful, but it was only on the inside. I couldn't share it, let it out. I did the best I could and said, 'Yeah, it's the pits.'

Emma looked at me blankly for a moment and then returned her gaze to Theo. I suddenly felt overwhelmed and couldn't stay in that room any longer. 'Come on,' I said, 'I've got to get out of here.'

I saw a flash of surprise in her eyes before she nodded and said, 'Okay. Do we need to tell Detective Killand?'

I walked over and tapped on the window. Both Killand and the woman looked at me and I saw the detective wind up his conversation and move towards the door. Emma and I were halfway to the exit when he emerged. 'All done?' he asked.

'All done,' I replied. I held the door for Emma and exited as the detective reached us.

Outside we stood by the unmarked car and spoke briefly about what happened next. 'The coroner said he wants a post-mortem,' Killand said. 'Unless you object they'll get onto it straightaway. The circumstances are unusual and he would like to identify the cause of death.'

I looked at Emma and said, 'No, we don't object. We want to know the cause of death too. Isn't that right, Emma?'

She nodded. 'Yes, we need to know what happened out there. We need to know whether it was an accident or if it was a ...' she stumbled momentarily on the word, 'if it was a ... if he took his own life.'

Killand nodded sombrely. 'I understand. It will take a few days but we'll get in touch as soon as the autopsy's completed.'

'Thanks, Detective,' I said. I held out my hand. 'I guess we won't take any more of your time. We can catch a taxi to the airport from here.'

'Yes, thanks, Detective,' Emma echoed, also shaking his hand. 'We appreciate your help.'

'No worries,' he replied. 'You're flying straight home?'

'No,' I said. 'Emma's coming with me to Auckland and we're going to Blue Ocean Seafoods this afternoon. We made the effort to come here and thought we might as well carry on and see them while we're together.'

Killand frowned slightly. 'We were quite thorough in our interviews. I don't know what else they could tell you.'

I said, 'I don't either. But we want to ask them and find out.'

He nodded. 'I understand. But you have to realise this is an ongoing investigation. I'm asking you to not do anything that might jeopardise it.' As he turned away he said, 'Have a good trip home. We'll be in touch.'

CHAPTER 7

While planning our trip to Dunedin we'd agreed that we should include a visit to Blue Ocean Seafoods in Auckland. Theo had fallen off their ship, and if anyone knew what happened then it should be them. I also wanted to meet the smooth-talking Callaghan bloke who'd spilled the beans on the discovery of Theo's body.

The office of Blue Ocean Seafoods was near the harbour. Not the warehouse and container part of the harbour, but the Viaduct Harbour, home of the America's Cup, trendy cafés and boutique offices. It was early afternoon by the time the taxi navigated the heavy traffic from the airport into the city and dropped us off between an Audi and a Range Rover. We walked the short distance to the office building, appreciating the light breeze off the water. The address we were looking for was low rise, six floors of modern architecture, lots of glass and views across the waterfront. We entered and looked for the building directory. Blue Ocean Seafoods had the top two floors, with reception on level four.

We exited the elevator and walked across the reception area to the counter. The carpet captured the translucent cobalt colour of the open ocean in sunlight. Photographs on the walls showed fishing vessels at work, some in rough seas, others tied up at brightly lit wharves. A glass case in front of the windows to the right contained a model of a longliner. Perhaps it was the one that Theo had sailed on.

'May I help you?' The receptionist smiled and looked at us expectantly. She was in her thirties, old enough to deal with any situation that arose and young enough to offer a welcome and still mean it.

I smiled back and said, 'Good afternoon. We'd like to see Mr Callaghan.'

The wattage of her smile dimmed momentarily and she asked, 'Do you have an appointment?'

'No, I'm sorry. We just dropped in. I'm Adam Stone and this is Emma DeSilva. I'm Theo Stone's brother. He's the man who was lost overboard on one of your vessels a few weeks ago.'

'Oh, of course, I'm so sorry. We were all shocked when we heard about it. I know it's a cliché but we really do feel like a family here. We're very proud of our safety record. Your brother's loss was a real tragedy.' She played with her keyboard for a moment and then looked up at us again. 'Mr Callaghan's schedule is absolutely full today, but let me give his PA a ring.'

'Thanks. We'd appreciate any time he can give us.'

Emma and I moved away and stood near the glass cabinet. In a few minutes, another woman came out of a door to the left of the receptionist's desk. She was older, maybe forty, and her well-trimmed hair and expensive business attire projected an air of efficiency and organisation. She conferred with the receptionist for a few seconds and then walked over to us. 'Mr Stone?' She held out her hand. 'I'm Carol Adams, Mr Callaghan's PA.'

'Nice to meet you,' I said. Her hand was slender and strong with a crisp, dry grip. 'This is Emma DeSilva, Theo's partner.'

'Ms DeSilva,' she offered Emma her hand as well. 'I'd like to say it's a pleasure to meet you, but I'm not sure that's appropriate in the circumstances.'

'Thank you,' said Emma, 'we're still trying to adjust to the news of Theo's death. It's been hard.'

'Yes, I'm sure. Well, as Charlotte told you, Mr Callaghan's

schedule is full this afternoon. I don't suppose you could come back tomorrow?'

I exchanged a glance with Emma and said, 'I'm sorry, I know we should have made an appointment. We're talking to people about Theo's death, trying to understand what happened, and we already have other appointments lined up for tomorrow. We only thought about talking to Mr Callaghan at the last minute. We'd really like to see him today if we can.'

Ms Adams frowned, pulled out her phone and scrolled through it for a few seconds. She dropped it to her side and said, 'He has meetings all afternoon, but I'll have a word with him.' She made a patting motion with her free hand as she turned towards the door to the office area. 'Wait here. I'll let you know what he says.'

'Thank you,' I said as she left the reception area.

After a few moments Emma looked at me enquiringly. 'Appointments?'

I tried to look knowledgeable. 'Maybe not so much in the literal sense. More in the intended sense.'

She wrapped some of her hair around a finger and tilted her head. 'This interviewing is more complex than I thought. New dimensions.'

'Only one dimension. Facts.'

'Oh? I thought we were after the truth.'

'Don't get all idealistic on me. The truth would be nice, but for now, we'll settle for facts.'

Before Emma could reply, Ms Adams came through the door and gestured to us. 'Please come this way. Mr Callaghan would like to see you.'

I let Emma lead and together we followed Ms Adams through the door and down a corridor. It was tidy, but unlike the reception area, it was entirely functional – no art, no carpet, no expensive lighting. About halfway along the corridor Ms Adams stopped and knocked on a plain wooden door.

We heard a voice say, 'Come in.' Ms Adams smiled at us, opened the door and motioned for us to enter.

The room was modest for the CEO of a company with revenues of hundreds of millions of dollars. The desk was plain but solid and well-made from a dark hardwood. It stood in front of floor-to-ceiling windows with a view across the harbour. The desktop held a computer monitor, several piles of papers, and a nautilus shell. There were two pieces of marine-themed art on the walls. The man who rose from his chair behind the desk was average in height, neatly dressed in dark trousers and a pale blue shirt with no jacket or tie. His hair was greying and cut short. His eyes were pale blue and his face showed the lines of his years at sea. Overall I had the impression that the man, like his office, was functional, not pretentious.

Another man had been sitting in one of the chairs across the desk and he also stood as we entered. He was taller than Callaghan and his lean body was clothed in an expensive dark suit. He turned to face us and I saw he had a gleaming white shirt with an open collar, no tie. Gold rings flashed on two fingers as he adjusted his cuffs. He looked closer to fifty than forty, with heavy dark eyebrows and clear grey eyes. He had a strong jaw and salt-and-pepper hair. He turned back and extended his hand to Callaghan. 'David, thanks for the briefing. It's always good to know we can count on you to deliver.' He had a gruff voice and spoke with a hint of an accent I couldn't place.

'Alexander,' said Callaghan, 'I'm sorry your visit had to be so brief. It would have been good to take you out of the office. We need to look for some kingfish like those you caught the last time you were here.'

'I'm sorry, too, my friend. Alas, sport must wait for another time.' Alexander nodded as he stepped past us and left the room.

'Mr Stone, Ms DeSilva,' Mr Callaghan said as he came around the desk and extended his hand towards me. 'I'm sorry you had to wait. That was our Russian agent in Vladivostok. One of our biggest customers.' That explained the accent.

'That's okay, Mr Callaghan—' I began.

'Please, call me David,' he said.

I nodded. 'David, thanks for seeing us at short notice. You can understand that Theo's death has been a shock. Emma and I went to Dunedin today. We identified Theo's body and spoke with the detective in charge of the case. He told us everything he knew, but he didn't have much information. We're trying to understand what happened to Theo. We're hoping that perhaps you can tell us more about how Theo died. Some facts about the voyage, the crew, the conditions at the time of his death – anything that might help.'

Callaghan gestured towards two chairs in front of his desk. 'Please, have a seat. First, would you like something to drink?'

We sat and both asked for water. He spoke briefly on the phone before facing us across his desk. He studied us for several moments before speaking. 'As I said on the phone, I'm very sorry for your loss. The death of a brother and a partner,' he shook his head, 'it must be a terrible thing.' He swept his arms across his desk as though clearing it before talking about Theo. 'But you didn't come here for condolences. I made space in my schedule to see you, but I can't give you much time.' He leaned back in his chair and his gaze moved above our heads. 'We were of course devastated by his death. Fishing can be a hazardous business, but we pride ourselves on our safety record. As a result of the accident, we're having an internal review and that information will be given to the police. You say you've spoken with them?'

'Yes, we spoke with Detective Killand earlier today. I think you said he spoke with you as well? He didn't mention anything about your review.'

Callaghan waved a hand. 'I guess that's not surprising. Anyway, the report's not finalised but I can summarise the highlights for you.' He tented his fingers. 'Your brother boarded the *Polar Princess* in Dunedin on the 20th of November. They sailed for the Ross Sea that evening. As always the plan was to be in the Ross Sea, ready for fishing when the season opened on the first of December. The transit was uneventful and they started fishing on opening day.' He looked at us and asked, 'Neither of you has been to the Ross Sea?' When we shook our heads he continued, 'Well, the one thing we've learned in the years we've been fishing there is there's nothing *normal* about the Ross Sea. It's a demanding place to fish. But within those parameters there was nothing unusual about Theo's voyage. The weather and ice were favourable and the fishing was good. I understand your brother and the other observer worked well. They recorded the catches and tagged and released the required number of fish.'

There was a soft knock on the door and Ms Adams entered with two glasses of sparkling water and a cup of coffee on a tray. She handed the glasses to Emma and me and put the coffee on Callaghan's desk. After she left he looked at me. 'You're a fisheries observer, aren't you?'

'Yes. And a fisherman at times.'

He smiled. 'A fox and a hound? That must be an interesting life. Then you're no doubt familiar with the rules governing vessel operations.' He swung slightly and looked at Emma. 'But you aren't as familiar with fishing, are you Ms DeSilva? Perhaps I should explain some of the strict regulations that govern our operations in the Ross Sea?'

Emma said, 'I know Theo was one of two observers on board. I know generally what an observer does. That's about it.'

'Fishing in the Ross Sea is managed by the Commission for the Conservation of Antarctic Marine Living Resources, commonly known as CCAMLR. It was established in the 1980s to conserve marine life in Antarctic waters. Kiwis developed the Antarctic toothfishery in the Ross Sea in the mid-nineties. Operations in the early days were, umm, a little loose, but now only approved vessels are allowed to fish there and the fishing is closely monitored.'

Callaghan's face became animated as he warmed to the subject. 'As you said, Emma, fishing boats are required to have two observers on board. Their role is largely scientific rather than regulatory. They are responsible for tagging and releasing some of the toothfish, recording the bycatch, and reporting other incidents such as seabird deaths. Every vessel fishing in the Ross Sea radios a report of their daily catch to CCAMLR. This gives the regulators a way to monitor how close the total catch for the season is to the catch limit for the area. On the voyage in question, the catch limit was reached in about five weeks. There is a small amount of toothfish quota available in New Zealand's

EEZ – Exclusive Economic Zone – so the captain of the *Polar Princess* decided to continue fishing there on the way back to port.'

I interrupted, 'Was that unusual?'

'No, he's done it before. He fishes some features near the Bounty Islands before returning to Dunedin.'

'The Bounty Islands,' I said. 'Where Theo's body was found.'

'That's right. We've found a few locations near the islands where toothfish congregate. It's not as reliable fishing as the Ross Sea but it's been worth the detour.'

He sipped his coffee and sat back in his chair. 'On the way to those fishing grounds there was a storm. Bad, eight-metre swells and wind over 50 knots, but not exceptional. The Roaring Forties and Furious Fifties deserve their reputation. There was no danger to the ship. The captain headed into the wind, dead slow, and they were riding it out.'

This time Emma interrupted. 'They weren't fishing?'

'No, they were still transiting to the fishing ground inside the EEZ. All the gear was on board. No one was allowed on deck. It would have been uncomfortable but the crew are used to that.' He spun his chair to the left and looked out the windows, clearly thinking about the events of that night.

He faced us again and said softly, 'It was night. Pitch black. Rain. Hard rain. Your brother went to the mess about ten o'clock for coffee and a sandwich. The other observer, Phil Coetzee, was there and appears to be the last person to have seen him alive.' He took a breath and continued, 'Theo wasn't seen at breakfast. This was unusual, so Mr Coetzee went to look for him. Your brother wasn't in his cabin. Mr Coetzee made a quick tour of the ship, looking in the obvious places, but didn't find him. He then went to the captain and told him his concerns. Captain Kennicott organised the crew and thoroughly searched the ship. There was no sign of your brother. There seemed to be nothing missing in his cabin, no sign that something had happened to him. The captain notified the appropriate authorities and us immediately. He searched the area they'd traversed during the night as best he could but found nothing. There was nothing more that could be done and we instructed him to return to port.'

56RAY WOOD

Callaghan was silent for another moment. 'You have to remember this is the Southern Ocean. Virtually no vessels are operating down there. Something happens there and you're on your own. Survival in those cold waters is a matter of minutes. Something goes over the side, it's gone. And it's not very likely to wash up on a beach. The nearest beach is in New Zealand or Chile, more than a thousand kilometres away. With one exception – the Bounty Islands, a cluster of rocks in the middle of nowhere.'

He looked solemnly at Emma and me. 'So you can imagine our surprise when we heard that a body had been found by a scientist on the Bounty Islands. The chances of that happening are infinitesimal. We heard about the body a few days after the *Polar Princess* berthed. We and the police had already started our enquiries into Theo's disappearance. Those didn't stop. It was important to get everything on the record while it was fresh in people's minds. But there was this question now. Was that Theo's body? And if it wasn't him, then who was it? And where had he come from?'

Callaghan looked at us, his pale blue eyes flitting back and forth, then continued, 'The scientist brought the body back to Dunedin on the boat he'd chartered for his expedition. They reached port on the 19th of January.' He paused. 'I'm sorry. I know this is hard on both of you.'

I replied, 'No, it's okay. It's what we need to hear.'

'There's not much more to say. We've talked to everyone on the vessel and no one knows anything. As far as I know, the police haven't learned anything significant, either. It's looking as if we'll never know how he ended up in the ocean.'

Emma and I were quiet for a while. Then I asked, 'Your investigation didn't discover anything new? There's still no clue about what happened in his cabin? Or anywhere else on the ship?'

Callaghan shook his head. 'I'm sorry. Nothing has come to light. We don't know what happened, but it was stormy and it was probably an accident.'

'There was no sign that he was upset or depressed or anything like that?' asked Emma.

Callaghan shook his head again. 'Absolutely not. That was one of the police lines of enquiry, but there is no evidence that this was anything other than a tragic accident. I know this is a terrible loss to you both but, believe me, it's been a blow to the company as well. The observers aren't our employees, but there's a special bond when you sail on the ocean together. This is the first fatality we've had on one of our ships in seventeen years. We're looking at our procedures and will do everything we can to make sure it doesn't happen again.'

I was silent while I thought about what he'd told us. Finally, I said, 'Let me get this straight. You think Theo's death was an accident, that there's nothing suspicious about it. That there's nothing unusual about an experienced sailor like Theo going outside in a gale, in a violent storm, against instructions from the captain, and going overboard. Is that correct?'

Callaghan was also silent while he considered what I'd said. Then he nodded and said, 'Yes. That sums it up. I understand that you are angry and want someone to blame, that you have trouble accepting that his death was an accident. Unfortunately, we will probably never know exactly what happened that night. Now that we have a body we may learn more, but it's likely some aspects of his death will never be explained.'

Callaghan was still the smooth talker I'd heard on the phone. Everything he said sounded honest and sincere, but there was something about him I didn't like, some undertone that didn't ring true. Theo's death had dented my tolerance for bullshit and condescension.

'Unexplained my ass,' I snarled. I'd kept my temper under control as long as I could, but it boiled over for a second. I clamped my lips together and composed myself. 'I don't believe my brother would go on deck in those conditions. Not unless there was a bloody good reason to do so. I think there was something funny going on. You may be satisfied, but we're going to keep looking until we find out what it was.'

Callaghan stared impassively at me. He shrugged slightly and said, 'That's entirely up to you. And Ms DeSilva. I assure you, you're wasting your time. Just because you don't like what I say doesn't make it untrue. But by all means, do whatever you have to do to satisfy your concerns. Don't hesitate to call on us again if you have any more questions. We remain dedicated to discovering the truth.'

I looked at Emma. She was staring at Callaghan with a cold, fixed gaze. She glanced at me and said, 'I don't think there's any more to say today. Do you, Adam?'

I stood up. 'No, I think that's it. Thanks for your time, David. It's been useful.'

Callaghan moved around his desk and shook hands with us as we walked to the door. 'No problem. If there's anything I can do for you, just ask. I mean it.'

Back on the sidewalk we stood and looked at the harbour. We could hear the tink, tink of rigging hitting the masts of sailing boats and the squawk of gulls circling overhead. There was the usual faint harbour smell of salt, rust and tar. Foot traffic on the quay was light and, despite the fine day, there was only a scattering of customers seated outside the bars and restaurants. Emma looked at me and asked, 'Drink?'

'Whisky, definitely whisky after that lot.'

We had one drink and then another at one of the bars that dot the Viaduct Harbour area. 'After I got that call from him, I searched the web to see what I could find out about Callaghan,' I said.

'And?' asked Emma.

'Under that urbane exterior and Rolex watch he's a labourer. He started as a deckhand, became a skipper, and eventually got into management. He didn't get that weathered complexion sitting at the board table. He's been CEO for five years and the company's profits have soared. From what I've read, he's taken some chances, but they've always paid off.'

'So, with that kind of background why is he so ... creepy?'

'Don't know. I'd say manipulative rather than creepy, but I know what you mean. He wants us to believe Theo's death was an accident. He wants it very badly.'

Emma studied her glass and said, 'I don't care what he said about how much they value their employees. Callaghan struck me as the kind of guy for whom a dollar is always the bottom line. Is there some insurance angle? If it wasn't an accident, then are they liable for something?'

I thought about it for a while but made no progress on the puzzle. 'Could be,' I ventured. 'Or if it wasn't an accident then maybe he's afraid of prosecution by the police. Not just because he doesn't want a fine or to go to jail. To a self-made man like him, reputation is as important as money. He wouldn't want anything to jeopardise his image as a high-flying businessman.'

It was late afternoon and the sky had clouded over, threatening rain. We hadn't known whether we could see David Callaghan that day, so had planned for Emma to stay with me and fly back to Napier the next day. We caught a taxi and picked up Indian takeaways on the way to my house. A few drops of rain sprinkled the windscreen, and just as we arrived it started to rain in earnest. We dashed to my front porch, reaching it not soaked to the skin but pretty wet.

I unlocked the door and gestured for Emma to go inside. 'Your bedroom's to the left. The shower's at the end of the hall. I'll grab you a towel.'

'Thanks,' she said with a smile. 'A towel would be great. I've just had the shower!'

The rain drummed on the iron roof as we ate the takeaways at the kitchen table. I opened a decent red and we were using my best wine glasses – actually my *only* wine glasses. With two flights and two interviews, it felt like we'd had a long day.

We finished the food and there was some wine left when I proposed a toast. 'To you, Emma. I don't know if we're any closer to figuring out what happened, but I wouldn't want to keep looking without you.'

Surprisingly, she blushed. 'Thanks, Adam, but it's a team effort.' She took a sip of wine and added, 'Theo would be glad we haven't forgotten him.'

I wanted to reach out and hug her, but knew it was the wrong thing to do. We tidied up the kitchen and went to bed early.

CHAPTER 8

Two weeks later we caught early flights to Dunedin and a taxi took us to the central police station. A young constable showed us to a meeting room. It was a different one from our first visit but had the same arrangement of table and four chairs and institutional paint scheme. We didn't wait long before the door opened and Detective Killand entered.

'Mr Stone, Ms DeSilva, good morning.' We shook hands and sat back in our chairs. Killand again offered drinks, and when we declined he took a seat.

'Thanks for coming,' he said. 'I could have sent you the coroner's report or had one of our Auckland officers speak with you, but I think it will be better if we go through it together.' He opened the folder and handed us each a thin document, stapled in the top corner. 'This is a summary of the coroner's findings.'

'A summary?' I queried. 'We requested the full report.'

'Well, of course.' Killand shifted in his chair. 'The full report is very long. All of the important things, the conclusions, are here.'

'I don't care,' I said. 'We want the full report. We were told that as next of kin we have the right to see the full report.'

His face swung from resigned to faintly hostile. 'Hmm. Okay. I'll see what I can do. I may have to courier it to you.' He made a noticeable effort and resumed his detached manner. 'Anyway, while you're here, why don't we go through this summary? I'd hate for you to have wasted your trip.'

Emma and I exchanged a look and she said, 'Fine. Take us through it.'

He picked up the document and opened the cover to examine the first page of the report. 'Because of the unusual circumstances, the coroner asked for an autopsy to identify the cause of death. Unfortunately, that took some time and delayed the release of his report.'

'Yes, we're aware of that,' said Emma. 'What is his conclusion?'

'Well,' Killand cleared his throat, 'the pathologist concluded that your brother, and partner,' he said with a nod to Emma, 'died of accidental causes.'

'Accidental causes?' I said in frustration. 'What does that mean? He fell off a ship in the Southern Ocean, for God's sake. Did he drown? Did he die of exposure? What the hell happened?'

'You'll see in the report that it does not appear that he drowned. The autopsy found evidence of several injuries to the back of his head. The captain testified that the seas were exceptionally rough that night and the ship was moving quite violently. No one was allowed on deck. The pathologist concluded that your brother, for reasons unknown, ignored that order, went on deck, slipped and hit his head. The blow killed him and the waves washed his body over the side of the vessel.'

I skimmed through the summary report while the detective was talking. 'But none of that's here,' I said. 'It says it was an accident and that there was an autopsy, but there's no discussion of what the autopsy found.'

'Isn't there?' Killand said, looking through his copy. 'I'm sure that's a mistake.'

'Yeah, I'm sure too,' said Emma. 'We don't care about this summary. We want a copy of the complete coroner's report and the autopsy.'

Killand looked uncomfortable again. 'That could take some time …' his voice trailed off.

'We don't mind,' I said. 'We have plenty of time. We'll wait.'

'Hmmph. I'll see what I can do.' Killand stood up and looked earnestly down at us. 'Look, you're not the first people to be unhappy about an investigation. I've seen it a hundred times. But you have to understand that the world is messy. Sometimes things don't fall into neat categories. There are loose ends, things we don't entirely understand. But that doesn't mean our conclusions are wrong. That doesn't mean that people are lying. All it means is we haven't found all the facts. In this case, everything indicates that your brother's death resulted from an accidental fall. It was tragic and unnecessary and unexplained. To move forward, you have to accept there are things we don't know – might never know – and that his accidental death is a fact.'

Neither Emma nor I responded, and he turned for the door with a shrug. Before he could open it I said, 'Well, there's one thing we agree on – we haven't found all the facts. But unlike you, we haven't stopped looking.' Killand started to make an angry retort, but I lifted my palm placatingly and said, 'Sorry. We'll wait outside. It's much nicer out there than in here. If you text us when the documents are ready, then we'll collect them from your desk officer.'

Killand frowned but didn't say anything. He escorted us to the lobby and disappeared back into the building. We went outside and paused on the pavement.

'Jesus, Adam,' said Emma. 'That was a waste of time. But did you have to antagonise him? He could be the only person with the authority to push Blue Ocean hard enough to find out what happened.'

'Yeah, sorry, but he really pushed my buttons. I think in his mind the case is already closed.' I looked around and spotted a bench in the shade of a large tree in front of the station. 'Let's sit over there while we wait.'

On the bench, Emma stretched out her legs and tilted her head back. 'I don't get it. One minute Killand seems to be helpful, and then the next he's trying to stop us from doing anything. He's not actually saying or doing anything useful. And that autopsy summary was bullshit. There was more information in the newspaper report on Theo's death.'

'You're right,' I replied. 'He seems to be doing everything possible to keep us in the dark.'

We were silent for a long time, each lost in our thoughts. Emma brought me back to the present when she said, 'Well, the good news is that it's unlikely Theo committed suicide. But the bad news is we still aren't sure what really happened.' She ran her hands through her hair. 'What do we do now? Are we going to stop asking questions?'

I turned and looked at her. 'What do you want to do?'

She scuffed her shoe back and forth on the concrete path before replying. Small wrinkles formed between her eyebrows and she started to speak, 'I don't kn…' She halted suddenly and her face turned stony, then she continued, 'Fuck it. I can't stop now. I want to know what happened to Theo. I don't trust Callaghan. I don't know if Killand wants to find out what happened, or if he only wants to get the case off his books. I think we're the only ones we can count on to look for the truth.'

We looked at each other for a long time. Eventually, I nodded and said, 'Okay.' I took a breath and repeated, 'Okay. We carry on. But Callaghan and Killand told us to stop, and I don't like getting on the wrong side of a powerful company and the police. We have to keep asking questions, but we've got to be careful.'

Emma said, 'I agree. But that's a risk we have to take. If we're right then Blue Ocean has something to hide, and I'm not sure official channels are going to discover what it is. I don't think we're going to get anywhere unless we provoke a reaction, get them to make a mistake and reveal what's going on.'

'Does the provocation start where I think it's going to start?'

Emma grinned but there was no sense of humour in her eyes. 'I think we need to read the full report. Then we need to have a talk with the pathologist. And then I think we may have a few more questions for our good friends at Blue Ocean Seafoods.'

In the end, we didn't have to wait long for the report. Detective Killand sent me a text and we picked it up from the station desk. We found a café for lunch and spent over an hour reading the report. The pathologist's name was included. It took no time at all to locate his office.

———

The pathologist, Dr Klein, was neatly dressed in a white shirt, tie, dark trousers and white lab coat. He was tall and was probably in his mid-forties, though he looked younger. His hair was brown, shaggy over the ears, with a vague parting on the left. His hands played with a pair of glasses with thick black frames that looked as though they came from The Warehouse but probably cost more than my entire wardrobe. His wiry frame suggested a single-figure golf handicap but his knuckles and fingers looked to be at least as familiar with a shovel as a golf club. As a doctor, he was probably earning more than our combined incomes, but the spartan appearance of his office showed the health board didn't care; they weren't going to waste taxpayers' money on furnishings.

Dr Klein stood and smiled easily when we entered his office. He gestured to chairs in front of his desk. 'Please, take a seat.' Emma headed for the chair to the right of the desk. I sat in the chair to the left and put my daypack on the floor beside me.

The office was maybe four metres square with cheap carpet on the floor and two file cabinets to the left of the desk. There was the usual diploma on the wall, as well as a photo of a group of men on a mountain summit. A computer monitor and an A4 diary were on the desk. A small gold frame held a photo of a woman who I assumed was his wife.

Dr Klein sat, put down his glasses, tented his fingers and looked solemn when he said, 'I'm very sorry. It was a terrible tragedy, but quite a remarkable story.'

'Thank you for seeing us, doctor. This is Emma DeSilva. She was my brother's partner. I'd like her to be part of our discussion, if that's okay with you.'

'Of course, I don't know what I can add to what you already know, but there's nothing Miss DeSilva shouldn't hear.'

'Thanks,' I replied. 'We're sorry to bother you, but I'm sure you can appreciate how badly my brother's death has affected us. We're trying to understand how the man we knew ended up dead in the Southern Ocean.'

I reached into my pack and pulled out a folder. I held it up and said, 'The police gave us a copy of your autopsy report. They're satisfied my brother's death was an accident, but there are a couple of things we don't understand. We'd like to clarify a few points in your report if you don't mind.'

Dr Klein shrugged. 'Ask away. The report contains all of my observations and conclusions. I don't know what I can add, but I'll do my best to answer your questions.'

'Thanks, doctor.' I opened the folder and flipped through the pages until I found the first marked passage. 'Now, you say there was no sign of water in the lungs, and that this means Theo was dead before he went into the ocean. Is that correct?'

'Well, it's not quite that simple, but that was my conclusion.'

'What do you mean, doctor?' asked Emma.

'Diagnosing death by drowning is one of the trickiest challenges for a pathologist. There are so many variables that it is very hard to be absolutely certain of the cause of death.' Dr Klein paused for a moment and then continued, 'What we know is that if a person starts to swallow water then their larynx contracts to stop it entering the lungs. That means water often goes to the stomach first. After the person becomes unconscious, their larynx usually relaxes and water enters the lungs. However, in a few cases, the contraction doesn't relax and water never enters the lungs even though the person entered the water alive.'

Emma looked thoughtful. 'That doesn't sound very diagnostic at all. You're saying Theo could have entered the water alive and still not have had water in his lungs?'

'Yes, it's possible. But I didn't find water in either his stomach or his lungs. It would be unusual for that to have happened if he'd been alive when he entered the water, but not impossible. But that wasn't the only reason I thought he died before he went overboard. There was the head injury as well.'

I went to the next section I'd highlighted in his report. 'Yes, we wanted to ask you about that. In your report, you say you found a severe head injury and that this was the most likely cause of death, right?'

'Yes, that's correct. The body had been in the water for eight days. It had suffered the expected degree of decay and evidenced damage from being battered against the rocks of the island and minor predation. Most of those effects could be determined to have occurred after death, but there was an injury just below and behind your brother's right ear that appears to have occurred prior to death. The skull was broken, and it is likely he would have died instantly from this injury.'

'And you say that the nature of the injury is consistent with a blow from a hard, cylindrical object? Like a pipe?'

'Yes. A pipe or a steel bar or a wooden pole of some sort. Something hard. Maybe twenty-five to thirty-five millimetres in diameter. The steel railing on the ship would probably be about that size. I can't be more specific because the body was in the water too long to preserve any residue such as paint or rust from whatever hit him.'

'Sooo,' Emma said slowly, 'your conclusion is that he slipped, hit his head on something, possibly the railing, and that's what killed him? And his body lay on the deck until it was washed overboard?'

'No one saw the incident, so we'll never know for sure, but that scenario or something similar is consistent with my autopsy.'

'Okay, doctor, I think we understand that,' she said, 'but in your report you describe two injuries, not just the one that killed him. We're not sure how the other injury fits into that picture.'

'Other injury? Oh, you mean the other cut and bruising on the back of his head?'

'Yes. We don't understand how that injury fits into your narrative of how Theo died.'

Dr Klein looked puzzled. 'What do you mean?'

Emma looked at me and I said, 'Well, the description of the other injury to the back of his head in your report is consistent with it occurring before Theo died, correct?'

'Yes, it definitely was not the result of his body hitting the rocks on the island, for example. However, it would be hard to tell if the non-fatal injury occurred before or immediately after death.'

'But that other injury was a significant blow, wasn't it? Non-fatal, but still significant? Not what you'd expect if you just bumped your head on something?'

'Yes, it was a significant injury.'

'Would it have been enough to knock Theo out if he was conscious?'

Dr Klein thought for a minute before replying. 'You're asking me to speculate on something that is unknowable. But if I had to guess, then I'd say that although it was a heavy blow, it probably wouldn't have knocked your brother out if he was still alive when it happened.'

I looked at the doctor and said, 'Let me get this straight. If the non-fatal injury occurred after the fatal one then it would have had to have happened very soon after. If it occurred before the fatal one, then it could have happened at any time. Is that correct?'

'Not any time – there's no sign of healing, for example – but it could have been some time before the fatal injury.'

I shifted in my chair, looked at Emma and then said, 'That's what puzzles us, doctor. We don't see how it's possible for Theo to have had a second heavy injury after a fatal blow.' I stood up and started pacing the small space in the room. I gestured with my arms and said, 'Say Theo slipped and hit his head on the ship's rail, a blow that killed him. He hits his head and falls to the deck. How could he have sustained a second injury such as you described? He could slide across the deck with the motion of the ship, but it's difficult to see how he could get a hard blow on the back of his head while he's in that position. He's already fallen, he can't fall any further.'

Dr Klein shrugged again. 'Yes, I see what you mean. All I can—'

I held up my hand and interrupted him. 'And if the blow was before the fatal one, then how did it happen? Did he hit his head on something that caused him to fall and hit his head again? Perhaps on the rail? The non-fatal injury is on the back of his head. What could he have hit his head on? He may have backed into something, certainly possible if the ship was moving violently in the waves, but we can't see any place where that could have happened. We looked at the police photos and the ship doesn't have many areas open to the sea, areas where a wave might have washed him overboard. The recovery deck on the starboard side is a possibility, but nothing there is at the right height and position to have plausibly caused the injury.'

Dr Klein said, 'Yes, all I can say is that we weren't there, no one saw what happened, we can only speculate on the evidence we have. Maybe he fell once and hit his head, got up and fell again, this time with fatal results. I can speculate as much as you like, but we'll never know if it gets us closer to the truth.'

Emma and I looked at each other and then I turned back to the doctor. 'One final question, please. Is it possible that the injuries could have been caused by someone hitting Theo on the head with a pipe or bar?'

A sour look came over Dr Klein's face and he took a long time to answer. Finally, he said, 'Do you mean is it possible that your brother was murdered?'

'Yes, that's exactly what I'm asking.'

He shook his head slightly, obviously discomforted by the question. 'I'm afraid you'll have to ask the police. I've described the injuries and the type of instrument that made them. I have no way of telling whether they are the result of an accident or were delivered on purpose.'

'But you think it's possible—' I started but Dr Klein interrupted me.

'I'm sorry, many things may be possible, but it is my job to report facts. I might say those facts could be consistent with blows from an assailant, but it is pointless to pursue that discussion unless you have evidence suggesting that was the case.' He stood up and it was obvious the interview was over. 'Now unless you have any more questions about the facts in my report then I think we're done.'

Emma and I looked at each other and stood up. We shook hands with the doctor, and as we moved towards the door I said, 'Thanks very much for your time, doctor. It's been helpful.'

Dr Klein held the door for us and said, 'I don't think I added anything to what is in my report. But if it was useful to you, then I'm glad.'

Emma murmured, 'Goodbye doctor' as we left the office. The door closed behind us and we stood for a moment in the corridor, looking at each other.

'Coffee?' I asked.

'Strong drink. Lots of.'

We made it to the airport in time for our flight to Auckland but only had time for one drink.

'Why is nothing simple?' Emma complained. 'Why is nothing about Theo's death straightforward?'

It was only lunchtime but I sipped my whisky and reflected that the smoky taste was welcome after the morning's meetings. The meeting with Detective Killand had been a lesson in deflection. The meeting with Dr Klein had perhaps been more useful, but he was equally evasive and it had raised as many questions as it had answered. I nodded in response to Emma's comment and said, 'Yeah, despite all the forensic expertise it seems nothing's certain. Theo probably didn't drown, but he may have. He probably fell and died when he hit his head, but that doesn't explain the other blow to his head. A wave probably washed him over the side, but it may have been Santa Claus.'

I looked up at the departure board and saw that our flight was boarding. I savoured the last mouthful of my whisky and put the glass down on the table. 'So, does that mean a change of plan?'

Emma finished her drink and picked up her bag as she stood up. 'Not to me. Killand's doing things his way; we're going to do things our way. I still don't trust anyone but you.'

I picked up my bag and followed her towards the gate. Part of me was thrilled, but another part was anxious that I was the only one she trusted. It looked like it could be a very lonely, and exposed, position.

CHAPTER 9

We exited the elevator and walked across the reception area to the counter. The carpet still looked like the ocean and the gleaming windows still overlooked the harbour.

'May I help you?' The receptionist smiled, but there was no look of recognition on her face. We obviously hadn't made an impression on our first visit.

I smiled back and said, 'Good morning. We'd like to see Mr Callaghan.'

Before she could respond Ms Adams, Callaghan's PA, stepped out of the elevator. She took us in with a glance and held up a hand to the receptionist. 'It's all right, Charlotte. I'll take care of it.' She gestured as she walked to the door from the lobby to the offices. 'Please come this way. I'm sure Mr Callaghan would like to see you.' She led us down a corridor to an office with her name on the door and said, 'If you wait here for a minute, I'll check if he's available.'

We stood in the small office and didn't speak until Ms Adams returned. 'He can spare you a few minutes. Please follow me.'

She led us to the office we'd been in before and knocked on the door. Without waiting for a reply she opened the door and stepped aside to allow us to enter. The room was exactly as we'd seen it on our previous visit. Callaghan was wearing an expensive suit and a cream shirt, again with no tie.

'Mr Stone, Ms DeSilva.' He stood and extended his hand across the desk. He shook hands with us and then gestured towards the two chairs in front of his desk. 'Please, have a seat. I know you've made an effort to come here today. How can I help?'

I glanced at Emma. She nodded encouragingly and I said, 'Thanks, David. We're sorry to interrupt your busy day, but we've spoken with Detective Killand and the pathologist about the autopsy results. And frankly, we're more confused than when we started.'

Emma took over. 'Have you seen the pathologist's report?' Callaghan shook his head. 'We'll send you a copy. The pathologist says it was an accident. Detective Killand says it was an accident. But to us, it doesn't add up. Theo died before he went overboard. He had two head injuries, both received at the time of death, and we can't see how that's possible if he died because he slipped and fell. We've looked at the photos and there's no place on the ship where he could have hit his head twice on something and then been washed overboard.'

Callaghan's look of mild interest didn't change. I said, 'So we have a problem, David. We think that someone, or maybe everyone, is lying. And if that's the case then we wonder why? If Theo's death wasn't an accident, then who was responsible? Who could have benefited from his death? Try as we might, the only answer we can think of is Blue Ocean. So what we want to know is, what are you trying to hide, David? What is more important than Theo's death? That's why we're here. We wonder if you have any thoughts on our problem?'

Callaghan didn't rush to answer. He swivelled slightly in his chair and looked at us. He put his hands on his desk and I could see his knuckles whiten as he clenched his fists. I then saw his hands relax and he said, 'I resent your accusation that I'm lying, and I'm sure Detective Killand and the pathologist would resent it as well. But I'm willing to overlook your offensive accusations because I sympathise with your grief; I understand your desire for closure. However, I have to question your judgement if you don't believe the autopsy. You don't trust the conclusions of a highly trained medical professional and an experienced detective because of some queries you have about blows to the head?' He shook his head and continued, 'Your concerns are predicated on the assumption that Theo's death was not an accident. Despite what you say, there is absolutely no evidence his death was anything else. It was a tragic accident. Theo's death unfortunately confirms that fishing is a dangerous business. I assure you, his death has nothing to do with Blue Ocean. We have nothing to hide. We are a respectable, profitable business. We have cooperated with the authorities and will continue to assist them with their legitimate investigations. I wish you well, but I hope you will listen to the police and their experts and find solace in their conclusions.'

After a long silence it was apparent he wasn't going to say more. 'That's it?' I asked. 'All you can say is, trust us, it was an accident?'

Callaghan shrugged. 'Unlike you, I believe the professionals. We have no evidence that proves, or even suggests, they are wrong.'

Neither Emma nor I spoke for a long time. Finally, I stood and said, 'Thanks for your time, David.' I looked at Emma and said, 'Ready to go?' She nodded and stood. I looked at Callaghan and said, 'Don't get up. We know our way out.'

———

After the door closed Callaghan stared unseeingly out his windows for a long time. Then, with a sigh, he picked up the receiver and made a phone call. 'Alexander, we need to talk. Adam Stone and Emma DeSilva were just here. They're still asking questions ... No, I don't think that's a good idea ... No, I know who he's talked to. But he doesn't know shit ... Loose end? Wait a minute, Alexander. We're on top of this thing. There's nothing for anyone to find ... but ... but ... I'm telling you I think you're making a mistake ... Okay ... Okay ... You do what you have to do. We'll try to pick up the pieces.'

He hung up the phone and stared out the windows. He rubbed his temples with his fingers and sighed. *Fuck Theo Stone*, he thought. *Fuck Adam Stone and that DeSilva bitch.* He sighed again. He wanted to think *Fuck Alexander Ivanov*, but didn't dare.

CHAPTER 10

I looked around the room and, other than Emma, there was almost no one I recognised. The body had been released from the morgue on Monday and I'd organised a funeral service for Friday. Emma and I arrived in Dunedin early Friday morning and went straight to the funeral parlour. I'd chosen one at random, close to the town centre. I'd let the agent who organised the fishery observers know about the service, and Emma and I had called the few of Theo's friends we knew. A dozen men and two women were scattered among the seats, their sombre clothes brightened by the sun shining through the stained glass windows at the end of the room.

It was probably the shortest funeral service I ever attended. The funeral director ran through a standard welcome and then Emma and I spoke briefly. No one else came forward, and the director wound up the service. A couple of observers and two of Theo's mates from university helped carry the casket outside to the hearse.

The parking lot was shielded by trees and the light breeze brought the scent of delphiniums and tuberoses from the garden next door. We'd arranged to have Theo's body cremated. Neither of us wanted to go to the crematorium, so we went to the pub with a few of the people who'd attended the funeral and told stories about Theo for a couple of hours. About 4 p.m. I got a text from the funeral director that Theo's ashes were ready, so we left the pub and went back to collect them.

While we were in the pub I convinced Emma to spend the weekend in Auckland before going back to Hawkes Bay. Fortunately, the planes weren't full and we were able to catch an evening flight to Auckland. On the way to my house we got the taxi to stop so we could get Turkish takeaways.

———

Even with the windows down, the car was hot. I rested my elbow on the window sill and felt the heat of the sun-warmed metal burning my skin. Fortunately, it was late afternoon and the sun was in the west, behind us, so we didn't have to squint into its glare. I could still feel the salt on my skin and the faint glow on my face from too much time in the sun. Emma sat beside me in my car, looking relaxed in a loose T-shirt and shorts, sunglasses hiding her brown eyes. The afternoon at the beach had been therapeutic, washing Theo and Blue Ocean out of our minds for a few hours.

The first thing I had done when we'd reached my house the previous evening was to put the box containing Theo's ashes in my bedroom closet. A pinot noir from Central Otago went well with the takeaways, and after dinner we talked until late. We talked about the funeral and what to do with Theo's ashes, agreeing that dispersing them at sea would be best. Neither of us was satisfied with the outcomes of our meetings with Killand and Callaghan. We'd followed Emma's strategy and pushed Callaghan hard, but there was no reaction, no sign he was concerned about us. We were still convinced that there was more to Theo's death than an accident, but we had no fresh ideas of how to proceed. The bottle of wine was long finished when we said goodnight.

On Saturday we got up late and went out for brunch to a place that served eggs Benedict and great coffee. Over the meal I suggested we drive to Piha Beach and spend the day there. Emma was reluctant at first, I think she saw anything that wasn't aligned with our investigation as an unnecessary distraction, but she agreed when I pointed out there wasn't anything productive we could do on the weekend anyway. We took our time and arrived at the beach in the early afternoon. We swam and ate a picnic and generally enjoyed the sun and the sea. I tried not to be too obvious but I could hardly take my eyes off Emma's one-piece swimsuit. We held hands in the surf and lay close together on the hard-packed sand. I felt like our relationship might be becoming more than two people sharing grief. Neither of us had much of a tan, so after a few hours we decided we'd had enough sun and packed up to return to Auckland.

The road between Piha Beach and Auckland winds through the Waitakere Ranges. Heavy native bush on both sides of the road broke the afternoon into dazzling sunbeams and cool shadows. The radio was playing *One By One* by the Black Seeds and Emma sang along, her hair blowing in the breeze coming through her window.

A black four-wheel drive ute had followed us up from the beach and was perched on my tail, so close that the Toyota emblem looked as big as a family-sized pizza. The vehicle had large bull bars on the front, also painted black. The windscreen was tinted, and all I could see was that the driver was a man. The road was narrow and windy and there were few places to pass or pull over.

After several kilometres of his tailgating, I said, 'The joker behind us is in a hurry. He's right on my bumper and it's making me nervous. I'm going to let him pass when I get a chance.'

Emma looked over her shoulder and said, 'Asshole. What's the rush? It's only a few minutes until we're out of the mountains.'

I saw that the shoulder widened on the corner ahead. I signalled I was going to pull over and said, 'Okay, buddy, off you go.'

Our car nosed onto the shoulder and slowed. The next thing I knew, there was a loud crunch and a mighty lurch as the ute slammed into our rear bumper. I clutched the steering wheel tightly and stamped on the brakes and looked around frantically, trying to figure out what was going on. Emma started screaming and threw her hands against the dashboard as, tyres smoking from locked brakes, we accelerated off the shoulder and over the edge.

I woke when the paramedic cut me free from the seat belt. Fortunately, we'd only fallen about seven metres down the bank and the car was still upright. The scrub and small trees had slowed our fall and probably prevented fatal injuries. I sat unmoving in the car seat. A mass of shredded shrubbery and branches intruded through the broken windscreen. The exotic herbal smell of the mulched vegetation almost overwhelmed my bruised senses.

My aches and pains told me I was still alive and relatively uninjured. With an effort, I ignored them and turned to look for Emma. The passenger door was open and her seat was empty. 'Emma!' I called, though my voice was a weak croak.

'Easy,' the paramedic said. 'Your girlfriend's fine. Or is she your wife?'

My head hurt and I was having trouble making sense of what had happened. 'No, not my wife,' I muttered. 'Not my girlfriend, either.' I shook his hand off my shoulder. 'Just let me out. I need to see Emma.'

He stood back and watched carefully as I turned sideways and started to ease myself out of the car. The whole front was a mess and much of the glass was gone. I swung my legs out the door and tried to stand up. I suddenly felt dizzy and toppled forward, hitting my head on the door frame. 'Shit!' I said forcefully as I collapsed back into the driver's seat.

'Easy,' said the paramedic, 'take it easy. Nice and slow. Here, you can do it, but I'll just put my hand here in case you slip.'

He reached out and lightly grabbed my right elbow. This time I felt steadier and stood up smoothly. For some ridiculous reason I felt immensely proud of this achievement. I looked around as quickly as I could, though this was not very quick as my neck hurt like hell and I didn't feel very steady on my feet. I saw Emma sitting on a blanket just up the slope from the car. Another paramedic was talking to her. The guy with me helped me stagger the few metres and I sat down abruptly next to her. I looked anxiously at her and asked, 'Emma. Are you all right?'

To my surprise, a small smile creased her face and she said,

'Compared to what? Being shot out of a cannon? Being mauled by a Bengal tiger?'

I reached out and put an arm around her shoulders and pulled her awkwardly to me. 'No, you nut,' I said. 'Compared to normal?'

'Ah. Normal. Hmmm.' She looked away, thoughtful. 'Normal. Since I've met you I'm not sure I know what that means.' She looked back at me and pulled gently on my beard. 'But not to worry. I was just going through my complaints with the paramedic and the list is quite short. Mostly bruises and sore muscles, the odd cut from the glass, but nothing serious.'

She pulled away and sat looking at me. 'And you, Adam, how are you? You look like shit, but it's hard to tell if there's any change from your usual condition.'

I grinned ruefully and moved my shoulders and twisted my body gently, feeling the deep aches that surely foretold some spectacular bruising. 'Thanks for the kind words. I think I know how you feel. The seat belts and airbags saved our lives, but I'll be bloody sore tomorrow.'

The paramedics spent the next twenty minutes making sure we weren't concussed or suffering from internal injuries. They asked us our names, today's date, the name of the Prime Minister – I behaved myself and answered their questions correctly. They seemed disappointed we didn't need a defibrillator or a tracheotomy but graciously helped us up to the road. By then two police cars were at the scene, and we spent another thirty minutes making a statement about the accident – after they had breathalysed both of us.

'No, we'd been swimming, not drinking.'

'Yes, the ute was a black Toyota with bull bars on the front.'

'No, we couldn't provide a description of the driver. Or a licence plate number.'

'Yes, we're sure the truck didn't hit us by accident.'

And so on and so on. At about 7 p.m. they finally offered to take us home. The paramedics had wrapped us in blankets for the shock, and we were grateful for them as the day drew to a close and the air cooled. The police didn't want to let us take our things out of the car in case they were evidence, but we convinced them that was highly unlikely and recovered our phones and other essentials.

'Here you are, Mr Stone, Ms DeSilva,' said the driver when we pulled up outside my house.

'Thanks, officer,' I said and opened the door. Emma crawled across the back seat, got out, and stood beside me on the footpath. I bent down and looked at the two constables sitting in the front seat. 'What happens now?' I asked.

The cop in the passenger seat looked at us, his sunglasses glowing in the evening dusk like insect eyes, and said, 'Your car will be taken to our lab for analysis. They'll let you know when you can collect it.'

'Collect it?' I said. 'You're joking. It's a write-off.'

He shrugged. 'Not our problem. They'll be in touch when they've finished collecting evidence.'

———

On Monday morning at 9.30, a taxi dropped us at the central police station in Freeman's Bay. It's a modern three-storey building, angled like a boomerang. A sergeant came and collected us as soon as she got the message that we were there to make a statement.

When she saw us in the lobby she strode straight up to us and introduced herself. 'I'm Sergeant Wero.' She looked fresh and neatly pressed. Shorter than Emma and solid rather than slender, I could see her playing rugby sevens or defending the goal in hockey. She had long, wavy black hair that was tied with a scrunchie at her neck, dark brown eyes and a scattering of freckles across her cheeks.

Emma and I introduced ourselves and the sergeant said, 'Please, come this way.' We followed her to an interview room and sat at the table. She opened her notebook and gestured to a file beside it. 'I read what the reporting officers said about your car accident, and I have some preliminary forensic information. We'll finish the forensics on your car in a couple of days. Someone will call and tell you where to collect it.'

'As I told the constable,' I said, 'it's a write-off. It's not going anywhere.'

The sergeant took a sip of her coffee and regarded me steadily. 'Nevertheless, Mr Stone, you will have to remove your vehicle from our yard. I'm sure if you talk with your insurance company they will arrange it.'

'Jesus,' I said. 'Okay. I'll talk to them. But what can you tell us? What did the forensics reveal?'

'Not much, I'm afraid. No one's come forward to say they saw what happened. There's nothing at the accident scene that tells us anything about the ute. The bull bars didn't leave any distinguishing marks on your car. We're looking at all black Toyota utes, but I've got to tell you, I'm not optimistic. They're the biggest selling vehicle in New Zealand, and black's the most popular colour.'

Emma snorted, something I didn't know she was capable of. 'So that's it? They're going to get away with it? Some asshole almost killed us and he's going to get away with it?'

Sergeant Wero looked at Emma. 'Ms DeSilva, it says in the incident report that you don't think it was an accident. Why is that?'

From her expression, I could tell Emma considered an appropriate but unhelpful response, but thought better of it. She opened and closed her mouth before saying, 'Well, primarily because the fucking truck deliberately pushed us off the road when Adam pulled over to let him pass. He rammed us and accelerated to make sure we went over the edge.'

Sergeant Wero made some notes and then asked, 'And who do you think did it? And why?'

We'd had plenty of time to talk about this over the weekend. There was no doubt in our minds who was behind the incident. I cleared my throat and leaned forward. 'We don't know who was in the truck, but we think they were working for Blue Ocean Seafoods. Or more precisely, were paid by Blue Ocean. As to why, that's something of a long story.'

Sergeant Wero sat back in her chair and crossed her arms over her chest. She frowned and looked sceptical. 'Blue Ocean Seafoods? I was expecting something more along the lines of the Mongrel Mob. Why would a respectable business want to attack you?'

So I told her: about Theo's death, finding his body on the Bounty Islands, our talks with David Callaghan and Inspector Killand, and the pathologist's report. I finished by saying, 'We're convinced the pathologist's report isn't consistent with accidental death. The two blows to the head can't be explained by a fall. We think he was hit twice by someone on the ship. The second blow killed him, and they threw him overboard so they wouldn't have to explain how he died. They never expected his body to be found. Now that it has, they're doing everything they can to cover it up.'

Sergeant Wero was silent for a long time. Finally, she said, 'There's no hard evidence in anything you've said, but I can see why you're not happy with the investigation of your brother's death. And I can see why you think that if his death wasn't an accident then someone from Blue Ocean might have run you off the road.' She tapped her pen on her notebook while she considered what we'd said. 'I need to read the reports about your brother's death. I'll give Detective Killand a call and get his take on what happened. I also need to have a chat with, what's his name? At Blue Ocean?'

'Callaghan, David Callaghan,' I said.

'Right,' she said, standing up. 'Is there anything else we need to discuss?' We shook our heads and she concluded, 'Thanks for coming in. We'll do everything we can to find the perpetrator of this crime. Someone knows what happened. We're going to find that person and follow the leads wherever they take us.'

The interview was at an end. I stood and held out my hand. 'Thanks for your time, sergeant. And thanks for taking us seriously. Good luck with your investigations. I hope you have news for us soon.'

CHAPTER 11

The minor cuts and bruises from the car crash healed quickly. I threw myself into my work, taking as many observer and fishing jobs as I could. Looking back, it's easy to see I was trying to run away from Theo's death. Work at sea can be all-consuming if you allow it to be. For me, time spent at sea was time spent not thinking about Theo and what I should do.

There was no problem getting work. I fished for orange roughy on the Chatham Rise, east of the South Island. I sailed to the west coast of the South Island, targeting spawning aggregations of hoki. I signed on to fish for southern blue whiting around Campbell Island, seven hundred kilometres south of the South Island. That was where I finally said goodbye to Theo, dropping his ashes over the side late one night. They poured from the box in a silver stream, dispersed by the wind before disappearing into the obscurity of the night and the ocean. I would like to have shared the moment with Emma, but when we talked about what to do with the ashes she said she didn't need to be there, she'd already said her goodbye.

In March, about a month after the car wreck, I received a call from Sergeant Wero. She reported that there was no progress on our attack. She'd read the reports relating to Theo's death and talked with David Callaghan. She wasn't satisfied that Blue Ocean was innocent, but she had no solid evidence to follow up. 'If they're guilty then they're either very lucky or very good,' she said. 'We're not going to give up, but I'll be honest with you – unless we get a break then we've got nothing to pin on them.'

I reported the conversation to Emma and I could tell it was a blow for her. She told me she was confident that the police would eventually find something linking Blue Ocean to Theo's death and they'd be brought to justice. Learning that the police investigation, despite their resources, had discovered nothing more than we had was a disappointment to us both.

Between voyages, I spoke with Emma often and went to Napier to see her once. I desperately wanted to talk about Theo and us, but didn't know how to begin. In my mind, Theo was a ghost that haunted my relationship with Emma. She told me she'd been doing research into Blue Ocean and the Ross Sea fishery, but had found nothing even remotely suspicious. She was always warm and friendly, but there was an empty space, too, and I sensed that, like me, she was drifting towards an unknown shore.

———

In late October, I returned exhausted from the Southern Ocean. Everything had gone wrong and the crew were a surly lot who made the voyage interminable. It's remarkable how much difference a bit of humour can make when things are tough, and how much worse it seems when it's not there.

I'd just had a long, hot shower and after briefly contemplating the empty fridge I was considering what takeaways to get for dinner when the phone rang.

'Adam? Is that you?' Emma's voice lifted my spirits immediately.

'Emma! Great to hear from you. How are you?'

'I'm fine.' There was a brief pause and then she said, 'No, actually I feel like shit. I need to see you. Can I come to Auckland?'

'Hey, of course you can. What's the matter? What's happened?'

I could hear the strain in her voice when she replied. 'Nothing.

Nothing's happened. That's the problem. I'm stuck. Theo's dead and I'm stuck. I don't believe his death was an accident. Until I know what happened, I can't move on with my life. I go to work, I see my friends, but it's all bullshit. He's in my mind every day, and I won't be able to get rid of him until I know how he died.'

Her words resonated with me. I realised I hadn't been able to have a meaningful discussion with her for the same reason – until I found out what had happened to Theo, I couldn't open myself to anyone. My obsession with work was a mechanism to stay numb, to withdraw from all relationships, to avoid feelings about anyone or anything lest they resurrect my grief at Theo's death.

I took a breath and before I lost my nerve I said, 'Emma. Please come. As soon as you can. I'm stuck, too. I need your help. We need to figure out what to do.'

'I know we were run off the road on purpose. I don't believe it was a random act of aggression. It has to be related to Theo, doesn't it? What do you think?' As I waited for her reply, I studied her face. There were smudges around her eyes that hadn't been there before.

We were sitting in my lounge, both with large whiskies. I'd picked Emma up at the airport and driven her to my home. She'd settled into the spare bedroom and I'd made a chicken stir-fry for dinner. We washed the dishes and went into the lounge. Emma sat on the sofa and I poured whisky before slouching in the armchair. Neither of us knew how to start. I'd finally broken the ice by focusing on the car wreck.

Emma shrugged. 'I can't see any other option. We said we wanted to provoke a response. We got in Callaghan's face, all but accused him of being responsible for Theo's death. Then someone ran us off the road. Tried to kill us. I don't believe in coincidences. You've got to think it's connected.'

'You're right,' I agreed, 'but I don't get it. We've asked questions. We have lots of suspicions. But other than the second injury on Theo's head we haven't found anything even remotely supporting our suspicions. Why would anyone want to kill us?'

'They might not know how little we have. Or maybe there really is something to find and they're afraid that if we keep looking we'll find it. Maybe they're willing to do anything to keep us from finding it.'

I could still remember the soreness in my shoulders, arms and chest from the crash. 'If someone is trying to tell us to stop, then I think I got the message. They've had a go at us once and I'm not sure I'll survive a second try.' I looked pensively at Emma and continued, 'Who knew we were together in Auckland? How did anyone know we were at Piha Beach?'

'Well, I told a couple of my girlfriends I was going with you to Theo's funeral in Dunedin. But I didn't decide to come to Auckland until after the funeral. Other than Callaghan, who saw us in his office, I don't think anybody knew I was in Auckland. How about you? Can you think of anyone who might have known what we were doing?'

I shook my head. 'Nope. Like you said, we decided to come to Auckland at the last minute.'

'When we arrived at the Auckland airport I got a text from Detective Killand asking if I'd found any more of Theo's stuff at my place. He's evidently still looking into the case. I texted him back and told him I'd have another look when I got back from Auckland. So he knew I was here. But I didn't tell him what we were doing. And anyway, he's a cop.'

'Detective Killand,' I repeated slowly. My thoughts were a jumble. 'He tried very hard to get us to stop asking questions.' I rubbed my forehead, trying to ease the pain behind my eyes. 'Nothing we've found out makes any sense. I don't like it that the only people we can think of who knew where we were are Callaghan and Killand.'

'But nobody, not even them, knew we were going to the beach.'

'Yeah, but assume someone knew we were going to be in Auckland. It wouldn't have been hard to watch the airport or Blue Ocean's office or my house and pick us up. Neither of us thought about being followed. Someone could easily have followed us from the city to the beach without us knowing it. They could have picked a suitable spot on the way there and then rammed us on the way back.'

'Fuck.' Emma drained the last of her whisky and put her glass down on the coffee table.

I got up to get the bottle and returned to sit beside her. I poured us both another drop and tried to think. The headache was a distraction. As was Emma. She'd showered when we got home and her hair smelled like green apples and tea. I'd used the same shampoo so I guess my hair must have smelled the same, but it smelled a lot better on her.

I ran my hand over my beard and said, 'We need a plan.' Before Emma could interrupt I went on, 'I know, we thought we had a plan – we'd ask questions and provoke a response. But that's not actually a plan. That's a hope, maybe a strategy. Callaghan and Blue Ocean are behind this somehow, but they've been too clever for us so far. We've taken all the hits and have nothing to show for it.'

'So what do we do?'

I took a sip of whisky and opened my mouth, sucking in air and feeling the alcohol burn. 'I'm not sure. We need to think it out. You had the right idea, provoking them, but we haven't executed it properly. They're still hiding behind their façade of respectability. We need to get on the offensive. We need to figure out things we can do, things that will give us new facts.'

'Ideally without getting run off the road again. Or worse.'

'Indeed. Does anything come to mind?'

'Hmm, let's think about it.' Emma paused as she swirled the whisky slowly in her glass. 'Let's assume we're right and Blue Ocean's responsible. Then the question is, why would they kill Theo?'

'Theo was a fisheries observer. He would never be a threat to them unless he was in the wrong place at the wrong time. Unless there was something he saw or heard that was illegal.' I took a sip of whisky and tried to remember what Theo had told me about his work. 'I think the only time he had any interaction with Blue Ocean was when he was on the *Polar Princess*. Is there any other way he was likely to have appeared on their radar?'

Emma shook her head. 'I only knew him for a short while, but as far as I know, he'd never been on one of their ships before, or had anything to do with them until he went south.'

'Then what could have happened on the *Polar Princess* that led to his death?'

We looked at each other and were silent. After a while, I said, 'Right, we have no idea. So what do we do?'

We were quiet for another long interval before Emma spoke. 'If it's impossible to find out what happened on the ship, then we have to look somewhere else.' She looked towards a far corner of the room, trying to formulate her thoughts. 'I'm fumbling, here, Adam, but what if whatever happened was about the company, not the voyage?' I looked blank and waited for her to go on. 'What if we assume that whatever happened to Theo was part of something bigger? What if he saw something big the company's doing that's illegal? You know, something more important than a health and safety issue or quota violations or a few dead seabirds?'

She paused and I tried to catch the thread of her thoughts. I said, 'You mean what if Theo's death is only the tip of the iceberg? That the company's got more to hide than the circumstances of his death?'

Emma looked at me, excitement in her eyes. 'Yes, that's what I mean. It's a hypothesis we can work with. We can dig through their records and look for something they're trying to hide. Something that might have given them a reason to kill Theo.'

'Okay, what does that mean for our plan? Do you know anything about searching records? I sure don't.'

Emma smiled for the first time since the car wreck. 'No, but I know someone who does.' She pulled out her phone and stood up, saying, 'No time like the present. I'll see if he can help us.'

As she walked towards the front door I said, 'Confidential?'

I wasn't sure, but I thought I saw her blush. 'Ex-boyfriend.' She opened the door and stepped out onto the porch.

While she was outside, I thought more about what she'd said. Something niggled at my mind and I struggled to get it into focus. As

Emma opened the front door and came back into the lounge I remembered what it was, and saw the course of action it suggested.

'I spoke with Connor,' she said. 'He's agreed to meet us.'

'Connor?' I asked. 'The ex-boyfriend?'

'You'll like him. He's a computer programmer. He has no social skills, either.'

I thought about that for a moment, and then shook my head and moved on. 'Emma, I've thought of something else.'

She held up a hand. 'Wait. While I was talking with Connor, I had another idea.'

'Another boyfriend?'

'No,' she smirked. 'A cousin, actually. His name's Gordon Crawford. He's a reporter, an investigative journalist.'

'A reporter? Emma, we're dealing with a very powerful company. A very secretive company. We need to be invisible until we figure out what's going on. If a reporter gets involved, then anything we discover could appear on the front page before we're ready.'

Emma explained, 'That's exactly why I think Gordon would be useful. He wrote that story about the racehorse scandal a year or so ago.'

I shook my head. 'Never heard of it. I must have been at sea.'

'From what I remember, a local vet was working with a Chinese gang to test drugs that affected a racehorse's performance. Gordon did some clever investigating that led to the discovery of where they were hiding out. He was there at the end when a bunch of people were killed.'

'Killed? Bloody hell, Emma. We don't need some trigger-happy cowboy working with us.'

'No, no, he didn't kill anyone. I was just saying – he's been around, seen some pretty scary shit. Gordon's not going to be intimidated by Blue Ocean or anyone else.' She took a small sip of whisky and added, 'And don't worry about anything being published before we're ready. Gordon and I have a wonderful relationship; he does exactly what I tell him. Anyway, I wasn't thinking we need his reporting skills so much as we need his investigative skills. Maybe most of all, we need someone else who knows what we're doing.' Emma's face got serious. 'I'm not going to let these bastards get away with it, Adam, but the car wreck? I'm scared. I want to know that if something happens to me – to us – that there's someone who knows the story and will nail whoever's behind all this.'

I thought about what she'd said. 'Me too. I'm scared. What you say makes sense. But if he agrees to help—'

'He'll agree,' Emma interjected.

'*If* he agrees to help,' I continued, 'then he's going to do it on our terms. He does exactly what we say. He doesn't talk to anyone unless we agree. He doesn't write anything for the paper unless we say so.'

'Great. I'm sure that won't be a problem. I'll give him a call and set up a meeting. The last I heard, he'd been promoted to a job in Wellington.'

'Okay, so are you finished? No more ideas? No uncle or auntie who should also be helping?'

Emma smiled and shook her head.

I paused to taste my whisky, suddenly reluctant to broach my idea with Emma. 'Well then. You know how earlier you said we can't know what happened on the ship? What if it were possible?'

'What do you mean? We've pursued every lead, and I don't believe in time travel.'

'Yeah, but I think there may be a way. What if I went on the *Polar Princess*? I'd be right there, where Theo was. I could be on the lookout for anything out of the ordinary, anything that Theo might have noticed.'

For the first time, I saw Emma angry. 'That's about the dumbest idea I've ever heard. They're not idiots. They know you're Theo's brother. They'd know why you'd be there. They'd make damned sure there was nothing for you to see. And if you did happen to see something then what could you do? There's no one you could call for help. You could ... you could end up like Theo.' Her voice broke for a second and she looked away. She regained her composure and looked back at me. 'They've killed one person I love. I won't let them kill another.'

I was stunned. Had I heard correctly? This woman who had taken my heart just said she loved me? I stared back and forth between her eyes, searching for doubts or hidden meanings. But her steady gaze only echoed her words.

Slowly, carefully, I leaned forward and kissed her. I kept my eyes open, ready to retreat at the first sign of uncertainty, of protest. But her eyes drifted closed and her lips were soft and they slowly parted to mine. The next moment we were in each other's arms, holding, touching, caressing. There was no more discussion that night.

———

'I've got to go on that ship.' We were having breakfast at my kitchen table. The sun was shining through the windows and the whole room glowed with its warm light. Or perhaps it was just the happiness that filled me after the previous night.

I'd been wrong. I didn't need to find out what happened to Theo before I could open myself to someone else. Emma had shown me I could experience both love and grief without compromising either. Did Emma feel the same? I wasn't certain. She'd lost the future and I'd lost the past. I didn't know if what we'd shared meant as much to her as it did to me, but I knew she'd been happy for at least one night.

Despite the lack of sleep, I didn't feel tired. Emma had offered to cook breakfast, but I insisted that she was my guest. This seemed like a good excuse to have a cooked breakfast in the middle of the week.

Emma's fork paused on the way to her mouth. 'No, you don't. We talked about that last night. And anyway, why would Blue Ocean let you get within a mile of the *Polar Princess*? You've all but accused Callaghan of killing Theo.'

'Two reasons. First, if I'm on the *Polar Princess* then I can't be somewhere else causing trouble. They can keep an eye on me and show me what they want me to see.'

Emma interrupted, 'Wait a minute. If you really think that then what's the point in going? You'll have no chance of finding out anything useful.'

I shrugged, 'That's where the second reason for going comes in. These guys are arrogant assholes who think they're better than everyone else. There's a chance that arrogance will lead to a mistake. Or they'll think if I see something then they'll be able to manage me.'

Emma forgot about breakfast. 'Manage you? The way they managed Theo? These guys are killers, Adam. Do you want to go over the side like Theo did?'

'Killing is bad for business. They don't want another body any more than we do.'

Emma was silent, clearly unhappy. Finally, she shook her head and said, 'It's either a waste of time, or the risk that you'll get killed is too high. I can't agree to you going.'

I swallowed my mouthful of eggs and replied, 'We agreed we have to do something. I don't think it would be a waste of time, and I think we can mitigate the risks.'

'Mitigate? As in you'll only be lightly killed?'

'No, mitigate as in satellite communications. These days it's easy to stay in touch. Garmin makes a device that would allow us to send text messages back and forth. It's easy and it's cheap.'

Emma was quiet for a moment. 'Maybe. But that would only let me know if you discover something. Or if you think you're in danger. It wouldn't do any good if they decide to kill you.' I kept quiet while she took a bite of her toast. She wasn't discarding the idea out of hand, which was encouraging as it might mean she was thinking about how to make it possible. Eventually, she said, 'What about this? If you go, then I'm thinking mitigate as in having another boat at the Bounty Islands as back-up.'

That was totally out of left field and caught me by surprise. 'Back-up? What for?'

She shrugged. 'I have no idea. Maybe we'll want witnesses? Right now, I'm concerned about you being alone in the Southern Ocean with those guys, those killers. Look what happened to Theo. If they decided to kill you then you'd be totally on your own, there'd be no one anywhere nearby who could do anything.'

I pushed my food around my plate. I wasn't sure that a boat near the Bounty Islands would be much help if something happened while I was hundreds of kilometres away in the Ross Sea, but if it meant Emma would agree to let me go on the *Polar Princess* then maybe it was a good idea. 'Assuming we could find a boat,' I asked, 'how would we afford it?'

'Fuck, Adam, I don't know. How much is your life worth? If you go, then we'll find the money.'

We were silent again, neither one looking at the other, both afraid of how events were unfolding. Finally I said, 'Okay. If we can find a boat then we'll send it to the Bounties. We'd need someone we can trust on board. Someone who knows what's going on and can make decisions for us. You need to stay here. I need to know there's someone onshore who has my back.'

'That makes sense. But who do you have in mind? There's only me and you.'

'No, there's your cousin Gordon. Or there *may* be your cousin Gordon. Sending a boat to the Bounties is another reason to make him part of the team.'

Emma nodded and said wryly, 'That would be interesting. He hates boats.'

We'd finished eating so I stood up and cleared the table. I was rinsing the dishes in the sink when Emma said, 'Adam, this plan so far? It's all focused on Callaghan, on Blue Ocean.'

I stopped and turned to look at her. 'Yeah, so?'

Emma clasped and unclasped her hands on the table. 'Last night we were talking, about Callaghan and Killand, and how they were the only ones who knew where we were.' She stopped and swallowed. 'Adam, what do we do if Killand is in on it?'

I thought for a long moment before replying. 'Then we're fucked.'

CHAPTER 12

I held the door for Emma and we entered the café. It was ten o'clock and reasonably busy. It was a modest size, ten small tables, and had a pleasant though unimaginative décor. A lanky guy with glasses was sitting by the window. He stood up when Emma entered and waved. Emma smiled and we moved through the tables to join him.

'Emma,' he said and hugged her.

'Connor,' she replied. She gestured to me, 'This is Adam. Adam, Connor.'

'Pleased to meet you,' he said as we shook hands. He had a firm grip but wasn't trying to make a point with it.

'Coffee?' I asked. 'What can I get you?'

'Flat white, thanks.'

I looked at Emma who responded, 'Cappuccino, please.'

I went to the counter and ordered. By the time I returned Emma and Connor were seated and chatting amiably. I put the coffees on the table and took a seat next to Emma.

'Adam,' said Connor, 'Emma says you have a project for me.'

I took a sip of coffee and looked at Connor before replying. 'I hope so. Has Emma told you anything about why we're here?'

Connor shook his head so I told him the story. Everything, from Theo's background as a fishery observer, what he was doing in the

Ross Sea, the meeting with Detective Killand, the pathology results, our conversations with the CEO of Blue Ocean Seafoods, the car wreck.

Connor nodded a few times but didn't interrupt me. When I was finished he said, 'Okay. Your brother died while on a fishing trip. You're still upset, think maybe he was murdered. But I don't see what I can do. I'm not a doctor or a policeman. I look at computer files. I don't see how I can help you.'

'I don't either,' I replied. Connor looked puzzled at this and I hurried to continue, 'I mean, I don't know for sure how you might help, what you might find. But I think it's worth having a look.'

'You've got me really confused now,' Connor said. 'Look at what?'

I twisted my coffee cup and looked at Emma before answering. She patted my leg under the table. I said, 'Okay, this is the deal. We think my brother was murdered. We're not sure how, but that may not be important. The big thing we don't know is why. Why would anyone want to kill him? He was a fishery observer. His job was routine. Some crews don't like observers but they wouldn't kill one. Emma will explain in a minute, but we don't think he was killed because of his job. We think he may have been killed because of something he saw.'

Emma leaned forward and took over. 'Killing someone is a big deal. Whatever the motive was, we don't think it was something like reporting the incidental catch of seabirds or health and safety infringements. It has to be something bigger than that, something important.'

Connor said, 'Not a crime of passion? Getting it on with the captain's wife? Blood to the head, knife in the back, that sort of thing?'

Emma shook her head. 'I don't think so. Theo and I were … close. I'm sure he wasn't seeing anyone else, so that's not a motive. And he was a nice, easygoing guy. I can't think of anything he might have done that would make someone want to kill him. Can you, Adam?'

I shook my head in agreement. 'Nope. He could be outspoken and could piss people off, but enough to want to kill him? I can't see it.'

Emma sipped her cappuccino and continued. 'We've learned a lot about fishing for toothfish in the Ross Sea from our interviews and research. I'm sure there are plenty of rules that get bent or broken, but it's not the Wild West out there anymore. Companies like Blue Ocean are monitored and measured and audited at every step. That's why guys like Theo and Adam are on board. The companies are filmed when they unload the ships. The processing plants account for every fish. Most of the toothfish are exported so they're monitored again when they leave the country.'

She paused for another sip and Connor asked, 'But you think that despite all these checks there's still something going on.'

My estimation of Connor went way up. I said, 'That's right. If we assume that my brother's death wasn't an accident or something equally unlikely such as a crime of passion, then we think the reason for his killing is most likely in the company's books. He saw something or learned something that told him Blue Ocean was not just catching toothfish. That made him a threat, and if the threat was big enough then it could have gotten him killed. We think if something is going on other than catching toothfish then there will be evidence in their financial records. But we don't know what to look for or where to look.'

Emma added, 'That's where you come in. All of Blue Ocean's activities and finances are on public record somewhere. In computer files – just what you're an expert in. Somewhere there may be something that doesn't add up; something that raises a red flag. Maybe a small flag, but that may be all it takes to figure this out.'

'Let me get this straight,' said Connor. 'You want me to hack into Blue Ocean Seafoods. Look at their finances, their operational records, their sales figures. Anything I can find. And look for anomalies. Is that it?'

'Yes,' I said, 'and don't forget that it's an international company. It has a subsidiary in Vladivostok that handles overseas sales. It seems a long shot, but if we're going to do this then we need to look at everything.' I hesitated for a moment and then said, 'These guys play for keeps and we need your best work. When you're done we need to know for sure if Blue Ocean Seafoods is clean or dirty. *Maybe* isn't going to be good enough.'

Connor's expression didn't change. 'Whatever it takes?'

I hesitated. How far were we willing to go? Was I prepared to give a hacker the green light for actions that might bend, if not break, the law? There was no doubt. I nodded in response.

No one said anything until Emma asked, 'What do you think, Connor? Do you think you can do it? Will you help us?'

Connor swirled the last of the coffee in his cup, finished it and set the cup down. He looked at Emma for a long time. 'You know I loved you, don't you?' he asked.

I could see Emma blush. She nodded but didn't speak.

'I'll do this for you,' he said. 'Not because I loved you, but because it's what I do, and it could be interesting.'

Emma reached across the table and covered his hand with hers. 'Thanks, Connor. 'You're ...' she stumbled for words and then said quietly, 'Thanks.'

Connor sat up straight. 'Don't thank me yet. You haven't seen my bill.'

'Don't worry about that,' I said. 'We'll pay whatever it costs. After hearing what we've said do you have any idea how long it might take?'

Connor thought for a moment and replied, 'Getting the data shouldn't take long. Vladivostok isn't as open as New Zealand, but I should be able to get everything I need. The thing is, I have no idea how long it will take to search the data for something useful. We may get lucky and find something the first day. Or it may take days of looking and thinking and testing. Usually, though, a couple of weeks are enough if there's something to be found. If it takes longer than that, then either there's nothing there, or it's so well hidden that it might never be found.'

'Okay,' I said. 'Thanks, Connor. We really appreciate your help.'

We stood and made our way through the tables and out the door. On the sidewalk, Connor and I shook hands, and he and Emma hugged and kissed cheeks. With a small wave, Connor swung his satchel onto his shoulder and walked towards the bus stop at the corner.

CHAPTER 13

David Callaghan looked up as his PA showed me into his office. 'Adam, it's been a while. How are you doing?'

I walked to his desk and didn't offer to shake his hand. 'Pretty well, everything considered.' I gestured at the papers on his desk and remarked, 'I know you're a busy man. It wasn't easy to get an appointment.' I folded my arms across my chest. 'I said some things I regret the last time I was here. I'm sorry. I haven't yet got over Theo's death.'

Callaghan looked at me, his pale blue eyes unblinking. Then he put his fancy fountain pen on the desk, clasped his hands together and leaned forward. 'I know this isn't a social call. Have you found what you're looking for? Is there something I can do for you?'

I avoided his first questions and answered the last one. 'You're right; it's not a social call. I have a favour to ask. Last time we were here you said to let you know if there was anything you could do to help. Well, there's something you could do.'

'Really? What is it?'

'I want to sail as your scientific representative on the *Polar Princess*. I know you often send someone along to help the observers manage the CCAMLR paperwork, to avoid hold-ups in the fishing. I want the job.'

Callaghan frowned slightly and picked up his pen. He studied it for a moment and then said, 'You want to sail on the *Polar Princess*? After what happened to Theo? After what you've accused me of? You're sure?'

'Yes, I'm sure. I need to sail on her. I need to share Theo's life, share that last voyage. I can never be there for him, never know what happened, but sailing on the *Polar Princess* is the closest I can come to it. It feels as if that's the only way I can let him go.' I looked away, then back at Callaghan. 'The things I said ... I was out of line. I'm asking for your help, your understanding. You have no reason to do me a favour, but I'm asking for one anyway.'

'Hmmm,' Callaghan considered me cooly. 'It's not my decision, you know. Our Chief of Operations decides who sails on the ships.'

'I know, but you're the boss. I'm sure he'd agree to your recommendation.'

'When's the sailing date?' He flipped through the pages in his diary. 'Hell, it's only a month away. He may already have hired someone.' He studied me for another few moments. 'This wouldn't be a compassionate trip. You'd be held to the same standards as anyone else. You understand that?' He saw me nod and said, 'All right, I'll see what I can do. No guarantees, mind, but I'll have a word. If he's already hired someone, then that may be it.'

'Thanks, it would mean a lot to me. I want to put this behind me and move on with my life.'

He stood up and walked around his desk. Once again we avoided shaking hands. We both knew why I wanted to be on that ship. As he ushered me towards the door I asked, 'When do you think I'll know? About going south?'

Callaghan opened the door and said, 'Soon. I'll make enquiries today.'

I thanked him again and made my way out of the building to the wharf.

After I left Callaghan returned to his chair and stared out the windows. Puffy white clouds floated in the cornflower blue sky. Stylish boats were nestled up to their berths or skipped across the harbour. The scene didn't soothe him.

———

I met Nigel at a coffee shop on George Street, the main street of Dunedin. I'd asked Detective Killand for Nigel's number, but he hadn't been willing to share it. 'What do you want to talk with Mr Pierce for?' he'd asked.

'Look, Detective, I'm looking for closure. I want to talk with anyone who had anything to do with Theo's last days.' I was looking for information, but I knew closure was something public servants were big on.

The phone was silent while Killand thought. Finally, he said, 'I think you're bullshitting me, but I'm damned if I can see why.' I heard him sigh and then he continued, 'I'll pass your number on to Mr Pierce and tell him you want to talk to him. But if he agrees, then all you talk about is finding the body and bringing it back. Got it?'

'Of course, Detective. What else would we talk about?' I asked innocently.

When Nigel called I asked if we could meet. 'I've spoken with Detective Killand and read all the reports about my brother's death and the recovery of his body. I'd like to talk with someone who was there – who saw his body.'

'Yeah,' said Nigel, 'I was there. But there's nothing I can tell you. Your brother was dead long before I saw him. We got him on board and immediately put him in a tarp. I hardly saw the body.'

'I understand, that's okay.' I hesitated momentarily and then added, 'Actually, there's something else.' Despite my earlier confidence, I remembered Killand's warning and felt nervous. 'I don't know ... we're not sure ... I want to talk about chartering your boat. I'd like you to keep it confidential, at least for now. Detective Killand's sensitive about who I see and what I do.'

After some more discussion, Nigel reluctantly agreed to meet me. Emma was busy at work, and we decided she didn't need to attend this meeting. My flight to Dunedin was uneventful and my taxi dropped me off early. I found a table near the front window and watched pedestrians pass by outside. I hadn't met Nigel but I had no trouble identifying him from his brief description of himself. The man who walked into the coffee shop was tidily dressed in pressed trousers and a check shirt, and there was no mistaking the short grey hair, the level eyes in a nut-brown face, and his hard, sun-tanned hands. He wasn't a big man, but he moved with confidence.

I stood and we shook hands. I felt the calluses and the tendons beneath the skin, evidence of someone used to hard manual labour. 'What can I get you?' I asked.

'Flat white, no sugar.'

I ordered at the counter and returned to the table. 'Thanks for agreeing to meet me. It's good to put a face to the name I've read in the reports.'

'No problem. Happy to help. But as I said on the phone, there's nothing I can add to what I've already said.'

We sat back when the waitress arrived with our coffees and took a minute to take a sip and look at each other.

'Look, Nigel, I won't lie. Detective Killand warned me to only talk about recovering the body. But I agree with you: I don't think there's much point in talking about that.' I paused to take a sip of coffee before continuing. 'What I want to talk about is your boat. The *Storm Petrel*? Something the detective might not approve of.'

Nigel gave a small smile. 'I've met Detective Killand. I suspect there are many things he might not approve of.'

I returned the smile and met his gaze. 'I, that is, we … I mean, Emma and I are working on this together. Have you met Emma DeSilva? Theo's partner?'

Nigel shook his head.

'Well, I won't go into details, but we've been looking into Theo's death. And we think something's not right. Someone's not telling the truth. We think Theo was murdered.'

That got Nigel's attention. He lifted an eyebrow as he took a sip of coffee.

'The only possible motive we can see is that Theo discovered something about Blue Ocean Seafoods, the company that owns the ship he was on, something they didn't want known. Something they were willing to kill him for.' I finished the last of my coffee and set the cup back in the saucer. 'The thing is, we have no idea what it might be. Emma and I have come up with a few things we can do to try and find out. One of them is for me to sail on the *Polar Princess*. We figure if I'm on board then I might see something that's a clue to what Theo discovered.'

Nigel said, 'Hmmm. Interesting idea. Probably something that would give the detective kittens.' He thought for a moment and then said, 'I understand why you might want to go, but do you think you'll learn anything useful? If they know you're on board, it seems highly unlikely they'd do anything suspicious.'

I shrugged. 'You're probably right. Maybe it's a waste of time. But we won't know unless I go.'

'Fair enough. But what does this have to do with me? And the *Storm Petrel*?'

'Emma decided the only way she'd agree for me to go was if we had some sort of backup, in case something went wrong. I'll have some basic satellite communications, but if anything happens, it's unlikely that any other vessel would be anywhere near us. That's where you come in.'

I paused and looked at Nigel. His face didn't give anything away but I could sense he was unconvinced. 'Our idea is you'll take your boat back to the Bounty Islands and wait. On the remote chance that something happens, you'll be days nearer me than anyone else. We have no idea what might happen, what you might do, but we figure if something does happen then you'll be there.'

'Look,' he replied, 'I'd like to help but what you're saying is pretty vague, and I'm not sure I want to get involved with potential murderers. I couldn't take your money without a better idea of what you want. And anyway, those longliners can be gone for months. There's no way I could be at sea that long.'

'I understand, but we're not expecting heroics. We hope nothing happens and you have a nice holiday watching the birds. If we need you then we think it would be sufficient for you to find the *Polar Princess* and let them know someone else is aware of what's going on. I don't think there's any real chance of violence. The duration of the voyage is no problem. We'll only need you for a couple of weeks. Theo went overboard at the end of the voyage, and I figure if anything happens this time then that's when it will occur. We're making lots of assumptions – that's just one more.'

Nigel stared at me and then said, 'When would this be?'

'The *Polar Princess* is scheduled to depart in late November. The ship will be in the Ross Sea for about six weeks. If it keeps to the same schedule as last year then it will sail to the Bounty Islands in mid-January to fish for a week or so before returning to Dunedin. We'd like to charter your boat for two weeks in the middle of January.'

'Let me think about it,' he said, standing up. 'I'm not wild about the job. But I don't have any other charters at that time, either. I won't keep you waiting. I'll make a decision and let you know straightaway.'

'Great, thanks, we hope you'll help us.' We shook hands and I watched him leave the café.

CHAPTER 14

Connor sat behind his desk and hit keys on the keyboard. 'Parts of it were easy, parts were hard. In hindsight it's obvious. Putting it together should have been simple, but at first I was as blind as everyone else. That was my consolation; no one else had seen what was going on either.'

He'd called me and told me he had something to show us about Blue Ocean Seafoods. Emma had flown over from Napier and she and I were in Connor's office, a bare space crowded with computers. We were seated with Connor behind his desk, looking at his computer screens without comprehension.

Before we started he handed a thumb drive to Emma and said, 'Everything I found is on here. Don't lose it.'

Emma looked dubiously at the drive. 'Thanks, Connor. But what did you find that was so important I had to fly here from Napier?'

Connor pulled up a chart on his screen and started pointing to the boxes. The centre box was labelled *Blue Ocean Seafoods*. 'The first thing I did was look at the corporate structure of Blue Ocean Seafoods. They're a publicly listed company with the usual variety of investors, from Mom and Pop to large pension funds. It all looked kosher, but I decided to dig a bit deeper and found something interesting. The shareholdings of a façade of small respectable companies are actually controlled through a network of interlocking corporate entities by Stepan Sokolov, a Russian oligarch. Through these intermediaries, Mr Sokolov holds about 28 per cent of the company, not enough to control it outright but more than enough for his needs.' Connor took a pull on his can of Red Bull before continuing. 'Mr Sokolov is based in Vladivostok. He made his billions in fishing, mining and forestry. We'll come back to him in a moment.'

Emma asked, 'And this is relevant to us? To why Theo was killed?'

Connor shrugged. 'It's relevant to understanding how Blue Ocean Seafoods operates. It may or may not be relevant to the other thing.' He paused and then continued. 'Back to my story. Blue Ocean Seafood exports most of its toothfish catch to Russia, marketing it through a company called Sustainable Seafood Trading. Sustainable Seafood is a joint-venture operation between Blue Ocean Seafood and Venture Holdings. Venture Holdings has a complicated structure, but if you look far enough you find, guess who?' He looked back and forth between us and said, 'Bingo – Stepan Sokolov.'

I said, 'So Blue Ocean and its subsidiary are tied up with a Russian oligarch. So what? I'm sure other companies are as well. That's probably the only way business is done in Russia.'

Connor pushed his hair back from his forehead. 'Yeah, yeah. Hang on. Let's review what happens to the fish. Blue Ocean Seafoods sells its toothfish to Sustainable Seafood Trading, located in Vladivostok. The fish are frozen and packed at the factory in Timaru. The packing is monitored and the boxes are monitored and everything is tickety-boo. The boxes are put in a container and sent straight to the port. There the waybill is checked, they're loaded on a ship and taken to Russia. The boxes arrive in Vladivostok. They clear customs and go to the Sustainable Seafoods warehouse.'

'Sounds pretty tight,' Emma observed.

'It is. Everything's monitored, there's absolutely no opportunity for tampering.'

'So where's the scam?' I asked.

'Hiding in plain sight.'

'Come on,' said Emma. 'Stop being cute and just tell us what's going on.'

'It's not surprising no one's noticed anything unusual. Unless you were looking you'd never think anything was wrong. I dug into Blue Ocean's accounts, looking at everything I could think of. I checked import records, export records, the accounts of other companies. It took ages but eventually I noticed that Blue Ocean is paying more to ship its fish than other companies are.'

'What do you mean?' I asked.

'Well, the rate varies somewhat depending on factors like the availability of containers and ships, but on average Blue Ocean is paying about 10 per cent more to move its fish. That may not sound like much, but in a competitive market, that's a lot. Every dollar spent on expenses like freight comes off the bottom line, and companies are always looking for ways to trim them.

'That made me curious, so I looked a little deeper. By digging through waybills and invoices I discovered that the reason Blue Ocean is paying more is that it needs more containers to ship its fish than its competitors do. For some reason, they're getting fewer fish in their boxes than their competitors are. That is, if their competitors ship one thousand kilos of fish in fifty boxes, then Blue Ocean ships the same amount of fish in fifty-five boxes. More boxes mean more containers, more containers mean more costs.'

'Sorry,' I said, 'I understand what you've said, but I don't understand what's going on. Who cares if they're using more boxes?'

Connor looked very pleased with himself. 'I think the boxes have been modified to carry something other than fish. If we lived in Colombia then I'd guess they were carrying drugs, but as we live in New Zealand there aren't too many options. It's unlikely to be milk powder so I'm guessing it's cash. I think Blue Ocean Seafoods and Sustainable Seafood Trading are running a money laundering scheme.' Connor beamed at us, then looked disappointed when we didn't immediately share his enthusiasm. He asked, 'Do you know anything about money laundering?'

Emma and I looked at each other. 'Not much,' I said.

'Don't worry, the basics are all you need to know,' Connor
explained. 'Crooks often end up with large amounts of cash. Their
business isn't usually the type of operation supported by Visa or
Mastercard. They don't want to declare that cash as income because
they can't explain where it came from, and equally important, these are
the type of people who really, really don't want to pay tax on it. So
they work out a scheme to move that cash into the legitimate financial
system, cleaning or "laundering" the dirty money. Over the years
criminals have worked out hundreds of ways of doing it. Laundering a
big amount of money, like we're looking at here, could cost 20 to 30
per cent of the gross.'

'Shit,' I said, 'that must hurt.'

'It's a cost of business. If I'm right, and Blue Ocean has found a
clever way to get cash out of the country, then they still have to convert
it from New Zealand dollars to a more widely traded currency or
product. Changing it to US dollars, euros, gold or diamonds is going to
cost them, but it's much easier in a kleptocracy like Russia than it is
here.'

I thought about what Connor had said. 'Okay, I think I get it. But
10 per cent of each box doesn't sound like a lot of money.'

'You're right, each box doesn't carry a lot of money. But there are a
lot of boxes. Based on the size of standard fish boxes and the volume
of fish they export, I estimate that they may be exporting about two-
and-a-half tonnes of cash. If I'm right, then these companies are
laundering more than two hundred million dollars of dirty money a
year.'

Emma and I looked at each other in astonishment. She was the first
to find her voice. 'Two hundred million? Dollars?'

'Yep. The amount of illegal money generated in New Zealand is
estimated to be well over a billion dollars a year. Most of that is
laundered through local businesses, but if I'm right, then a lot of it is
going to Russia.'

'Damn, Connor. That's good work,' I said.

Connor's face got serious. 'Yeah, but you guys need to be careful.

Very careful. Two hundred million dollars is serious money. Definitely enough to kill for.'

Emma looked worried. 'This is way bigger than I expected. Should we take this to the police?'

Connor looked a little sheepish. 'I forgot to mention something about my investigations.' He paused, licked his lips and said, 'Not everything I've reported to you is strictly speaking, um, publicly available.'

Emma's worry increased. 'You mean, you—'

Connor held up a hand and interrupted her. 'Yeah, I hacked a few of their confidential files.' Both Emma and I started to talk but he carried on over us. 'Hey, wait. You said I should do whatever was necessary. I did what was necessary. The public stuff wasn't giving me what we needed. There were bits and bobs, but nothing concrete. I poked around a little and started finding things that were useful, and I guess I sort of just kept going. But don't worry, I was very careful. Their security's not top of the line, and I'm sure I didn't leave any tracks.' He looked down at his keyboard and then back up at us. 'But it means it might not be a good idea to share everything we know with the police.'

We were all silent for a while. Finally, I sighed and said, 'You're right. We can't go to the police. Not yet. You've got to give us a list of what you found in the public records, and what you found in the confidential files. Eventually we're going to want the police, and we'll need to know what we can tell them.' I looked at Emma and said, 'I'm still puzzled. This is great stuff, but it's all about exporting fish *after* they've come off the ship. I don't see a connection to the *Polar Princess* and Theo.'

Emma shrugged. 'I don't either. But a day ago we didn't know about money laundering. This makes me more optimistic that you may find something on the *Polar Princess* after all.'

After that, our conversation dried up. Connor stood and Emma gave him a long hug. Neither of them said anything as he left.

———

David Callaghan was working through the board papers when his phone rang. He picked it up and immediately recognised the husky voice of Alexander Ivanov. 'David,' the voice asked, 'is this a good time?'

'Of course, Alexander. It's always a pleasure to talk with you. What can I do for you?' The last thing Callaghan wanted was to talk with Alexander Ivanov, but that was something he could never admit.

'I know you're busy, so I'll come right to the point. It's about our friends. Again.'

Callaghan sat back in his chair and ran his hand through his hair. Of all the things he didn't want to talk to Alexander about "our friends" were highest on the list. The Russian was determined to pursue a course of action that, to Callaghan, seemed reckless and likely to fail. For all his urbane appearance and behaviour, Callaghan thought Alexander was, at heart, just a thug. But that was one more thing he could never admit – unless he was willing to accept the potentially fatal consequences.

Eventually, he said, 'Our friends are only a problem because of your paranoia and rash behaviour. If you'd been patient, they would have given up long ago and got on with their lives. As it is, Stone has proved remarkably lucky, surviving the little accident you arranged for him. But I assure you, we have this contained. We've hired Stone to come on the next voyage of the *Polar Princess*. He doesn't know anything, and we'll have him under close observation the whole time. The woman will do nothing by herself. If we control Stone, then we control the situation.'

'I am well aware of your opinion, David, but I'm not so sure that these two are not a threat. I was speaking with our accountant in Vladivostok this morning, and he informed me that someone has been snooping around our accounts.'

'What do you mean? Our accounts are public documents. We have nothing to hide.'

'Perhaps I should have said files rather than accounts. The files containing the off-the-books financial information about our enterprise. We have alarms set to monitor access to them, and some of the alarms have been triggered. Those files are sensitive, definitely not public documents. Our accountant is still tracing the intrusion, but so far he can only say it came from New Zealand.'

'Look, Alexander, files or no files, as far as our friends are concerned there is absolutely nothing to worry about. The death on the *Polar Princess* has been officially buried. And you know as well as I do that our company records are clean. If it was Stone and DeSilva who somehow found sensitive files in Vladivostok – and that's a big if – then I'm sure it was part of some random search, part of their refusal to admit defeat. They know nothing about business. They wouldn't know what those files were. They are mosquitoes buzzing around your head, nothing more.'

'I don't believe in your perfect world, David. I believe in human beings. In Russia, you learn that there is always something to find if you look hard enough, dig deep enough, ask the right person the right questions.' Alexander paused and Callaghan waited impatiently for him to continue. 'You think Adam Stone is a mosquito. That may be so, but even mosquitoes carry fatal diseases. There is too much at stake to take these risks. I don't want Stone asking any more questions. I don't want Stone on the *Polar Princess*. I want this to end right now.'

Callaghan said nothing for a long time before replying. 'I've told you before that I think you're making a mistake. I want our friends to go away just as much as you do. But your actions only draw attention to us. Repeated attacks on them cannot be disregarded as an accident or a coincidence. More attention might lead to official questions about our activities. If you persevere down this course then you have to finish it. There can be no more mistakes.'

'Don't worry my friend. Stone has been lucky so far. But his luck has run out.'

The phone went dead in Callaghan's hand, Alexander offering no goodbye. He replaced the receiver and looked down at his desk. The board papers would have to wait. There was no way he could concentrate, knowing that Alexander Ivanov was on the loose.

CHAPTER 15

It was blowing like forty bastards and raining when we landed in Wellington. I was glad I'd worn a coat; the temperature was at least five degrees colder than Auckland. We had no bags, so we headed straight for the exit and caught a taxi into town.

It was mid-morning and the traffic wasn't bad. The harbour came into view as we got to the large roundabout at the north end of the runway. The colourful fibreglass rods of the wind sculpture in the centre of the roundabout were getting thrashed by the northerly gale.

'Pretty wild,' I said to the driver.

He shrugged. 'Not so cold as yesterday.'

I looked at Emma and she rolled her eyes and tried to wrap her jacket closer around herself. The taxi took the road around the waterfront. The wind funnelled across the harbour and the spray from the waves flew across the road. As we came around a point, Wellington's compact downtown came into view, surrounded by hills. Even in the grey light and horizontal rain, it was at once plain and attractive, exactly in scale with its location. The taxi wove its way through the one-way streets and pulled up outside a modern building.

'This is it?' I asked.

'Camden House, yes,' said the driver.

I paid and Emma got out on the curb side. The wind almost blew the door out of her hand, but she held on and closed it after I exited. We dashed for the doorway and were only somewhat wet by the time the doors swept open and we entered the lobby. We checked the building directory and saw that the news service Gordon worked for, Hot Wired, was on the fourteenth floor.

We took the elevator and stepped out into a hall. A sign directed us to the left. We followed the hall to a glass door with Hot Wired on a plaque alongside it. We opened the door and entered.

Emma led the way to the reception desk and was greeted by a young woman. 'Can I help you?' she asked.

'Yes,' said Emma, 'we have an appointment with Mr Crawford.'

The receptionist typed on her keyboard and studied her screen for a moment. 'Ms DeSilva and Mr Stone?'

We nodded and she said, 'You're a little early. Have a seat. I'll give Mr Crawford a call.'

'Thanks,' said Emma. She sat in one of the armchairs while I strolled around the reception area, studying the photos on the walls. They were impressive, large-format prints of dramatic news events throughout the South Pacific. We had only been waiting a few minutes when a man entered the room from the corridor to the right of the receptionist.

I guessed he was about forty, good-looking rather than handsome, brown eyes and brown hair tidy off his ears. He had a beard shadow and although he could probably afford to lose a few kilos, he looked reasonably fit. As soon as he saw Emma his eyes lit up and he said, 'Emma! It's great to see you.'

They exchanged warm greetings, and then Emma introduced me. 'Gordon, this is Adam. He's Theo's brother.'

I came forward and shook Gordon's hand. His grip was warm and he held my hand while he said, 'I'm very sorry about Theo, Adam. I only met him a couple of times, but he was a hell of a guy.'

I nodded. 'Yeah, he was that.'

Emma said, 'Actually, that's why we've come to see you, Gordon. About Theo's death.' She looked around the reception area and asked, 'Is there someplace we can speak privately?'

'Sorry,' said Gordon, 'of course. Let's go to my office.' As he directed us towards the corridor he asked, 'Would you like anything to drink? Sandra makes a great long black.'

We both declined and he gave the receptionist a wave and ushered us along a short corridor lined with more photographs. 'You haven't been to my office, have you, Emma?'

'No, I rarely come to Wellington. But you haven't been here long, have you?'

Gordon laughed. 'Nope. About a year. I was offered the chance to head the office and accepted. Justin himself flew to New Zealand to talk to me, and it's hard to say no to him.'

He saw our blank looks. 'Justin? Justin Mappe? The Silicon Valley kid who's shaking up the news industry?' Emma and I shook our heads and he continued, 'Justin made a zillion dollars doing something very clever and it's now an integral part of just about the entire Internet. He dabbled in a few things and then decided that it was time to drag the news business into the twenty-first century. He founded Hot Wired and in just three years he's set up offices in more than thirty-five countries.'

'Sort of a techno Al Jazeera?' I asked.

Gordon grinned. 'More like a Californian Rupert Murdoch, without the controversy and multiple wives. He's got several threads in his business model – wholesale, retail, subscriptions, pay-as-you-go – I don't know if it's profitable yet, but sales are growing fast.'

The corridor ended in a large room with glass walls to the left and right. The space was occupied by half a dozen desks with multiple computer screens and the usual clutter of pens, pads and photos. Four of the desks were occupied: two men and two women, all young and all ordinary looking. No obvious geeks, radicals or socially challenged gonzo journalists.

Gordon led us across the space to a door in the glass wall on the left side of the room. 'We're still small, but we have a great team here. Justin pays well so, in terms of staff, we get the best of the best. These are early days but I think we're starting to make our mark.'

We went through the glass door into his office. The door shut behind us and the hum of computers and the soft noise of people at work disappeared. Emma looked around the room and murmured, 'A step up. From reporter.'

Gordon moved behind his desk. 'Managing Editor, New Zealand.' He laughed heartily and observed, 'That means fuck-all these days. In an office this small everyone puts their hand to everything. Take a seat.' He gestured towards the outer work area as he sat down. 'I need to be part of the team, but even so, there are times when I need privacy. The glass gives me both.'

While I glanced around the office Emma leaned forward in her seat and said, 'Gordon, thanks again for seeing us. Adam will explain more in a minute, but the thing is, we're in a bit of a bind and think you could help. Like I said, it's related to Theo's death.'

Gordon leaned back in his chair and spread his hands. 'Go ahead, I'm all ears. I've blocked out the entire morning, so take as long as you need.'

Emma looked at me and I started talking. For the third time, I told the entire story, as I'd told it to Sergeant Wero and Connor: Theo, the voyage to the Ross Sea, what we'd learned from Detective Killand, what we'd learned from the CEO of Blue Ocean Seafoods, the pathology results. Gordon's eyes widened and his body went still when I told him about the car wreck. I paused at that point and said, 'Maybe I could use some water after all.'

'Of course,' said Gordon. 'You, Emma?' She nodded and he spoke briefly into his phone. We didn't say anything for the few minutes it took for the receptionist to deliver three glasses and a pitcher of water. 'Thanks, Sandra,' Gordon said as she left the room. He poured glasses for each of us and sat back in his chair.

'That's quite a story,' he observed. He looked at Emma. 'Thank God you're all right. Were you injured?'

'A bit, but nothing serious. We were lucky, though. I'm sure they were trying to kill us in the car wreck.'

'*They*? You've told a story with a cast of thousands. Who do you think *they* are? Who wants to kill you?'

Emma hesitated, so I said, 'We think Blue Ocean is behind it. Probably Callaghan. They're the common thread. There's one more thing we need to tell you.' I took a breath and recounted Connor's story about Blue Ocean Seafoods, Sustainable Seafood Trading and Stepan Sokolov. I explained how the fish were exported and the number of boxes and how that might mean they were being used to carry cash as well as fish. I finished with Connor's estimate that they could be laundering two hundred million dollars a year, and cautioned Gordon that some of Connor's investigative techniques weren't entirely kosher.

Gordon's eyes widened at the mention of two hundred million dollars, but he didn't say anything. I guess investigative journalists don't really break a sweat for anything less than a billion. He swivelled slowly in his chair and thought about what we'd said. 'Damn, Connor sounds like someone we could use.' He paused and then said, 'It sort of makes sense. If you're right then they have a big motive.' He was silent for a moment then asked, 'How good is this Connor chap? Do you really think he was able to get that information without leaving his fingerprints all over the place?'

Emma explained, 'We asked him that and he said it's almost impossible to leave no trace at all, but unless there's an audit, no one will know he was there.' She raised her hands and lowered them again. 'All I know is he's very good.'

'Let's hope so. If two hundred million dollars is at stake, then the motive for keeping a lid on what happened to Theo is very high, and the danger to you and Adam just as high.' Gordon looked back and forth at us before continuing, 'But why are you here? You haven't come to tell me a story. What do you want from me?'

Emma cleared her throat and said, 'We're here for several reasons. First of all, I trust you, and we need someone besides us whom we can trust. If our lives are in danger, then we want to know that if something happens there's someone else who knows what's going on.' She took a sip of her water and continued, 'Second, we may want your investigative and reporting skills. There may come a time when we need to publicly expose what's happened, to tell the story of why Theo was killed.'

'Fuck yes,' said Gordon enthusiastically. 'Are you kidding? We could write the story you told me today and put the heat on these bastards.'

'No, Gordon,' said Emma. 'No story, not yet. If we move too early then the people at the top may be able to hide or destroy the evidence we're looking for, and we'll never figure out what's going on. We want to work with you, but you have to work with us. We'll let you know if and when there's a story for you.'

Gordon rubbed his hand across his eyes and sighed. 'Only for you, Emma. It goes against everything I believe, but if that's the way you want it, then okay, no story unless you say so.' He held up a hand and said, 'But if there *is* a story, then I get it first. An exclusive.'

'You've got it, Gordon.'

'So is that it? Doesn't sound like much.'

I rubbed my hands together and said, 'Actually, there are two more things. First, the fish boxes. Connor's figured out what's probably happening but there's no evidence to support his theory. We don't think there's any way to intercept a box and see if there's money inside, either in New Zealand or Vladivostok. We don't have enough information yet to go to the police and convince them to get a warrant to look at the boxes. But we think it's worth going to the company that makes the boxes, see if anything they tell us corroborates Connor's theory.'

'Hmmm,' said Gordon, 'that could work. And you'd like me to ask those questions?'

Emma responded, 'A good reporter can find a reason to ask anyone anything.'

Gordon smiled wryly. 'Well played, Emma. Setting me up so if I fail then it's because I'm a bad reporter.' He reached for his glass of water. 'Okay, I can do that. But you said there are two things you want me to do. What's the other one?'

Nigel had called a few days before our trip to Wellington and said he was willing to sail to the Bounties. He mentioned a price and I didn't haggle. Money couldn't buy what we wanted from him if things turned to custard. We had a boat and now we needed someone on it. I smiled at Gordon and asked, 'Are you a good sailor?'

Gordon almost choked on his water and sputtered, 'What? Am I a good *what*?'

'Sailor. Like in small boats. In a big ocean.'

He growled at Emma. 'You know I hate boats.'

'But Gordon,' she said sweetly, 'I remember how much you used to like going sailing on Lake Taupo in the summer.'

'You know that was only because I was hot for Rebecca Davis. I lost my lunch every time we left the wharf.'

'Well, maybe your sea legs have improved. We'd really, *really* like you to find out.'

Gordon gave Emma another look and sighed. 'What? What do you want? How bad can it be?'

'Well, we've decided that Adam should sail on the *Polar Princess*, like Theo did, and see if he can figure out a motive for Theo's death.'

'You want me to sail on the *Polar Princess*, too? You're crazy! It would be cold. And smelly. And small. And ... and ...'

'Actually,' I said, 'fishing boats aren't smelly. The fish are fresh and everything's kept spotlessly clean. And they're not small. Not like the boat we have in mind for you.'

Gordon looked back and forth between us, disbelief on his face. 'Smaller? Smaller than a fishing boat? No. No way.'

'Yeah, it's a beautiful boat. A yacht, actually. Almost twenty metres long. Well, at least fifteen. We're told it's very comfortable in rough seas.'

'Rough seas? Jesus. Where do you propose I go in this "yacht"?'

'The Bounty Islands,' I said. 'They're about—'

'Yeah, I know where they are,' Gordon said. 'They're a thousand fucking miles from anywhere.'

'About seven hundred kilometres, actually. They're supposed to be spectacular,' Emma said brightly. 'Incredible bird life. And seals. Lots of seals. Great fishing.'

Gordon's face turned pale. 'Let me get this straight. You want me to go to some godforsaken rocks in the middle of the Southern Ocean, in a toy boat. To do what?'

'Well,' I said, 'to wait.'

'To wait? What for?'

'We don't know. We're not sure. That's why you'll be there. In case I need you. There'd be no one else.'

'No way. Uh-uh. Not in a million years.'

'Gordon, do you want this story or not? If you do, then the only way you're going to get it is to get your ass onto that boat.' Emma was leaning forward and shaking her finger at Gordon. She sat back in her chair and looked intensely at him. I was willing to bet this wasn't the first time Emma had intimidated Gordon and got him to do something she wanted.

Gordon buried his head in his hands and mumbled, 'Fuck. When would you want me to leave?'

CHAPTER 16

Even with earmuffs on, the noise of the factory was loud. And it was hot. Gordon's shirt stuck to his back with sweat and his scalp was damp under his hard hat. He was thankful the tour was almost over.

Gordon had shown up at the factory in Petone, across the harbour from Wellington, introduced himself to the receptionist and asked to see the production manager. It took about twenty minutes before a short, round man with a receding hairline came into the lobby and extended his hand. 'Cyrus Hopkins, Mr …?' he said.

'Crawford. Call me Gordon.' He took out his wallet and added, 'Here's my card.'

Hopkins looked at the card. 'Right, right. Gordon Crawford. Managing Director. Impressive. What can I do for you?'

'Thanks for taking the time to see me, Mr Hopkins. The receptionist told you that I work for Hot Wired, the new digital news network? I hope you've heard of us. We have offices all over the world. I'm trying to raise the profile of New Zealand, publish stories about what a great place it is. It's hard to do when we're competing with the royals, football stars and the odd civil war and famine, but we're trying.'

Hopkins smiled and said, 'Good on ya. The country needs all the help it can get.'

Gordon explained, 'We're developing a series on New Zealand entrepreneurs. Not the usual tech groupies that everyone already knows about. We're looking for people who are doing clever things that don't get the recognition they deserve. I ran into the CEO of Blue Ocean Seafoods the other day, and I think he's the sort of guy we're looking for. He said they're doing something very innovative with the packaging of their fish for export, and that if I wanted to know what it was all about I should come and see you. So here I am.'

'Well, Gordon, that's great. Those guys at Blue Ocean certainly have some new ideas. We make the polystyrene boxes that everyone in the industry uses for their fish, and I've got to say we were pretty surprised when David came along and said they wanted to try something different.'

'David Callaghan? The CEO? He came to see you?'

'Yeah, sure. I think the whole thing was his idea. Mind you, we don't know the whole story. Only what David told us. But if what he says is true, then the industry's looking at a new ballgame in terms of packaging – when he releases the intellectual property.'

'David was a bit vague on that, Cyrus. Can you tell me what's different about Blue Ocean's packaging?'

Cyrus shook his head. 'Only what we needed to know. I shouldn't say anything, but since David sent you to see us then I guess it's okay. They've got a new insulation material that's cheaper and better than polystyrene. They can't use it for the whole box, but they add it to the box once it's made. David says it will reduce their need for refrigeration and pay for itself tenfold.'

'Add it to the box? How do they do that?'

'We've never seen the stuff, Gordon, so I don't know exactly what it is. But Blue Ocean puts it in the bottoms of the boxes we make. They say it makes a hell of a difference.'

'Bottoms of the boxes? What do you mean, Cyrus?'

'The design is the same as a standard 50-litre fish box, outer dimensions 800 by 320 by 300 mill. They've got us making a box inside a box. The sides and top and bottom of the outer box are half the thickness of a standard fish box, as are those of the inner box. The pieces are designed so that when the inner box slides inside the outer box there's a 60-mill gap between it and the bottom of the outer box. That's where they put the new insulation material, underneath the inner box.' Cyrus paused and ran his hand back across his scalp. 'As I said, we don't know what that material is, but it goes in that gap. I'll tell you one thing, it wasn't easy. Our designer was pulling his hair out trying to make something they were happy with.'

Gordon thought about this for a few moments. 'Sixty mill – six centimetres, right?' When Cyrus nodded he said, 'So let me get this straight. You send the boxes, with their inner and outer parts, to Blue Ocean. They put the new insulation material in the bottom of the outer box, insert the inner box, and then they fill the inner box with fish? And from the outside, it looks like an ordinary fish box?'

'Yeah,' Cyrus nodded. 'That's it.'

'Hmm. If it works then it sounds like exactly the kind of thing we're looking for. Thinking outside the box, if you'll pardon the pun.' Gordon pulled out his phone and said, 'Do you mind if I take your picture? And do you think I could take a few photos in the factory as background for the story?'

Cyrus beamed as though he'd just won the lottery. 'Sure thing, Gordon. Where do you want me to stand?'

After getting outfitted with safety gear – hard hat, ear muffs, bright orange safety vest – Gordon followed Cyrus into the factory. It was a large steel building with a high ceiling and exposed steel beams. Skylights let the summer sun in, supplementing the light from the large fluorescent light fittings hanging from the ceiling. The factory was immaculate: the floors were clean and everything was in its place. The front of the work area was filled with machinery, and Gordon could see in the distance tall stacks of finished products. He was momentarily disconcerted when he saw a worker lift one of these stacks, which looked as though it should be immensely heavy, and carry it to a waiting truck.

Inside the door, Cyrus paused by a large bin and picked up a handful of small translucent beads. 'Aren't they amazing? These little beads are the key to everything we make. They expand to fifty times their initial volume and can be formed into just about any shape you can imagine. And it's all done without chemicals so is environmentally friendly.'

As they moved through the factory Cyrus explained how steam was used to expand the beads in two steps. In the final step, they were put in a machine where they expanded to fill the moulds with a solid material that is 98 per cent air. The tour finished among enormous stacks of white polystyrene objects. Cyrus pointed to a stack off to their right. 'We don't have any of the Blue Ocean boxes in stock right now, but they look like those fish boxes over there.'

'You don't happen to have a photograph of them, do you?' asked Gordon.

'Maybe ... let me have a look.' Cyrus pulled out his phone and scrolled through his photos. 'No, no, no, earlier than that .... Yeah, here it is. Can I email it to you?'

'Sure. My email address is on my card.'

Cyrus pulled out the card, pressed keys on his phone and said, 'Done.' He then led Gordon back to the lobby.

Gordon put his safety gear on a table in the lobby and extended his hand. 'Well, Cyrus, thanks for your time. I'll have to follow up with Blue Ocean, but this could definitely feature in our series. If it does, then I'll be in touch to let you know.'

'No problem, Gordon. Give us a good word in your story.'

CHAPTER 17

Jayden was skateboarding on the footpath as I got out of the cab. 'Hey, Jayden,' I said. 'How's it going?'

'Good, Adam. I wasn't sure when you were getting back. I mowed your lawns on Sunday. They're a little long again.'

'Thanks, buddy,' I said, looking over the gate. 'They look fine. You've done a good job. Maybe you can give them a trim in the next few days.'

'You bet. No worries.'

I was walking up the path to my porch when Jayden called out from the gate, 'What's the matter with your electricity, Adam?'

I stopped and turned. 'Electricity? Nothing that I know of. Why?'

'A couple of guys were here this morning. I asked them what they were doing and they said there was a problem with your electricity. Their van said Harbour City Electricians, so I thought it was okay. They said they had a key.'

'They had a key?'

'Yeah. I watched them open the door. They used a key.'

'Thanks, Jayden. Thanks for letting me know.'

'Sure thing. See you later.' Jayden disappeared from the gate and then reappeared. 'Adam? There was something else. They had a big cardboard box. I couldn't figure out what an electrician would have in a cardboard box. Don't they have volt metres and wire cutters and stuff like that? It looked heavy.'

'Right. Thanks, Jayden. I'm sure they'll have left a note or something.' His head disappeared again and I heard him roll off down the footpath.

I couldn't think of any reason why an electrician would have a large cardboard box, either. I couldn't think of any reason why an electrician would come to my house. There'd been nothing wrong with my electricity before I left, and I hadn't asked for it to be looked at. So who had? What had the electricians done? How did they get a key? I was still puzzling these questions as I stepped onto the porch, used my key to unlock the door, and pushed it open.

One of the forensics team told me later that I was lucky the door missed me entirely. I wasn't sure if he was being funny or not. Sometimes those guys have a peculiar sense of humour. Just because the door missed me didn't mean I was uninjured. The glass from the door got my right arm, but fortunately it didn't go into my face. The blast blew me off my feet and I hit one of the porch columns with my left shoulder before landing on the lawn. I sprained an ankle and was deaf for quite a while.

Jayden was the first person on the scene. He's 40 kilos soaking wet, but he managed to drag me away from the fire. He was first because his mother stopped to ring 111 before running next door to my house. She helped move me further from the flames and got me into a comfortable position. After the trauma of the car wreck, my body decided this abuse was totally unfair. All I wanted to do was sleep. I could hardly move my head but my eyes kept going back and forth between my burning house and Jayden's worried face. I don't remember much of the immediate aftermath of the explosion, but I have a vivid memory of watching sparks spiralling up like orange fireflies and disappearing into the night.

I couldn't hear Jayden or his mother or the flames or anything else, so it was a surprise when I saw the red and blue flashes of emergency lights. The next thing I knew bulky men in yellow jackets, black trousers and helmets were dragging hoses across my lawn and pumping water onto the flames.

My sense of time was as wonky as my hearing, but it seemed to take no time at all to put out the fire. By then the police and an ambulance had arrived. A young paramedic was assessing my vital signs and my hearing was starting to return. Once she concluded I was likely to live, she started removing the glass from my arm. There was a small, searing pain every time she nudged one of the shards with her tweezers. My arm was oozing blood as though I'd been attacked by leeches. Jayden and his mother watched from nearby, a look of morbid fascination on Jason's face and concern on his mother's.

'Mr Stone?' One of the uniformed policemen stood in front of me. He sounded as though he was at the end of a tunnel, but I could hear him. I nodded but didn't answer.

'Sir, we'd like to talk to you. Is this a good time?'

'Is this a good time?' I asked. 'Does this *look* like a good time?' He recoiled slightly, and I suspected that I may have raised my voice – which I justified to myself because my hearing was still impaired.

'I'm sorry, sir. But it's very important. Sergeant Wero would like a word.'

'Thank you, officer. Please tell Sergeant Wero that I will try to see her after this young woman has finished dressing my arm. Unless I still feel like shit, in which case she can make an appointment with me tomorrow.'

The officer moved away. I reached out to Jayden with my uninjured left arm. We shook hands awkwardly and then I pulled him into an equally awkward hug. He looked embarrassed but proud, too. 'Thanks, Jayden. You saved my life.'

'No. You probably would have been okay. The fire wasn't that big, really.'

'Thanks to your mother's quick work.' I looked up at her and said, 'Thanks, Mary. Quick thinking.'

She smiled a little shakily. 'Couldn't let a neighbour down.'

I gestured towards my house. 'How bad is it?'

She frowned. 'Looks a mess but I don't think it's too bad. The fire crew got here before it could spread. Your front room's pretty much trashed, but the rest of the house should be okay. Some smoke and water damage, probably, but nothing major.'

The paramedic finally finished extracting glass splinters and bandaged my· arm. I didn't talk to Sergeant Wero that day. Mary insisted that I spend the night with them. Jayden and I had fun talking about skateboarding and fishing over dinner.

CHAPTER 18

I met Sergeant Wero the next morning. I'd retrieved some clean clothes from my house, ignoring the crime scene tape that had been strung around it. I gave the clothes a good sniff. They smelled slightly of smoke, but I figured they'd be fine after being out in the fresh air for a while.

I entered the central lobby of the police station and asked for Sergeant Wero. After a short wait, she appeared through a door and led me back to a meeting room. 'Coffee? Tea?' she asked.

I wasn't sure about coffee in a government department but decided to give it a try. 'Coffee,' I said, 'black, no sugar.'

She made a call and gestured for me to take a seat. The room was similar to the meeting room we'd been in before – plain table with four chairs, stress-reducing paint scheme – but this one had a small desk with a telephone.

We sat at the table and waited for the coffee. Sergeant Wero wasn't the sort of woman who needed to make small talk. She gestured towards my bandaged arm. 'All good?'

I lifted it. 'Yeah, not too bad.' I flexed my shoulder and added, 'Some other bits aren't so hot, but the arm's okay.'

The coffee arrived and we each took a sip. I was impressed – it was real coffee, not instant. Sergeant Wero shifted in her seat and opened her notebook. 'Thanks for coming in this morning, Mr Stone. I hope this won't take long. Before we talk about what happened yesterday, I'm sorry to report that we've still made no progress on finding the person who ran you off the road. We've looked at dozens of Toyota utes, but none show any sign of damage, and most can be proved to have been somewhere else when your accident occurred.'

'Accident,' I repeated with some irony. 'Going too fast and skidding off the road is an accident. What we experienced was attempted murder.'

Sergeant Wero looked at me patiently. 'I'm sorry. I didn't mean to belittle what happened to you.' She tapped her notebook with her pen. 'We can discuss semantics, or I can finish telling you about our investigations.'

I suddenly felt small and petty. 'Sorry, Sergeant. It's been a tough week.'

She gave a small nod. 'So far, the ute is a dead end. I talked to Mr Callaghan and Detective Killand. They're both adamant your brother's death was an accident.'

'No—' I started to respond but Sergeant Wero held up a hand and stopped me.

'Callaghan insisted Blue Ocean had no reason to kill your brother; that they are a business with nothing to hide. Killand stands 100 per cent behind the pathology report. I don't know whether he has no imagination or chooses to ignore other possibilities.'

She paused and I said, 'About Blue Ocean. We've done some digging and found some things of interest.' I told her about how the toothfish go from the fishing vessels to the shops in Vladivostok. While I did so I was thinking rapidly about how much I could say about the information Connor had discovered illegally. I continued, 'We found some other information, unconfirmed, that suggests Blue Ocean is laundering money to Russia. We think Theo may have stumbled onto that scheme somehow.'

Sergeant Wero looked unconvinced. 'Money laundering? How? You've just told me how every step of their export is monitored.'

'We have an idea how they're doing it but need more information. If we find something, *when* we find something, we'll give it to you straight away.'

The sergeant looked at me and shook her head. 'I'm not sure I'm happy with you digging into Blue Ocean. They may have tried to kill you twice. Do you really want to risk a third time?'

I didn't know what to say, so kept quiet.

She sat back in her chair and crossed her arms. 'Off the record, this is a fucking mess. I don't know whether to congratulate you on being alive, or arrest you for obstruction of justice. If you know something relevant to a police investigation then it is your duty to inform me. Now, is there anything else you want to tell me about money laundering?'

After a long silence, she sat forward and flipped through her notebook until she found the page she was looking for. 'Okay, let's talk about what happened yesterday. I've read the report from the officer at the scene, and I only have a couple of questions.'

'Shoot.'

'Okay, first, to make sure I understand what occurred, can you tell me in your own words what happened?'

So I went through it all: seeing Jayden, him telling me about the electricians, the cardboard box, the key, the explosion. When I finished I said, 'Now, what can you tell me? What exploded in my house?'

Sergeant Wero cleared her throat and turned to a new page in her notebook. 'We'll get to that in a minute. I just need to follow up on what you told me.'

So we spent twenty minutes going over it again and again. No, I wasn't aware of anything wrong with my electrical system. No, the only people who had a key to my house were me and my neighbour, Mary. No, I didn't think Mary would give my key to anyone else. No, I had no idea what was in the cardboard box. No, I had no idea why they would have a box. No, I don't know why I ducked when I opened the door.

'Just one more question,' she said. 'We saw no sign of a barbeque at your house. Do you own a barbeque? Or a heater? A gas heater?'

I stared at her for a moment. 'Okay, that's enough. I want to know what's going on. I don't own a barbeque. I've never owned a barbeque, or a gas heater. Tell me what you know or I'm leaving.'

Sergeant Wero looked at me for a moment. 'Our forensics team went through your house, looking for the cause of the fire.' She paused then said, 'It wasn't hard to find. There was a gas cylinder inside your lounge. The kind used for portable barbeques. The valve was open. There was a switch connected to the front door. When it opened it created a spark. Well, you know the rest.'

I thought about this for a minute. I thought back to the moment I opened the door. Had I sensed something? I'd gone through that door a thousand times. Had Jayden's story of the electricians triggered a heightened level of sensitivity? Had I felt something, some small resistance, something that told me to duck? I didn't know. And it didn't matter. For whatever reason, I'd moved from the doorway in the instant that the explosion occurred and had survived. If I hadn't, I'd be dead. 'Now wait a minute,' I said. 'You're saying someone entered my house with a gas cylinder and rigged it to blow up when I opened the front door?'

'We're not saying anything just yet, Sir. Our investigations are ongoing. But we've checked with the young gentleman next door and he says the cylinder could have been in the box the so-called electricians took into your house. It doesn't look like an accident. I have to ask, particularly in light of our previous discussion – could this be related to your brother's death and the car crash?'

I felt her gaze on my face. I thought about Theo's death. I thought about being run off the road and having my house blown up. Part of me, the rational part, desperately wanted to go back to my ordinary life and leave the whole matter to the police. They are the professionals, right? They've got the skills and experience and resources to find out what happened to Theo. Realistically, what could Emma and I do? A couple of amateurs up against very powerful people. People who'd sent a message to me twice. We should stop being so stubborn, so dumb.

But another part of me knew that the police were never going to succeed. Despite the links to Blue Ocean, Sergeant Wero was no closer to solving the car wreck than the day we first spoke with her. And now this. If the "electricians" were as professional as the guy who ran us off the road then they wouldn't have left any evidence that would tie them to the explosion.

I thought about our plans. In the cold light of day, they struck me as futile, unlikely to achieve anything other than provoke another attack on us. But ... I reviewed our logic and concluded that nothing had changed, we had at least as great a chance to succeed as the police. And neither Emma nor I was the type of person who wanted to sit and wait.

In the end I said, my voice rising, 'Of course they're related. Blue Ocean's behind it. Callaghan's behind it all. No one else has a motive. You've had this information for months and have made no progress catching him. I've survived two attempts by these bastards to kill me. What are you going to do about it?'

I had to give the sergeant credit, there was no visible reaction to my outburst.

She tapped her pencil and looked thoughtful; perhaps she was taking my question seriously. 'You may be right, but doesn't it strike you as odd that if Blue Ocean is behind the attacks they've made no effort to make them look like an accident? They are the only ones with an obvious motive. Why would they risk drawing the attention of the police?'

'I don't know. Maybe they thought they wouldn't fail. Maybe they're arrogant and think they can operate outside the law. And maybe they're right. Do you have any evidence that points in their direction? Without proof, there's nothing we can do.'

'There is no such thing as the perfect crime. Whoever attacked you must have made at least one mistake.'

I was tired of going around in circles. 'I'm sorry, Sergeant, there's nothing more I can tell you.'

She must have thought there was more I could tell her because she picked and poked at me for another hour but made no useful progress.

As I was leaving she said, 'Thanks for your cooperation today. We may want to speak with you again.'

'You've got my phone number. Call when you've tracked down those electricians. Or the guy who drove us off the road.' We shook hands and I caught a taxi to the airport.

CHAPTER 19

Emma met me at the airport. We hugged and kissed and held each other. Neither of us spoke; our emotions were too overwhelming. We finally broke apart and stood holding hands, just looking at each other. We grabbed my bag and walked outside to her ute.

Once in the ute, it was as though a spell was broken and the words rushed out. Rushing, colliding, interfering, tumbling over one another: *I thought I might not see you again, I thought I was going to die, It was awful, It was terrible, I was scared, I was scared, I was scared.*

Emma drove straight to her house. We made love. We didn't make it to the bedroom. I held her against the wall, her legs wrapped around my waist.

We ate a late lunch or early dinner in her kitchen. She did something with chicken, red pepper, aubergine and other bits and pieces. 'Get a bottle of wine,' she said, pointing to the pantry. 'Something good.'

I found a chardonnay that looked likely to be up to the challenge. 'Aubergine,' I said. 'This is a new experience for me. I don't think I've ever had an aubergine in my fridge.'

'You're living on the edge now,' she replied. 'You never know what may come next.' She gave me a wicked smile.

'Next? There might be a next?'

'Ummm,' she mumbled around a mouthful of chicken. 'Next. You know. It's what comes after.'

'Huh. I was still savouring first and now you're telling me there might be after?'

She stood up and walked around the table and sat on my lap. I had to push my chair back from the table to give her room. It wasn't a hard choice.

We eventually finished our meal. We put the dishes in the dishwasher and took our glasses and the remains of the wine to her lounge. We sat on the sofa, our legs pulled up and our feet entwined. It was starting to grow dark outside. We left the lights off and watched the shadows envelop the room.

'I don't think we're moving any closer to understanding why Theo died,' I said. 'I don't think we're closer to understanding anything.' I sipped some wine and tried to organise my thoughts. 'Let's review what we know.' I ticked points off on my fingers. 'One – Theo is dead. Two – there's shitloads of money involved. Three – seriously violent people are behind it, willing to kill us.'

Emma said, 'Four – thanks to Connor we're convinced that Blue Ocean is laundering money. Gordon probably confirmed how they do it.'

'Well, our plan's working – sort of. We know Blue Ocean's dirty, that's part of what we want to discover, but we can't prove anything. We still can't tie them to Theo's death.'

Emma stretched and said, 'Guess that's up to you, Adam. If you can get on the *Polar Princess*. No pressure.' She stood and pulled me to my feet. 'Enough business. Time for pleasure.'

We didn't think about Theo, the *Polar Princess* or Blue Ocean the rest of the night.

———

Two days later I got a call from Blue Ocean's Chief of Operations. He told me I could sail on the *Polar Princess* as the scientific representative for the company, if I still wanted it. I assured him I was still keen on the position, and he told me when and where to board the ship.

I called Emma. 'I just got a call from Blue Ocean. I'm on the ship.' She was silent for so long that I said, 'Emma, it's what we wanted, isn't it?'

'Yes, yes it's what we wanted. Just be careful, Adam. Come back to me.'

Before I left to join the ship in Dunedin, I finalised plans with Nigel and Gordon. Nigel assured me that he would be ready and that the *Storm Petrel* would be on station in mid-January. He had organised most of the food and equipment he'd need for the voyage, and his crewman, a guy named Hare Driscoll, would help him load it and prepare the boat for sea. We discussed how to keep in touch using the Garmin satellite communicators. Nigel said he'd have a backup in case one failed. He was in good spirits when we ended the call, more positive than I felt. But he wasn't sailing on the *Polar Princess*, either.

Gordon was also surprisingly upbeat for someone who professed to hate going to sea. I could tell that he had become more excited about the story and, like any good reporter, wasn't going to let hardship or discomfort get in his way. We went over our expectations of him once more – he was responsible for making decisions on Nigel's boat. I reviewed the use of the satellite communicators. We didn't say it in so many words, and I hoped like hell I'd never need him, but my life could be in his hands.

I still wasn't exactly sure what help the *Storm Petrel* could be, but I had begun to feel reassured knowing it would be there. There were so many unknowns about my forthcoming voyage that I didn't even know what I should worry about. But Theo's death was always in the back of my mind; I wanted to find out the truth, but I also wanted to come home.

I wished Gordon well and said I hoped I didn't see him until we docked in Dunedin. I slept poorly and the next day flew to join the *Polar Princess*.

PART II

SOUTHERN OCEAN

CHAPTER 20

The taxi dropped me off at the wharf security office and, after a short wait, a van pulled up and drove me to the *Polar Princess*. She was a longliner, very different from a bottom trawler or a crab boat with their large open decks aft. She was about fifty-five metres in length, slab-sided in the stern with a bridge structure midships and an open foredeck with a mast and crane. There was a large opening in the starboard side of the vessel where the longline was recovered. The upperworks were white and the hull was an icy green. I thanked the van driver, grabbed my duffel bag, and walked to the gangway. The tide was out and the deck of the ship was not much higher than the wharf. A brisk wind cut across the harbour, blowing wispy clouds across the pale blue sky, and the tang of salt was strong in the air.

I climbed the gangway and was met by a large Maori bloke. He had clear brown eyes, dense dark eyebrows, a nose that had seen more action in the scrum than the ref had, and neat ears tucked back against his skull. His long black hair was tied in a ponytail. Despite the cold, he was dressed in a singlet, canvas trousers and rubber boots. His arms were corded with muscle and heavily tattooed with Maori designs. He grinned, held out a meaty hand and introduced himself when I stepped onto the deck. 'Call me Ishmael.'

'Ishmael my ass. You look more like fucking Queequeg.' I smiled back and gripped his hard hand.

'Yeah, well Ahab will always be Ahab, but who the fuck are you?'

'Adam Stone,' I said.

There was no obvious sign but I sensed a subtle change in his demeanour. 'Stone, eh?' he asked, tilting his head slightly and squinting with one eye. 'Any relation to Theo Stone?'

'Brother.'

'Solomon,' he responded. 'Tamati Solomon. Bad business, your brother. Knew him.' He shook his head and looked at me quizzically. 'Observer too?'

'Scientific rep for the company.'

'Been to the Ross Sea before?'

'Nope.'

He looked me over and his eyes missed nothing. He grunted and said, 'I'll show you to your bunk.'

I followed him aft into the superstructure. The passageway was gleaming white with eight doors along its length. He led me to the furthest aft door and opened it. He stood aside and said, 'Welcome home.'

I went inside and looked around. The *Polar Princess* could carry twenty-four crew plus officers and observers. The cabin was well laid out, with a double bunk bed behind the door, a desk in the far corner and two comfortable chairs. There was a bag on the top bunk so I dropped my duffel on the lower one and turned back to Tamati.

'Who am I sharing with?'

'Finn. Deckhand.'

'Good guy?'

Tamati shrugged. 'He's okay.'

'What about the observers?'

'Not here yet.'

'Know them?'

Tamati paused for a second before answering, 'I hear the local observer's a guy named Martin Malone. I don't know him. The other guy's Phil Coetzee, from South Africa. He's done the trip a few times.'

I raised an eyebrow to invite more information. 'And? That's it?'

Tamati looked at me and then shook his head and turned back down the passageway. 'Head's across the passageway. Mess's below. Captain says we sail at 1600.'

I stuck my head out the doorway and said, 'Hey, Ishmael.' He turned. 'Thanks.'

The observers arrived together just before we sailed. Their berths were in the cabin across the passageway. I heard them talking and stuck my head in their cabin. 'Hey, I'm Adam Stone, the company science rep.'

The bloke nearest the door looked up with an easy grin. 'I'm Martin, the Kiwi observer.' He was slightly built with short brown hair. He nodded at the other man who was stowing his gear in a small locker. 'This is Phil. He's from South Africa, but don't hold that against him just because the Springboks are the rugby world champs.' Phil was taller, bigger, with short hair.

I shook hands with both of them. Phil gripped my hand harder than was necessary. His hand was strong but lacked the calluses I'd gained from months working as a fisherman. I didn't feel like playing his game, so let it ride.

I was on deck with the other crew members who weren't on watch when we let go the lines and eased away from the wharf. The blue sky had given way to grey overcast, brought by the unseasonably cold southerly breeze spilling across the city and into the harbour. It was mid-November but felt like August. A few people had come down to see us off. I was surprised to see Detective Killand standing towards the back of the crowd. Try as I might, I couldn't think of any reason for him to be there. His hands were shoved in his trouser pockets and, from the scowl on his face, I deduced that he still wasn't happy. Neither Emma nor I had told him I was sailing on the *Polar Princess*; as far as I knew, he thought I was pottering in my garden in Auckland.

I idly scanned the other faces and realised that among the half dozen Blue Ocean staff was someone else I recognised. I had to search my memory, but eventually I recalled where I'd seen that lean body and strong face – it was the Russian we'd met in Callaghan's office, the company representative from Vladivostok. I couldn't remember his name, but I was sure it was him. I wondered why a Russian fish importer would come to watch a ship leave port. Part of a hook-to-plate marketing scheme to document the origin of the fish? It seemed unlikely. I didn't think Russian consumers were that discerning. I had plenty of time to speculate as we slowly gathered way and the group on the wharf dispersed, but none of my thoughts were even close to the real reason he'd been there.

CHAPTER 21

I lay in my bunk and eyed the door. The toilet was across the passageway. I decided I didn't need it. Yet.

Even after all these years of going to sea, I usually feel queasy for the first day or so. This was the worst I'd felt in a long time. We'd rounded the headland and turned directly into the teeth of the southerly. The four to five-metre swells, driven by a wind straight from Antarctica, immediately had the *Polar Princess* pitching and rolling uncomfortably. Usually, the motion of the ship was less severe close to land and I had time to adjust to it. There was no time to adjust on this voyage.

Finn was watching videos in the rec room. His bunk was made and his gear was tidy, which was a relief. I hate sharing a cabin with a slob. Before we'd sailed, he'd entered the cabin as I was getting settled and held out a hand. 'Finn, short for Finley.'

'Adam Stone,' I replied.

He looked at me for a moment. 'Related to Theo Stone?'

'Yeah, I'm his brother.'

'Bugger. Sorry.'

I just nodded.

'Been south before?'

'Not to the Ross Sea.'

'Grows on you.'

The conversation petered out and, with a nod, Finn left the cabin. He seemed friendly enough but I sensed a reserve, something left unsaid. Maybe it was the contrast with Tamati's easygoing manner, but from this first impression, I didn't think Finn and I were going to be best mates by the end of the trip.

The voyage quickly settled into a routine. After a day I was used to the motion of the ship and felt fine. The wind dropped and we were soon steaming south through long, rolling swells which made for a much more comfortable motion.

It takes about a week to reach the fishing grounds in the Ross Sea. A ship designed for fishing is a complex, high-maintenance vessel and there was no shortage of tasks for the crew. The observers and I had no assigned duties until the fishing started. Martin and Phil spent most of their time in the rec room watching movies or shooting the shit with some of the guys Phil had sailed with before. I spent my time poking around the ship, talking to the crew, and thinking. It was weird, realising that I might be sleeping in the same bunk Theo had used. I wavered between certainty that what I was doing was necessary, and worrying that I should have let it go and stayed in New Zealand with Emma.

The transit took us eight days. The weather at these latitudes comes from the west or southwest. We were well south when a gale kicked up a choppy southwesterly swell, nothing unusual but it set the ship corkscrewing and slowed us down. I spent more time in my bunk when the ship was rolling – not because I felt bad but because simple activities like putting on your clothes, walking passageways, climbing stairs between decks, even sitting at the dining table, were uncomfortable and tiring. I knew from experience that it's easier to handle bad weather when you have something to do, something to focus on other than the vessel and its motion. I was more than ready for the start of fishing.

Tamati introduced me to some of the crew and I met others when I toured the *Polar Princess*, familiarising myself with the layout and where we'd be working. An observer's job can be lonely. On a good voyage, the officers and crew realise that the work we do contributes to sustainable fishing and they are helpful and supportive. Unfortunately, on some voyages, the crew resent our oversight of their fishing operations and the relationship can deteriorate and become confrontational or threatening. Several observers have disappeared at sea, though foul play has never been proven. One of the reasons Theo's death wasn't regarded as suspicious was his good relationship with the crew.

I had no problems with any of the crew on the *Polar Princess*, except one. For some reason, the bosun, Judd, took exception to me. He was a big man, about my size, with curly brown hair and an unkempt beard hiding a tanned, lined face. There was nothing physical or even directly confrontational that I could respond to, just a constant barrage of snide comments and half-heard conversations that let me know he didn't like me.

I'd been around enough that I was able to ignore his bullshit. He could say what he liked, but I didn't report to him and seldom even had to deal with him. However, a ship is a small place and there was no way I could avoid him altogether. And I was puzzled – was he just an asshole or was there a purpose to his nastiness? I had an ulterior motive for being on the *Polar Princess*. Was it making me paranoid? Was Blue Ocean using Judd to send me a message? Had he been instructed to let me know by his behaviour that he was watching me and everything I did? I eventually decided it didn't matter. I needed to keep my eyes open and look for anything that might shed light on Theo's death. I couldn't let the bosun or anyone else divert me from that task.

Martin was friendly enough, but Phil didn't say ten words to me on the voyage south. I'd never been on a ship with another observer, so didn't know what to expect, but his lack of engagement seemed unusual. Most of us are outgoing by nature. Observers try very hard to convince the officers and crew that we're not there to catch them doing something wrong. But it's almost impossible to entirely erase the us-versus-them attitude, and I was surprised that Phil didn't want to spend more time talking to one of the two people on board he could count on to have his back. I made an effort to communicate for the first few days, but I gave up when it became obvious he wasn't going to respond.

I was talking with Tamati at dinner on the seventh day at sea. We expected to reach the fishing ground the next day and there was an undercurrent of excitement running through the ship. I was having a second cup of coffee while Tamati had a second helping of dessert. By the time he'd finished, we were the only people in the mess. The smell of roast meat and vegetables was still in the air, and we could hear the cook banging pots and pans as he cleaned up in the galley. Tamati leaned back in his chair with a sigh. 'Man, I love that cheesecake.'

I nodded towards his XXL waistline. 'Yeah, and I can see it loves you, too. Those desserts stick around forever.'

Tamati grinned. 'You're just jealous. Your skinny ass wouldn't last ten minutes if you fell overboard. Everybody knows the story about the Icelandic fishing boat that sank. The only survivor was the guy who weighed 115 kilos.'

I laughed and said, 'Yeah, so what? What they don't tell you is he died six months later of heart disease and kidney failure.'

Tamati rubbed his hard belly. 'Maybe. But I bet he thought it was worth it.'

We were quiet for a minute. A metallic crash from the galley signalled the entry of the cutlery into the dishwater. I leaned forward slightly and said, 'Ishmael, can I ask you something?'

He smiled and said, 'Sure, as long as it's not my girlfriend's phone number.'

'No, nothing like that. It's just … I was wondering about one of the observers, Phil. You said you know him, from other voyages.' I played with my coffee cup for a moment before asking, 'Does he seem odd to you? Different? He sees me every day but says fuck-all. I've watched him here in the mess and he talks to the other guys. I don't think I've ever heard him laugh, but he seems to have normal conversations.' I scooted further forward on my chair. 'So what I'm asking, Ishmael, is there something wrong with me? Is that why he won't talk to me?'

Tamati's teeth made a bright flash in his brown face when he grinned. 'There's no doubt there's something wrong with you, but I don't think that's why Phil won't talk to you.' He examined his hands for a second and then said, 'I've been on two other voyages with him. He's an odd bugger. I noticed straight off that he's friendly as anything with the officers and bosun and a couple of the crew that are tight with the bosun. But he's got no time for anyone else. If you watch, I bet you'll see there aren't many other guys he talks to.' Tamati ran his hand over his long hair and added, 'It seemed odd at first but now I guess I'm used to it. It's just the way he is.'

'Thanks, mate,' I said as I stood up. 'It's good to know it's not just me he has a problem with.' I returned my coffee mug to the kitchen and went back to my cabin.

———

Other than becoming familiar with the ship and the crew, there wasn't much I could do on the transit; certainly nothing that would help me understand Theo's death. It didn't take long to learn everyone's name. Once we started fishing, I spent much of my time below decks, analysing the fish chosen for sampling and recording the results. I worked alongside the guys in the fish processing factory, but because we were all so busy I didn't get to know them well. It was the deck crew that I became more familiar with, the men I saw when I took a break or went on deck to watch the recovery of a set or to release a tagged fish. On deck, I had time to share a joke or a story with Roger, Gabriel, Jason, Finn and Levi. And they told me about their families and girlfriends and the Ross Sea.

On the transit, I made an effort to be on deck most mornings and evenings. Once we started fishing my free time would be much more restricted. I loved watching the sunrise and sunset at sea. It seemed both simpler and more dramatic because there were no landmarks, no hills or mountains or tall buildings. One minute the sun was there, the next it wasn't. I found the everyday act of an orange ball appearing or disappearing strangely therapeutic. Even on overcast days, I enjoyed seeing the line between the ocean and the sky form or vanish as the light waxed or waned. On a clear evening, I always looked for the green flash, a green spot briefly visible above the sun. I saw it once, long ago, but now my memory is uncertain – that is, I remember I saw it but not what it looked like. I tried not to think about how many other events in my life suffered a similar fate.

I was also fascinated by the diversity of life at sea. I'm no expert but even I could tell that the Southern Ocean was rewarding me with a new variety of birds on this trip.

I kept in touch with Emma via the GPS satellite communicator as arranged. This device used the Iridium satellite network to send and receive texts and emails. We had agreed that I would send a message at least every other day so Emma would know I was all right, or more frequently if I saw anything I needed to tell her. It was a tenuous link and I had little useful to report, other than the behaviour of Judd and Phil Coetzee. She wasn't able to share anything more than a brief summary of what she was doing, but it was enough to assure me that she was okay.

———

We arrived at our first fishing ground a few days before the start of the season. We were fortunate – we appeared to have the area to ourselves, there were no other vessels in sight or on the radar. We spent those days using the echo sounder to map the seafloor morphology and look for habitat where toothfish might be found.

Occasionally the ship would stop among the icebergs. This was my first experience of the quiet of the Antarctic. The ice provided shelter and there was no wind, no sound. If I spotted a bird or a whale or a seal it was also silent, adding to the eerie effect. At this latitude in December it never gets dark, something else I hadn't experienced before. Sitting in silence at midnight, watching the soft twilight play on the faces of the icebergs, made me feel both very small and very connected to the world around me.

Modern longlining for toothfish is simple in concept, a very large version of the set lines commonly used near shore. The ship deploys a line (the backbone), often many kilometres long, with baited hooks on short lines (snoods) at about one-and-a-half metre intervals. Fish are attracted to the bait, are caught by the hooks and are brought on board the fishing vessel when the longline is recovered. The *Polar Princess* and similar vessels use sophisticated technology to automate many of the fishing processes.

The backbone and hooks are stored in magazines, each typically holding a thousand hooks on 1.5 kilometres of line. The hooks are baited automatically by a machine as the line is deployed. Anchors are attached at each end of the backbone to keep it near the bottom. Downlines connect the anchors to buoys that float at the surface and allow the vessel to find and recover the longline after it's been deployed. The buoys can have lights, poles, a radio or a GPS location system to make it easier to find them, especially at night or in rough seas.

The *Polar Princess* slowed for the start of the first set. It was early in the season and the ice cover was extensive. We were fishing in the northern part of the fishing ground in about one thousand metres of water. The fishing set began by deploying a buoy line and anchor. Roger stood at the stern rail, ready to throw the floats overboard. They were hard floats with a light, flag and GPS unit attached. The first mate stood beside him, holding his walkie-talkie. This close to the ice there was almost no swell and the *Polar Princess* rumbled quietly beneath our feet as she continued on a course parallel to the ice edge.

I am always excited at the start of fishing. I'd put on my cold weather gear and stood on deck, out of the way of the fishing activities but able to watch what was going on. I get great pleasure from seeing skilled seamen making a tricky job seem easy. To port the icebergs stood among the fast ice, taller than the ship, translucent blue against the clear pale sky. To starboard, smaller bergs and brash ice stretched to the horizon. The reinforced hull of the *Polar Princess* easily pushed these fragments out of our path, leaving a ribbon of clear water in our wake.

The walkie-talkie squawked and the mate looked up and nodded and Roger pushed the buoys over the edge of the stainless steel chute. The downline unspooled smoothly as the buoys fell behind, bright

orange dots on the blue-black ocean. It took about ten minutes to let
out 1.5 kilometres of line, enough to allow the weights to settle to the
bottom and the buoys to stay on the surface regardless of the tides and
currents. While the downline fed out Roger and Gabriel made sure the
chain and anchor were attached to it and that the first segment of the
backbone was ready to be deployed. They stood clear as the last of the
downline pulled the chain and anchor rattling and clanking over the
stern, to drop with a splash straight into the icy water, dragging the
backbone with them.

As the vessel steamed ahead the backbone and hooks were pulled
through the automatic baiting machine and over the chute into the
water. The backbone was weighted so that it sank quickly, minimising
the time the baited hooks might attract seabirds. A few albatross soared
off the port side, cruising the ice edge, unaware of the steady stream of
tasty morsels flowing from the ship. Any birds that approached the
ship were deterred by streamers that trailed in the water over the area
where the baited hooks were still visible.

The first set was a short one, only a few kilometres long. As the
first magazine was emptied, Tamati connected the backbone to the line
in the next magazine and the deployment continued. The ship and crew
moved more slowly than normal on this first set, ensuring that the
equipment and gear were working smoothly and re-establishing the
routines for safe operations.

As the end of line approached, Roger and Gabriel prepared another
anchor and chain. They connected them by a downline to another set of
floats, similar to those deployed at the start of the line. When the end
of the backbone appeared they quickly attached the anchor and chain
and let the lot go down the chute. Ten minutes later, they watched the
buoys splash into the water and drop slowly astern. The mate spoke
into his walkie-talkie, telling the officer on the bridge to mark the
position of the end of the set. It had taken over an hour to deploy the
first line. As they got back into their routine the crew would be able to
lay a much longer line in the same time.

We let this set stay on the bottom for twelve hours before hauling it
aboard. While we waited the crew deployed three more sets.

When we returned to start recovery of the first set, the wind had shifted and caused the free ice to move across the line, making location and recovery of the set difficult. After careful navigation among the icebergs and the jumbled blocks and slushy clumps between them, the captain spotted the buoys from the bridge and slowly manoeuvred the ship until they were close off the starboard side. The recovery room, a large watertight room five metres long and open to the sea, was just for'ard of midships, below the main deck, several metres above the surface of the water. With the fishing gear and fish coming in over the side it was understandably a wet place, and the waves could sweep right through the room, engulfing the men working there with near-freezing sea water. That exposure to the ocean was why it was watertight, keeping the sea from entering the rest of the ship.

Jason had the best arm and was poised with a grapple and line. When the buoys were close he twirled the grapple briefly and hurled it towards them. The grapple hooks caught the downline and Jason quickly began to haul it in. When the buoys reached the side, two other deckhands grabbed the grapple line and helped him lift the buoys onto the deck. They quickly ran the downline through the main hauler and began to recover it. It took about thirty minutes for the chain and anchor to appear at the end of the rope. Two deckhands took them off the line, connected the backbone to the secondary hauler, and recovery of the backbone began.

The main hauler lifted the hooks and line from the seafloor and pulled them over a side roller and into the recovery room. Finn and Levi stood on either side of the main hauler, each with a long gaff in their hands. The backbone emerged steadily from the water, the first few hooks depressingly bare. Then the first toothfish appeared and the work began. Antarctic toothfish can grow to be more than 1.7 metres long and weigh more than 130 kilos. They are solid, heavy-bodied fish, dark grey in colour.

I looked over the side and saw several fish coming up through the water. The first fish was large, almost 1.5 metres. As it reached the surface Finn used the gaff to bring it on board and took it off the hook.

He put it in the stainless steel tray, where he cut its throat before shoving it down the chute to the processing line below decks.

From the recovery room, the hooks and line continued through the hook cleaner and secondary hauler to the room where they were reloaded onto the magazines. The recovery of the line was slower than its deployment, but it proceeded smoothly once the crew established a rhythm. It was a good haul, with more fish than bare hooks coming over the side. Once the line was recovered and the buoys and anchor were on board, the *Polar Princess* changed course and headed to the next set.

————

The next few weeks were more of the same: fish, eat, sleep, repeat. As the company science rep, I was on board to help the observers stay on top of the data recording. They were on twelve-hour watches, midnight to noon and noon to midnight. Instead of a fixed watch, I was on duty whenever I was required, usually at the end of a set. CCAMLR rules require observers to record a wide range of information about the voyage, the fish and the marine environment. The observers and I documented the fishing gear configuration, details of the fishing operations, catch composition, measurements of target and bycatch species, details of fish tagging, and vessel sightings. We only saw one other vessel during the voyage: a Korean longliner.

Most of my time was spent near the processing line: sampling, measuring, and dissecting the catch, and tagging fish for release. There is a requirement to dissect 1 per cent of the catch and, when the fishing was good, this was a large number of fish. The workload varied depending on the timing of the recovery of the sets and the success of the catch, but I was usually buggered by the time I fell into my bunk.

I often talked with Tamati during or after our watches. He was not well educated but was very well informed, and he held his own on discussions of just about anything. I particularly enjoyed our lively disagreements on politics, social justice, or rugby. Having a mate on a long voyage makes time pass quickly.

———

It happened very fast. It was about 2 a.m., but it never gets very dark at that time of year and visibility was good. The sea had come up a bit, swells about two metres, and the wind was blowing force 6, lashing the wave tops into foam. Clouds blew across the sky, whipped away to the east. The ship was lively beneath my feet, rolling and pitching a bit as we proceeded slowly close to the wind. The spotlights on the hauling deck made the heaving waves look silver-black as they rolled by the ship. The ice pack to starboard gleamed dully in the morning light.

We'd recovered two sets during the night and had just started recovery of a third. I had caught up with the dissection from those sets and decided to get some fresh air and watch the next set come on board. I went to the recovery deck, greeting the fishermen hauling the line as I entered. Tamati gave me a grin and Gabriel nodded a greeting, while both kept working at a steady pace. I was well out of the way, standing at the rear of the recovery deck, watching the backbone slowly lift dripping out of the ocean. Despite the weather, we were largely sheltered from the wind. Most of the spray from the waves flew aft, past me, but enough came aboard to keep my face wet. I wiped the salt water from my eyes and saw a toothfish emerge from the sea.

Its grey body glistened like steel in the harsh artificial light and it hung slackly as Gabriel caught it in the gills with his gaff and lifted it towards the deck. I looked down over the side and saw two empty hooks following the fish. Gabriel expertly took the fish off the hook, cut its throat and passed it through a chute and down to the factory. The backbone stretched as taut as a banjo string from the main hauler through the secondary hauler, dripping sea water as it passed over the recovery deck.

The first empty hook passed over the side and through the haulers to the magazine room. The second had just reached the side when I felt a vicious shove from behind. Taken unawares I staggered forward, towards the main hauler. Instinctively I raised my hand to steady myself, bracing against the rail near the main hauler. The next thing I knew the bare hook had penetrated my clothes, buried itself in my left biceps and was dragging me across the deck towards the secondary hauler. Toothfish are large fish and the hooks are seriously big, about eight centimetres long, with a gap between the shaft and the barb of about six centimetres. The hook went through my clothing and the barb was firmly embedded in my arm. But it wasn't the hook that concerned me; it was where it was dragging me.

I was frantic, but helpless. I couldn't get the hook out – even if I could get a grip on it the pull of the line ensured it would stay buried in my arm. And if I couldn't get the hook out then I was going to be dragged into the secondary hauler, in which case my arm would be crushed, or I could even be killed. My boots skidded on the wet deck as I desperately tried to do something – anything – that would save me. My arm was centimetres from the hauler when it stopped.

I looked around and realised that Tamati had hit the emergency stop button. Once he was sure the power to the haulers was off he moved swiftly to my side and put a big arm around my shoulders. 'Fuck, Adam,' he said. 'What are you trying to do? Lose your arm?'

'I just wanted to get a close look at what you're doing. Part of the observer's job, making sure the safety gear's working.'

Tamati reached into his pocket, pulled out his big folding knife and sliced through the snood connecting the hook to the backbone. As soon as I was free I shrugged off his arm and stepped shakily back from the line. I was in shock and couldn't feel the big hook. I started to tremble and said, 'I feel a little cold. I think I should go below for a few minutes.'

The emergency stop had triggered an alarm on the bridge and as I said this Captain Kennicott appeared on the recovery deck. He glanced angrily around the deck and said, 'What the fuck's going on?'

Tamati stepped forward and gestured towards me. 'Adam slipped and got a hook in his arm. I stopped the haul and cut him loose.'

The captain looked at the shaft of the hook protruding from between the fingers of my right hand. 'Right. Tamati, take Adam below. I'll send the mate down in a minute to see to that arm. You, Gabriel, you're on the primary hauler now.' He nodded to Finn, who had also run to the recovery room to see what had happened. 'And you,

you'll take over on the gaff.' He brought his walkie-talkie to his lips and said, 'Peters? All clear now. Reset the system. And once you've done that get the first aid box and go below to the mess. Stone's got a hook in his arm.' He clicked off the walkie-talkie without waiting for a reply. 'Anything else?' he asked and when everyone was silent he said, 'Then get back to work. We've got fish to catch.'

I sat on one of the padded benches in the mess room and waited for the mate. Tamati stood nearby, eyeing me speculatively. 'Ship was a little bouncy,' he said.

'Yes.'

'Nothing special, though.'

'Nope.'

'Deck was wet.'

'Yes.'

'Just clumsy?'

I hesitated. 'Probably. But getting shoved in the back may have contributed.'

Tamati raised an eyebrow and didn't say anything, so I continued, 'I was pushed. Hard. Into the line. I didn't even have time to think when it happened. But when you turned off the hauler I turned to look and there was no one there. The door behind me was open but there was no one there.'

'Someone doesn't like you.'

'Seems not.'

'Any idea who?'

I was silent for a while. 'It wasn't hands. I wasn't pushed with hands. I was shoulder-charged.'

'Damn, that was banned by the rugby board in 2006.'

I gave Tamati a long look. 'Yeah, whatever. But it was high up, just below my neck. Not many jokers could hit me high in my back with their shoulder.'

Tamati thought for a moment. 'Judd?'

'Dunno. He doesn't like me. But that doesn't mean he'd try to injure me.' We were both silent.

Then Peters entered the mess and plonked the first aid box on the table. He looked at my arm and said, 'Jesus, Stone, what have you done?'

I glanced at Tamati and shrugged. 'Slipped, I guess.'

Peters opened the box and rummaged inside for bandages and antiseptic and needle-nosed pliers. 'Silly bugger. Lucky all you got was a fishhook in your arm.'

Tamati stood and turned towards the door. 'I'll get back to work.' He gave me the thumbs up behind Peters' back as he left the mess.

Peters helped me remove my storm gear and jersey so he could get at the hook. He cleaned the area with alcohol and turned my arm this way and that, looking at it in different light. Finally, he took the pliers and gripped the shank of the hook. 'This is going to hurt,' he said.

He was right. I knew he was going to be right. Because of the barb, there's no way to pull a hook back out of flesh. The only way to remove it is to push it all the way through, cut off the barb, and then pull the shank out. It hurt like stink. I gritted my teeth and it was all I could do to hold my arm still while Peters did his work. I watched the point emerge from my skin. I wasn't aware that my entire body had tensed until I felt my muscles relax when he snipped off the barb. I felt hot and clammy and wished like hell I knew who had pushed me.

Peters dressed my wound and I flexed my arm as he repacked the first aid box. It was sore but the intense pain had faded.

'Thanks,' I said. 'Guess I'll get back to work, too.'

'Don't be a hero, Adam. If that gets infected, then you'll be in the shit. I'll change the dressing tomorrow.'

'No worries. This isn't the first time I've had a hook removed. I'll keep a close eye on it.' Peters disappeared up to the bridge and I grabbed a hot scone from the kitchen on the way back to the processing line.

CHAPTER 22

My arm healed quickly. If the incident in the recovery room had been an attempt on my life, then it had failed. If it was meant as a warning, then it was a roaring success. The accident made me more aware of my surroundings, more alert whenever I left my cabin. While I was healing I spent more time on the foredeck, watching the ice and the birds and the ocean and the sky. There was something about the light in the Ross Sea that I never tired of. When the sun was out everything looked brighter or sharper or clearer than normal. When it was cloudy, or the mist came down, then there was an air of mystery in the light, a sense of hidden wonders just out of sight. I understood why people who'd come here once wanted to keep coming back.

By this time I knew everyone on the ship, but, except for Tamati, we weren't friends. From the moment I'd met Tamati, I'd felt a connection, and I was pretty sure he felt it too. I was no closer to figuring out what had happened to Theo, but I was certain that Tamati had had no part in it. He was big and rough and a damned good seaman, and I was sure killing people wasn't part of his code.

Tamati would sometimes join me on the foredeck and we'd have desultory conversations, or sometimes just sit and look at the view. One day I asked him, 'How'd you get into fishing, anyway?'

'I'm Ngāti Mutunga, bro. It's what we do.' When he saw me

looking blankly at him he said, 'The Chatham Islands. I'm from the Chatham Islands. My family's been fishing and crayfishing for generations.' He gave a small smile and added, 'I guess I didn't learn much at school, but I learned heaps on the boats.' He raised his chin in enquiry, 'What about you?'

I laughed and said, 'Jacques Cousteau.' It was his turn to look blank. 'You're probably too young. Or, did you even have television on the islands?' I laughed again and ducked his swing. 'Seriously, there was this French guy on television. He sailed all over the world studying the oceans and fish and shit. My parents taped every one of his shows. We watched those programmes together, seems like a hundred times. He made the oceans look pretty cool, so that's what I did.'

'You chose your career based on some TV star?' He shook his head incredulously. 'Your brother, too, huh?'

I lost the smile and said, 'Yeah, my brother, too. Do you have any brothers and sisters?'

'Two sisters and a brother. All older. They're why I come to sea, bro!' he said with a grin.

———

As the summer progressed the pack ice retreated and we worked our way south, deeper into the Ross Sea. The icebergs provided an ever-changing backdrop to our operations: large ones, small ones, flat ones, pointy ones, funny-shaped ones – the variety was endless. I hadn't sailed in ice before and it took some time to get used to the noise. At first, we were in slush ice and small chunks of ice that slithered and clunked along the hull. As we got closer to icebergs we encountered larger blocks of ice that were much louder, banging and clanking along the hull as though we were sailing through a scrapyard.

The captain was cautious. He wasn't afraid to drive the *Polar Princess* through the ice, but he knew we were not an icebreaker and kept us well clear of serious trouble. In the past, some captains had pushed the envelope too far and had become stuck in the ice. As recently as 2015, an Australian fishing boat had been trapped and had to be rescued by an American icebreaker.

I never forgot why I was on the *Polar Princess* and watched every step of the fishing process, from deploying the line to putting the frozen fish in the hold. Everything we did seemed ordinary; I saw nothing even remotely unusual – unless you count fishing in one of the most amazing places in the world unusual. There was nothing that even remotely suggested a motive for Theo's death.

Sometimes, when I was outside, I'd lean against one of the six black boxes lashed to the foredeck. They were large, heavy-duty black plastic boxes with lights on rods sticking out of their tops. I asked Tamati what they were and he said they'd been told they were buoys, part of a global research programme into ocean circulation. He said Blue Ocean had volunteered to deploy them in the Ross Sea. 'Wow,' I said, 'that's bloody generous. I bet there aren't many opportunities to get buoys taken down here. Do you know what happens to them?'

'Nope. I guess they wash up somewhere eventually. We've been putting them over the side for the last three seasons.'

'Huh. I didn't get the impression that Blue Ocean was that philanthropic. Life is full of surprises.' In my next message to Emma, I mentioned the boxes and the beauty of the icebergs in our fishing area.

———

Towards the end of the trip, we were heading northeast, towards the Bounty Islands, as the *Polar Princess* had done when Theo disappeared. We'd had a good voyage, caught lots of fish. Once again, the captain wanted to finish the trip by targeting toothfish inside New Zealand's fishing zone.

We had our first real storm on that transit. We'd had some bad weather on the run south but nothing like this. The wind was force 9, a strong gale. It blew from the southwest without hindrance for hundreds, maybe thousands of kilometres. Eight-metre swells marched with it, spray blown from their crests by the furious wind. The birds that had accompanied us for most of the trip disappeared.

The captain turned the *Polar Princess* to head into the wind and we rode it out the best we could. Occasionally the ship would hit a wave, driving through it rather than riding over it, and the whole hull would shudder as if it had been struck by a giant hammer, the reverberation rolling up and down the ship for many seconds. No one was allowed on deck unless it was necessary for the safety of the vessel.

The *Polar Princess* was designed for weather like this. The storm wasn't dangerous, but it was certainly uncomfortable. Any movement through the ship required both hands to hang onto the rails along the passageways and stairs. You could find yourself climbing steeply along a passageway one minute as she fought her way up a wave, and the next almost running forward as she pitched bow-first down its back.

I'd gone to the mess for dinner, and when I returned to my cabin I opened the door and stopped abruptly when I saw Phil Coetzee on his knees in front of my bag. His head turned around to look over his shoulder at me, a look of surprise on his face. I could just see my Garmin communicator in his hands. 'What the fuck are you doing?' I said angrily. I stepped into the cabin and shut the door. 'Get out of my stuff!' I moved close to him and tried to grab the communicator.

I saw a look of fear flash in his eyes before he wrenched the communicator back and stood up to face me, his back to the bunk, fear replaced with triumph. 'You're fucked, Stone,' he said. 'You are so fucked.'

My anger was still building and I lunged for the communicator again, but it was a small space and he easily evaded my grip. His feet were firmly braced against the bunk and the next thing I knew he threw himself against me, knocking me off my feet and into the cabin door. The ship rolled and I slid down the door and lay looking up at him. I was so surprised that I stayed there for a second, unmoving, trying to figure out what was going on.

Phil stepped back and held up the Garmin. 'I see you've been spying on us. Telling everything to your girlfriend.' He flipped his finger to scroll through the messages. 'But there's nothing to tell, is there? Everything's hunky-dory on board the *Polar Princess*.'

'You bastard,' I said as I tried to get to my feet. But he kicked my legs out and I fell back to the deck.

'Unfortunately for you, devices like this are strictly prohibited by company policy. We can't have anyone giving away our fishing locations, can we?'

This time I got to my feet and stood with my back to the door. I wasn't injured; only my pride was hurt. Phil was about my height, but I had at least six kilos on him and I knew I could put him down. But that wasn't what I wanted, that would be no help at all.

I cursed myself for being so careless, so thoughtless. How could I have left the Garmin in a place where it could be found so easily? Admittedly, it was a small cabin with few options, but I should have found a better place than under my socks. Our whole plan rested on me being able to observe what happened on board the *Polar Princess* without anyone knowing that I was reporting back to Emma. Now that Phil knew what I was doing, our plan was blown.

'Fuck you. Since when did you become a stooge for Blue Ocean? Just give me the damned thing.'

He held it for a moment longer and then tossed it to me. 'It's all yours, Stone. For now. We'll see what the captain says when I tell him what you've been up to.'

I eyed him closely and shook my head. 'I don't get it. Why were you searching my stuff?' I held up the Garmin. 'You read the messages. You know I didn't say anything about fishing. All I'm trying to do is find out what happened to my brother. Why were you snooping? Why do you care?'

He smiled grimly. 'Maybe I'm nosy. Maybe I just don't like you.' The smile vanished and he went to the door, opened it and stepped into the passageway. I heard his footsteps recede towards the bow of the ship.

I looked at the communicator in genuine puzzlement. Okay, I shouldn't have had one, and sending messages to Emma was probably, strictly speaking, against company policy, but there had been nothing important to report for the entire voyage. I checked the call register and went back through the mundane messages I'd sent – weather, life on the ship, snapshots of the officers and crew, fishing operations, the buoy experiment, food, seabirds – nothing remotely related to Theo's death.

I put the communicator back in my bag – there was no point in hiding it now – and lay on my bunk, wondering if there was any point in continuing our plan. I was angry with myself for being so stupid. Callaghan and the others might have suspected that I wasn't just on the *Polar Princess* for "closure", but the discovery of my communicator certainly confirmed it. I lay with these negative thoughts swirling through my head for what seemed a long time, until Tamati burst into the room and shouted, 'Adam! Get up! You've got to get out of here!'

He crossed the cabin in one long stride, pulled my immersion suit down from the shelf where it was stored and tossed it on the deck. By this time I'd swung my feet to the floor and was sitting on my bunk, staring blankly at this Maori hurricane. 'Ishmael! Hey! What the fuck? What's going on?'

'Adam, there's no time. Get off your bunk and into this suit. Don't think, don't ask questions, just do it.' I had no idea what was going on, and getting into my immersion suit made no sense, but I knew Tamati well enough to realise that I should listen to what he said, had to trust him. So I dropped to the deck and started struggling into the suit.

Safety requirements stipulated that everyone on board was issued with an immersion suit and that we all practised using them as part of the regular safety drills. Immersion suits are a type of dry suit intended for emergencies. They are made from neoprene and provide insulation from the cold of the water if you end up in the ocean. They fully cover the hands, feet and head, and although they are designed for fast and easy donning, I've always struggled to get one on.

I probably can't multitask as well as Emma, but I can talk and put on an immersion suit at the same time. As I pulled the bright orange suit up my legs I said, 'Ishmael, talk to me. What the fuck's going on? Why am I getting into this suit? There's been no alarm.'

Tamati reached down and helped me get my arm into a sleeve. 'I overheard Phil talking with Judd. Something about you spying on the ship? A satellite communicator? Judd asked if you'd mentioned the boxes on deck in your messages, and when Phil said yes, Judd went off his nut.' Tamati helped me with the other sleeve and added, 'He went ballistic. He said he was going to kill you, that there would be no mistake this time, that your body would never be found. He was fucking scary, man. I ran straight here. You've got to get ready.'

'Wait, wait. That's scary all right, but why do I have to put this suit on? I'll go to the captain and tell him what's happening. He won't let Judd kill somebody.'

'Fuck, Adam, that's just it. Didn't I tell you? The captain was there! He agreed with Judd.'

A stab of fear shot through me and I was unable to draw the hood over my head. Phil had been right. I was fucked, I was so fucked.

———

I hate the Safety at Sea refresher courses. One of the requirements for observers is that every three years we have to go through one of these courses. The classroom work covers what you'd expect: flares, fire extinguishers, communications and so on. Then there are the practical exercises in the pool: floating, swimming and huddling in a group, tying knots underwater, boarding a life raft. The courses have a very simple, though unspoken, message – don't fall overboard.

It's the practical exercises that I hate. Not because they're hard, but because I get cold after being in the water for a few hours. I look forward to donning our immersion suits and floating around the pool because it's the only time I'm warm.

I'd never worn an immersion suit in water this cold. Most swimming pools are in the low-to-mid-twenties. We were north of the Ross Sea and although it was midsummer the water was still no more than 12° C. Swimmers can train for water this cold, but I hadn't trained for it. I *wished* I'd trained for it. I wished I was an Olympic swimmer. If I were an Olympic swimmer, then I wouldn't be a fishery observer and Theo probably wouldn't have been an observer, and I wouldn't have ended up here. But I wasn't an Olympic swimmer, and there was a good chance that I'd be out in the ocean for a long time. I tried not to think of it as "the rest of my life", but it was in the back of my mind.

Technically I didn't fall in – Tamati tossed me overboard. I'd broken the unspoken rule of my survival courses and abandoned a perfectly good, seaworthy vessel. In the end, the choice wasn't hard. If I stayed on board, I would die. If I went overboard, I would *probably* die. The difference might be only semantics, or it might be everything.

I finally got into the suit and Tamati helped me to my feet. 'Topside,' he said without explanation, then opened the door and headed down the passageway. I looked at my bag and could just see the communicator lying on top of my clothes. I wanted to send a message to Emma telling her what was happening, but it was too late. I could never operate the communicator with the immersion suit gloves on, and from what Tamati said, I had no time to take them off. I tore my gaze from my duffel bag and shuffled awkwardly behind him, struggling to keep the wild motion of the ship from throwing me off my feet.

We passed through the hatch and emerged onto the foredeck. The *Polar Princess* was headed into the wind and it hit us like an insane force, thrusting us back against the bridge structure. It shrieked, it howled, it pinned us like bugs against the cold steel. A single light on the front of the bridge shone down on us, the rain like silver tracer rounds blowing horizontally into our faces. Through the driving rain we saw four of the crew struggling with the black boxes that had been lashed to the deck. I was pretty sure one of them was Finn, but I couldn't tell who the others were. I saw only two boxes; the others must have already gone over the side. For a second I wondered why they were deploying buoys in this storm, but I had no time to ponder the answer.

Tamati was dressed in his usual singlet and canvas trousers, with a dark blue watch cap straining to contain his long hair. He was instantly soaked to the skin. We levered ourselves upright and staggered toward the port side, holding onto the safety rail along the front of the bridge structure. We were nearly there when, over the noise of the wind and waves, I heard a shout behind us. Turning, I saw Judd and Phil emerge from the hatch. Both wore heavy jerseys; neither had taken time to don storm gear. Judd was the first to see us. He yelled something that disappeared in the gale, grabbed Phil's arm and pointed in our direction. The rain slicked down his curly hair and ran off his beard. His fishing knife was in his hand and, even in this uncertain light, I saw the gleam of anticipation in his eye when he spotted me.

A wave suddenly rolled the ship to port and my feet slipped on the streaming deck. I slammed into Tamati and together we slid across the deck, fighting to stay upright, almost upright, and together we crashed into the port rail. We spun during the slide and I ended up outboard of Tamati and hit the rail first. The impact knocked the wind from me and I was trapped between Tamati's body and the rail. I couldn't move, couldn't think. I thought I heard Tamati shout, 'Man fucking overboard,' but the sound of the storm was tremendous and I may have been mistaken. The next thing I knew I was flying through the air, over the rail and towards the ocean below.

I fell for what seemed like forever, but was probably no more than a second. I hit the water on my back, shoulders first. I didn't sink far. One of the benefits of immersion suits is their buoyancy. In no time I was back on the surface, though this was a mixed blessing as the ocean was so rough that my face and mouth were immediately buried in spray. I gasped and flailed my arms, struggling to get onto my back and point my head as well as I could into the oncoming waves. I willed myself to relax, to flow with the waves, but it was impossible. I didn't turn on my emergency light beacon as the last thing I wanted was to be seen by someone on the *Polar Princess*, someone who was trying to kill me.

For a few minutes I could still see the ship. She didn't have many deck lights on, but there were enough to see Tamati, Judd and Phil standing at the rail, looking at the ocean, searching for me. The wind and waves quickly pushed me towards the stern. I turned my face away from them so they couldn't see it as a pale blob against the dark sea and watched the stern lights fade in the rain and blowing spume. There was no one at the stern rail. I watched the last light disappear with a tiny sense of relief and an enormous sense of dread.

There were no stars, no moon, no light to illuminate the ocean. I sensed the waves by the tilt and roll of my body, but it was never enough to coordinate my breathing with their passage. I gasped in air when I could and tried not to drown in between. The wind was fierce and blew spray off every wave. I unrolled the transparent face covering attached to the hood and fastened it in place with difficulty. It's remarkable how hard it is to do simple things when you're wearing boots and gloves inside a washing machine.

I had no real idea of the passage of time. It is difficult to describe my feelings once the adrenalin wore off, when the shock of falling and the panic of coping with the wild seas had passed. I had never felt such desolation. I had never felt so alone. Part of me – a large part of me – wanted to give up. What was the point? There was no hope. I was in the ocean, hundreds of kilometres from land, and the only vessel nearby had people on it who wanted to kill me. I could struggle as much as I liked but it would only prolong the inevitable. Eventually, I would tire. Eventually, I would sink. Eventually, I would die.

Fear is difficult to maintain for long. The flight response releases a flood of hormones that raise the heart and breathing rates, constrict the peripheral blood vessels, increase the blood flow to vital organs and muscles. But the supply of these hormones is limited and once they are exhausted, the body functions return to normal, usually leaving a feeling of deep fatigue.

I struggled over a nasty wave and was surprised to realise that I was no longer afraid. I was worried and uncomfortable and tired, but not afraid. People had tried to kill me, but I was still alive. There was nothing to run away from, which was just as well because I had no place to run to.

Despair, however, is different. Despair sits like an icy blanket on your heart. It doesn't weaken, it doesn't go away. It eats away at you like acid, making every action, every decision harder. But the spark of hope is hard to extinguish, and it's remarkable what the mind and body can adapt to. Fighting for breath, fighting to stay on my back, fighting the waves, straining to see in the darkness, fighting when there are no expectations, this became my new normal.

Most of my thoughts were devoted to the immediate needs of survival, but I did have time to think of the irony of my situation. We'd gone to great lengths to have a safety net in case I needed it, but none of us had considered that my emergency might be falling overboard. I pictured the communicator again and wished I'd been able to notify Emma or Nigel. But even if I had been able to send a message, what could the *Storm Petrel* do? I was a speck in the ocean; a black, violent, vast ocean. They might as well look for a grain of sand on the beach.

After what seemed like two lifetimes I was starting to feel the cold. It wasn't bad yet, but my body felt a definite clammy chill. I rose to the top of a particularly large wave and opened my mouth to grab a breath as I had done a thousand times before. But this time I saw a light flashing about a hundred metres in front of me. Or was it a light? I dropped into the wave trough and lost sight of it. My mind was growing sluggish and thoughts seemed to take forever. I'd only had a glimpse through rain and flying spray. Was it possible for a light to be here? Were my eyes playing tricks after so long in pitch darkness? Was I going crazy? I rode over another three waves before I saw the light again. The bearing and distance were about the same.

I dropped into a trough. I had no idea what a light was doing in the Southern Ocean, but even with my diminished mental faculties, it didn't take long to decide that whatever it was it offered more possibilities than my present situation. I turned so my head was pointing in the direction in which I'd seen the light and began an awkward backstroke. The waves broke into my face and breathing was even more difficult than before, but that hardly bothered me. The flame of hope flared slightly brighter and fuelled my struggles.

I swam for what seemed an eternity, at least half an eternity, before spinning around again and searching for the light. I was closer now and didn't have to be raised as high by the waves to see it. I'd missed the course by a few degrees and had to aim more to the right. It was still pitch black and other than the wildly swinging light I couldn't see anything; I couldn't make out what the light was attached to.

I adjusted my course and continued to backstroke. As I got closer, I was able to turn slightly and look over my shoulder and alter course until I was close. I was less than five metres from the light when I saw that it was attached to the top of a rod sticking up from a large black box – one of the black boxes I'd seen on the foredeck of the *Polar Princess*. The rod was a metre long. About fifty centimetres of the box was above the water. The motion of the box was sluggish, ignoring the smaller waves entirely.

I finally got close enough to touch it. It was hard black plastic, an industrial case – made to house a scientific buoy, I'd been told. The rod was in the centre of the top of the box. I grabbed it and pulled myself forward. The box was about a metre square, not big enough to lie on but big enough to get my head and upper body out of the water. Holding onto the box I felt immediate relief. I was no longer fighting for every breath, no longer working to keep my position in the stormy waves. The box sank under my weight until it was almost awash, but those precious few centimetres made all the difference between unrelenting struggle and relative ease. Waves still broke over me, the wind still drove spray into my face, but they were sporadic rather than relentless.

I looked more closely at the rod and saw that it was something functional, more than just a support for the light, probably an antenna. My mind had time to think again, to think about more than surviving the next wave, and the sense of dread began to ease.

It wasn't recognition of where the box came from that kindled my hope. It was the thought that a light and an antenna meant these boxes were meant to be recovered. I had no idea what vessel might recover them, and it seemed unlikely that buoys would be recovered soon after deployment, but hope isn't rational. I knew that if I could hold on long enough then I might survive. How long "enough" might be didn't matter. I managed to get most of my body onto the box by huddling in the foetal position around the antenna.

And I held on. I was utterly exhausted by the time I found the box. Much of me was out of the water, but nevertheless I felt the cold deepen and spread. Immersion suits are very good, but they can only slow down the loss of heat, not prevent it altogether. I held off sleep for as long as I could, but even the tossing of the waves and lashing of the spray couldn't keep me awake forever. The first time I fell asleep I woke as my body began to slip off the box. I snapped out a hand and grabbed the antenna and hauled myself back. The next time I fell asleep I woke when my head went under water. I gasped and inhaled a wave and thrashed until I was on my back with some semblance of control. I hadn't drifted far from the box. However, my fatigue was noticeable; my arms and legs were leaden and it was all I could do to paddle the few metres back to it.

I hauled myself up and huddled once again on top of the box. I felt disembodied, drifting in and out of consciousness. I was feeling cold; I wasn't feeling anything. I tried to think of tropical islands, sandy beaches, palm trees. But try as I might all I could think of was the frozen waste of Antarctica. I thought of Amundsen and Scott, trudging to the Pole. I tried very hard not to think of Scott.

As the boundary between dreams and reality began to fade I sensed a body lying down behind me and wrapping me in its arms. Emma. I could smell her hair and feel the warmth of her body along my back. I felt her hands encompass mine and close tightly on the antenna. A sense of contentment washed through me. If Emma was here then everything would be all right. If Emma was here then I would survive.

CHAPTER 23

At some deep level, I sensed a rhythmic thumping. Low, steady. Drums? Drums made no more sense than Emma lying behind me, but I was beyond making sense. It was still pitch black, the waves still tossed me like a cork, but the wind had dropped from a banshee scream to a wild howl. I struggled to regain consciousness. I didn't want to be conscious, to acknowledge the cold, the rain, the waves, the fear – but something deep inside dragged me back. I forced my eyes open. I saw my hands clutched around a metal rod, but I couldn't feel them. I knew I was lying on my side, but I couldn't feel my legs or my feet.

I was cold. So cold. I tried to lift my head but failed. I started to get angry. Of course I could lift my head. I tried again and this time I managed to lift it a few centimetres and looked out at the ocean.

Black. Waves. Spray. Nothing. The box was moving in the waves, spinning randomly at the mercy of their passage. I felt the box lift sharply up a large wave and spin to the left. I struggled to lift my head and looked again.

Black. Waves. Spray. Nothing. No, not nothing. Something. Something darker than the night. Something more solid than the waves. Something thumping, pulsing. Something close. My head dropped and I closed my eyes and held on.

————

I awoke. My whole body ached. But I was warm. I was wrapped in something soft. Nylon. A sleeping bag? I felt the sleek material against my body. I was naked in a sleeping bag. As I regained consciousness I realised I must be aboard a vessel. A light on the bulkhead gave enough illumination to see that I was in a small cabin. There were four bunks, two on either side. The vessel surged up and down through the waves, but the motion wasn't violent or alarming. I wanted to stay in the bunk, stay in the warm sleeping bag forever. But I needed to know what was going on. Where was I? Who'd rescued me? Where was the *Polar Princess*?

I'd just about gathered sufficient energy to escape the sleeping bag when a head appeared in the doorway. It had tousled hair and a week-old growth of beard on its face. 'Adam! You're awake!' the face shouted. It was followed into the room by a tousled body, the body of Gordon Crawford.

I croaked out a response and tried to roll over and go back to sleep, but Gordon wouldn't let me. He shook my shoulder and said, 'Adam! Get up. We're being chased by a ship and we need your help.'

I shook my head and tried to focus. 'Wait, wait. Where am I? What time is it? What's going on?'

Gordon started to unzip the sleeping bag. 'Adam, I still can't believe you're alive. Fuck. I mean, we got these strange radio signals. There was no message from you or Emma, and Nigel decided we should go and see what they were. We tracked them the best we could, and then we saw this light and headed for it. Shit, what could possibly have a light in the middle of the goddamned ocean? We went upwind and drifted alongside this thing and blow me down, it looked as if there was someone on top of it. We had to pry your fingers off the light before we could get you on board. And that was a bloody nightmare, believe me. I almost went overboard twice.' He looked down at me and gave me a big grin. 'And then, imagine our surprise when we discovered it was you. And you were alive.'

My brain was still somewhere on the Southern Ocean and I was suffering from information overload. 'Gordon,' I croaked. 'Gordon.' I wet my lips and asked more strongly. 'Where am I?'

'You're on the *Storm Petrel*. Your Plan B worked. We picked you up with that box. But no sooner did we have you on board than the radar picked up another ship. It turned towards us and hasn't changed course. It looks as if it's chasing us.'

'Hang on. You got the box? There's another ship out here?' I gave up my thoughts of rest and shoved the sleeping bag down my body. 'Where are my clothes?'

Gordon handed me trousers and shirt and socks. They weren't mine but they looked to be about the right size. I put them on and he handed me a heavy roll-neck woollen jersey, saying, 'Storm gear's by the hatch. Come on deck as soon as you can.'

He disappeared for'ard and I followed shortly afterwards. The motion of the small boat was very different from the *Polar Princess*, but fortunately the sea and wind were easing and I wasn't thrown around too badly. I was moving, but still felt incredibly weak. I desperately wanted to head back to the bunk and the warm sleeping bag but, with what seemed an inordinate effort, I donned wet-weather gear and boots and exited the cabin.

I stepped into the cockpit just abaft midships. It had a short roof, screens to reduce the spray coming on board, and benches that ran fore and aft on either side. A man in faded yellow storm gear stood at the large wheel just aft of the binnacle. He gave a bit of a nod as I entered the cockpit, but didn't take his eyes off the sail or the sea for long. Even in his parka I could see it was Nigel. His curly brown hair was plastered to his skull by the spray, and his thick eyebrows and scruffy beard hid most of his face. His dark eyes gleamed in the dim morning light.

Another man stood near the stern with a pair of binoculars in his hands. He turned his head when I entered the cockpit and nodded a greeting. He was also clad in yellow storm gear and swayed easily with the motion of the boat. He had a dark complexion, either Maori or Pacific Islander, and had a similar build to Nigel. He had short grey hair that contrasted with his thick, dark eyebrows.

Gordon sat on the port bench, the upwind side, and gestured for me to join him. The wind was still blowing hard, roaring through the rigging, and the waves were breaking heavily around us, their tops blown off by the wind. I lurched across the cockpit, sat and leaned close to Gordon and shouted in his ear, 'Where are we?'

'According to the radar, about six nautical miles south of the Bounties.'

I half-stood and tried to see over the stern. All I could see was the grey sea. 'And the other ship?'

'About three nautical miles behind us.' He nodded towards the man at the helm. 'You know Nigel. The guy in the stern is Hare. He's mate, crew, cook, everything else.'

I felt the *Storm Petrel* slew as it surfed down the back of one of the large southerly swells, and then felt the stern rise and the boat accelerate as the next swell caught up with us. I called out to Nigel, '6, 7 knots?'

'Near enough. Best we can do in these conditions.'

'And our friends?' I jerked my head to indicate the pursuing ship.

Nigel didn't turn to answer. 'Don't know. We can see on the radar that they're closing, but we haven't tried to work out their speed. In these waters, it's probably a fishing vessel of some sort. The waves make it hard to read the radar but from the size of the blip, I'd guess it was a factory ship. They can do at least 12 knots in a flat sea. In these conditions,' he looked aloft again and shrugged, 'maybe nine?'

I did the maths in my head and it wasn't pretty. If Nigel was right then they'd catch us in an hour, just about the time we reached the islands. 'What about the radio?' I asked.

Hare shook his head and laughed bitterly. 'Forget the radio. There's no way that's just another fishing vessel. Radio reception's crap in these conditions, but they've got some sort of jamming device. We can't send or receive anything.'

Nigel concentrated on handling the *Storm Petrel*. 'Radio wouldn't do us much good anyway. There's no other shipping anywhere near here.'

I said, 'It would be good if someone at least knew what's going on.'

'Yeah, well that's not going to happen. We're on our own.'

The clouds were right down and, although the rain had stopped, the wind and waves and spray kept the visibility low. We couldn't see anything in the wave troughs; from the crests, the horizon would have been about five nautical miles away, if we could have seen that far through the murk.

Gordon asked, 'Who are they? Why are they chasing us? What do they want?'

Nigel looked at me. I shrugged and said, 'Fucked if I know. You said you got the box? The one I was on?'

Gordon nodded and I said, 'All I know is that I saw those boxes getting thrown over the side from the *Polar Princess*. There were six of them.' I suddenly had a flash of insight. 'They're supposed to be buoys, part of a science project that Blue Ocean's supporting. But I think that's bullshit. Blue Ocean's not that kind of company. I bet those boxes are something else. I don't know what they are, but I bet the ship chasing us is here to collect them. I bet the antennae broadcast some sort of signal that allows them to track the boxes and pick them up.'

'Shit,' said Gordon, 'that would be the radio signals we received. They were tracking the boxes, so when we rescued you and picked up a box they knew we had it.'

Nigel added, 'They've been chasing us for hours. They must want it pretty bad.'

'What do you think they'll do if they catch us?' asked Hare, who'd been paying close attention to our conversation while he kept watch astern.

'I don't know,' I said, 'but they've gone to a lot of trouble to keep the transfer of the boxes secret. I doubt they'll say "Thanks, boys, see you later."'

Gordon looked worried. 'Are we going to give it to them? We could drop it back over the side and let them take it. The antenna's still on it. They could track it and pick it up.'

Hare said, 'Could we break off the antenna? That would stop the signal.'

I shook my head. 'They have us on their radar now, they don't need the antenna to track us. And I don't think tossing the box overboard would solve our problem. They tried to kill me to keep whatever's going on a secret. I think that my brother's death was also somehow related to those boxes. If they're willing to kill anyone who knows too much then secrecy is as important as the box, and they'll do anything to preserve it. Even if they get the box, they won't want us going home and talking about what's happened. Whatever we do I think they're going to try to kill us.' I looked around the cockpit at my three companions. 'On top of that, they've really pissed me off, and I want to know what's going on. I know that's not your concern and I'm sorry you're involved, but that's the way it is.'

'Damn,' said Gordon. 'When I said I'd help I didn't know this was what I was signing on for. I mean, it would be a great story but I have to live to write it.'

Nigel and Hare exchanged a look but didn't say anything. I could tell they weren't exactly happy, either.

'None of us did,' I said, 'but it's too late for second thoughts now.'

There was nothing else to say. We quickly slipped into a routine. Gordon monitored the position of the islands and the other ship on the radar. Nigel steered the *Storm Petrel*, urging every knot of speed out of the sails and diesel engine. Hare kept his attention on the ocean astern, looking for any sign of the vessel behind us. I shifted my attention between the ocean and the cockpit, keeping an eye out for anything that might be a threat, or perhaps help our escape.

We rose to the top of a wave and Hare shouted, 'There!' I looked where he was pointing. It took me a moment to locate it, but once I did there was no doubt; the other ship was dead astern and much too close.

We dropped into a trough and lost sight of the pursuer, but the image was still vivid in my mind. The ship was throwing huge washes of spray as it breasted the crest of a wave, and I could see the mast and A-frame corkscrew as it powered down the wave front. The hull was faded black and the upperworks dirty white, with orange rust stains. 'How far to the islands?' I shouted to Gordon.

He raised his head above the cockpit shelter and was immediately blasted by spray from a breaking wave. He wiped the water from his eyes and swung his gaze back and forth. I could just hear him shout over the noise of the wind and waves. 'The radar says they're less than two nautical miles to the northeast! But I can't see anything through this crap.' Then, just as I swung back to look astern, he cried out, 'Wait! I see something! Over there!'

I looked where he was pointing to starboard and at first saw nothing but grey waves, grey sky. I kept looking and suddenly the tip of an island separated from the water and sky and clouds, highlighted by the bright pulsation of waves breaking halfway up the steep cliffs.

Gordon looked closely at the radar and chart and shouted, 'I'm pretty sure the strong echo is Funnel Island. There's lots of interference, but I think I can pick out the smaller islands.'

Nigel snatched a glance to the northeast and said, 'I think you're right. That'll be the Centre Group. The Main Group will be just to the north.'

Gordon ducked back to the front of the cockpit and returned his attention to the chart and radar. 'Yeah, if we stay on this course, we'll pass just west of the Main Group.'

Nigel had to swing the wheel hard as the *Storm Petrel* slid down the back of another large roller. 'Good-o,' he shouted, 'I want to take her just west of Ruatara and Penguin Islands. A kilometre, or less. We'll have to keep our eyes peeled. There's a reef coming off the island platform there. Lots of rocks, shallow ground. Never properly surveyed. I think we'll make it. *Probably* make it. Maybe our pursuer won't.' He glanced over his shoulder and said, 'How far?'

Gordon answered, 'Less than two kilometres.'

After a quick look at the islands, I turned to look astern, and my eyes never lost sight of the other ship. It was visible all the time, still bulling its way through the seas. It was buttoned up tight; no one was crazy enough to be on deck in these conditions. I could see the bridge windows but couldn't make out anyone on the bridge. I judged her to be eighty or ninety metres long, a modest size for a commercial ship but enormous compared to us.

I stood as high as I could in the cockpit, clutching one of the stays to keep from getting thrown overboard, and surveyed as much of the ocean around us as I could. The pursuing vessel was only about a nautical mile astern. I could see the central group of islands clearly, lying almost due east, to starboard, bare grey rocks beaten by the stormy sea. The northern group of islands were visible off the starboard bow, also maybe a nautical mile to the northeast. I looked straight ahead and could see no sign of the rocks Nigel had mentioned, just column after column of waves marching past us, spray flying from their crests.

Our shouted conversation lapsed as we sped on. We were all pretty tense and there was nothing to say. Nigel altered our course slightly to north to pass closer to the islands. After ten minutes we could see that our pursuer had altered course as well.

Hare maintained his position, but the rest of us no longer watched the other ship. We knew it was less than a kilometre behind. All three of us stared desperately at the sea ahead, trying to spot any sign of rocks or shallows. I stared with all my concentration, but all I saw was an unending march of breaking waves.

Then, imperceptibly at first, we all sensed the change. The seas became more jumbled, the order imposed by their passage across thousands of kilometres of the Southern Ocean disrupted. There was nothing dramatic, but I was suddenly infused with a ray of hope.

Nigel sensed it as well. 'Eyes sharp now!' he cried.

Gordon was the first to spot something. 'Rock!' he yelled, pointing to the port side. 'Rock over there.'

I looked and could see the water boiling over an area of maybe an acre. Nigel altered course to starboard and we sailed on. This time it was my turn to shout, 'Rock! Rock two hundred metres to starboard!' Nigel looked and, without comment, adjusted course.

From then on it was a constant chorus of shouts and pointing and small changes of course. None of the rocks were properly above water; all were visible only by the effects they had on the waves. Some were shallow enough to cause the waves to break dramatically over them; others were deeper and distorted the waves' behaviour, pockets of greater chaos in a maelstrom, only visible if you were desperately looking for them. Hare joined us, and his experienced eyes often spotted subtle swirls from submerged rocks long before Gordon or I recognised them.

I glanced astern. The pursuing ship loomed over our little vessel and was less than five hundred metres behind us. I could read the name painted on the hull – the *Sergey Belov*. Despite the weather, someone had emerged from the interior and was standing in the bow holding a rifle. It was an insane thing to do. Not only was it extremely dangerous to be on deck; there was no way anyone could shoot from one wildly moving vessel and hit someone on another. But if there was ever a question about their intention it was answered by the appearance of an armed seaman. My heart sank. The ship was too big, too powerful, too committed to our destruction. We'd tried, but we didn't have a chance. They were going to run us down and destroy our boat and drive us under the sea.

Nigel was not distracted by the proximity of the other ship, or by the rifle. He remained focused on the ocean, the waves, the wind, the sails. The northern group of islands were almost abeam. The clouds were breaking up to the east and a shaft of morning sunlight shot down and turned the water ahead into a mirror.

I could see Nigel suddenly look hard to starboard, then to port and back to starboard again before bracing himself at the tiller and yelling, 'Hang on! Coming about!'

Hare jumped to release the boom, and I just had time to grab onto something before Nigel put the helm hard over and the *Storm Petrel* started a sharp turn to starboard. The boom swung around and Hare sheeted it home, the scrap of canvas hard as iron in the gale-force wind.

We were heading northeast, aiming to pass just north of the islands. I could see the boiling water close – too close – on either side as we threaded a way through the rocks. Nigel didn't take his eyes off the ocean as he shouted, 'Where's the ship?'

I looked aft and watched as the *Sergey Belov* started to follow our turn. 'She's turning with us!' I shouted.

'Inside?' Nigel shouted back.

I looked hard at our pursuer, judging angles. After less than a minute it was obvious they were trying to turn inside us and cut us off. 'Inside!' I yelled.

I swear I saw a grim smile on Nigel's lips, though if it was there it was gone so quickly that I could never be sure.

'Rock! Rock!' Gordon screamed and pointed off our starboard bow.

Nigel stared at it, judging speed and angles and wind and waves, and then changed course to sail closer to the rocks. I looked at the rocks and the broken seas and at Nigel and screamed, 'Rock! You're steering for the rocks!'

Nigel didn't even acknowledge me. He kept his hands on the wheel and his attention focused forward. I looked at Hare. He, too, was staring straight ahead. A large wave picked us up and we began to slide down its face towards those menacing rocks. I could see every nook and cranny. I could see the sharp grey edges, the seaweed thrashed wildly by the waves, the water flowing across the exposed rock faces as the waves receded. We slid down towards those dreadful rocks, nearly broadside to the wave, the sail flapping madly as it lost the wind.

At the last second, Nigel spun the wheel as fast as he could, trying to bring the *Storm Petrel* back on course. The world stopped, frozen in time: no wind on my face, the deck solid beneath my feet. I willed us to come around. I wanted to believe in God just so I could pray we'd come around. I stole a glance at the others and saw they were also immobile, their faces taut with unspoken fear. Then, like a miracle, I felt the deck shift beneath me, felt the sail fill with wind, saw Gordon's eyes wide with fright as the rocks loomed so close it seemed impossible we'd miss them.

We missed the rocks. But the pursuing ship did not. With a masterly piece of seamanship, Nigel hauled us back on course and we flashed past the deadly reef, so close I thought I could touch it. The crew of the *Sergey Belov* had tried to cut inside us, and when they realised their peril it was too late. They had nowhere to turn; nowhere to go – except onto the rocks. At the last moment, their bow lifted on a wave and then dropped onto the reef. This vast ship, this powerful ship, this relentless ship ... stopped.

The sound was colossal. It was like an enormous bell. It was like dropping a freight train from a great height. It was like the collision of planets. The noise went on and on, a continuous scream, a grinding and rending of tortured metal.

I couldn't look away. Gordon was equally mesmerised. Hare stood with one hand braced on a halyard and watched it unfold. Nigel eased the *Storm Petrel* around enough so he could sneak glances at the doomed ship. After a few minutes, he altered course again, back to the northwest, towards New Zealand.

There was no sense of celebration. We'd survived, we'd escaped being run down by the Russian ship, but we were too physically and emotionally drained to do more than sail away in silence.

Gordon was the first to recover. He looked back and forth between the *Sergey Belov* and Nigel. 'What, what about the crew?' he asked.

'Fuck 'em,' I said before Nigel could answer. 'Those bastards were trying to kill us. Did you see that rifle? If we go back they'll kill us and take our boat. Is that what you want?'

Gordon looked steadily at Nigel. 'Nigel? Is that what you think?'

Nigel looked grim and kept his eyes focused forward. 'There's no thinking about it, Gordon. Adam's right. I saw the rifle. You did too. Going back there wouldn't be safe. It was them or us. They just about got us. But they didn't. So, yeah, fuck 'em.'

'Hare?' Gordon looked at the seaman with pleading eyes.

Hare shrugged. 'We're alive. I want to stay that way.'

I watched the wreck slowly recede as we sailed away. Gordon was visibly upset. 'Shouldn't we radio somebody?' he persisted.

Nigel thought for a minute and then said, 'Nope. We won't radio. In fact, we were never here. We left the islands yesterday. And we've been having problems with our radio, so we won't hear them calling and have to turn around in case they transmit an SOS.'

'Which they will,' I said.

'Which they might,' Nigel corrected. 'If anyone's still alive, and if their radio's still working then they might send an SOS. But if they try to contact someone then it is more likely to be a message to one of their sister ships. Think about it. Wrecking a vessel on the Bounties is a total disaster for them. As well as losing whatever is in those boxes, they've got big problems rescuing the crew. Worse, they've brought attention to themselves – having to explain the wreck, what they were doing there.' He paused while he steered us down the back of a wave before adding, 'And maybe worst of all, they'll be in deep shit with the government and environmental groups for causing pollution in a marine reserve.'

'Yeah,' I said. 'If word of the wreck gets out then there will be questions about activities in the Southern Ocean. Questions which, if what we know gets out, could be quite awkward.'

Gordon nodded. 'Damn. That's where I come in. This is a big story. Huge. People need to know what's going on.' His face clouded. 'But how can I write the story without revealing our part in it? That we sailed away from the wreck? Didn't even check for survivors?'

I grabbed his shoulder and said, 'You can't. You can't write anything. Not now. Maybe not ever.'

'What? But, that's ridiculous. Don't you want these guys exposed? Don't you want to know why your brother was killed?'

'That's why you can't write anything. We told you from the start that you have to do what we say. Getting the guys responsible for Theo's death is the priority. Emma and I make the decisions, decide how to do that. Catching the small fry or writing headlines isn't important.' I paused then said, 'Can't you see? We still don't *know* anything. Some boxes are thrown overboard and picked up by another boat. What's in the boxes? Where's the link to Callaghan? We need more information before we can prove anything. One thing you can be sure of, they've been very careful to protect themselves, to hide all evidence of what they're doing. We need more than a smoking gun. We need a bullet to the heart.'

Gordon still wasn't happy. 'Look,' I said, 'we'll open the box when the weather settles. Maybe that will give us the information we need. I want you to get a story. I want you to expose these bastards. But if it's not done right, at the right time and in the right way, then it's all for nothing. Their fancy lawyers will slide them away, laughing at us. Is that what you want?'

Gordon sighed. 'Fuck. I'm not convinced you're right, but I'll go along with it. For now.' He pointed astern. 'People died back there. Maybe bad people, but they were still people. Bad or good, someday someone needs to tell their story.'

'Maybe someday,' I said, 'just not today.'

CHAPTER 24

We heard no Mayday radio call. The weather moderated as we sailed northwest and by dinner time all that was left was a brisk southerly breeze and a long southwesterly swell. We had taken turns at the helm during the day. At 6 p.m. I was piloting the *Storm Petrel* while Nigel fixed dinner. He came into the cockpit to tell me it was ready and engaged the autopilot device. Gordon had poured us all a stiff drink in big glass tumblers. We sat at the small table, and for the first time in what seemed like days I felt myself relax.

We finished dinner and were working on a second drink when Gordon said, 'That was pretty risky, Nigel. It turned out well, but we could have been the ones on the rocks.'

Nigel shrugged and took a sip of his drink. 'Maybe, but I gambled that we're better seamen than they were. You guys made the difference, seeing those rocks and all.'

Gordon nodded towards Hare. 'Hare's the one. He had the sharpest eyes.' Hare just smiled and leaned back against the bulkhead.

I looked quizzically at Nigel. 'That was your plan all along, wasn't it? Have you been through those rocks before?'

Nigel looked very tired then. He pushed his plate away with a finger and replied, 'No, I've never been through those rocks. I've sailed past them, though, so I had some idea what to expect.' He was quiet for a long time. We waited for him to go on. 'I started planning as soon as it was apparent they were chasing us. If we couldn't outrun them, then we didn't have many options. There's no way we could do something clever and evade them. Their radar kept us pinned like bugs to a board. It had to be something else, something they weren't expecting.'

Nigel took another sip of his drink and let it roll around his mouth before swallowing and continuing, 'We were lucky we were close to the Bounties. I thought about heading among the islands, finding water too shallow or passages too narrow for the bigger ship to follow. But they'd just have backed off and hung around until we ran out of food and had to leave. We had to get rid of them today, get rid of them for good. The only way I could see to do it was to run them aground. And the only place I could think of to do that was on those rocks west of the Main Group.'

Gordon watched the liquid in his glass move with the motion of the boat and said, 'Yeah, well, you cut it pretty fine. We're lucky they hit that rock.'

Nigel gave his faint smile and said, 'Luck didn't have much to do with it.'

'What do you mean?' asked Gordon.

'I saw that configuration of rocks coming up. I altered course and knew there would only be one person in a thousand who could resist trying to cut us off. They wanted us dead. They wanted it bad. It clouded their judgement.' Nigel put his glass down and explained, 'Once they were on that course, they were doomed. There were too many rocks ahead and they were going too fast to avoid them. All I had to do was get us out of the way and leave them to their fate.'

I stretched and felt the fatigue in my bones. 'You did a fantastic job,' I said gratefully. 'You have no idea how glad I am I didn't end up swimming again.'

Gordon smiled. 'You can say that again. Thanks, Nigel, you saved us, mate.'

I stood up and headed for the cockpit. 'There's one more thing we have to do.'

Gordon asked, 'Open the box?'

'Indeed, open the box.'

The box was too big to store below, so Nigel and Hare had lashed it to the foredeck. Fortunately, by evening the seas were calm enough for us to work there safely, though we all wore safety lines just in case.

In the middle of the Southern Ocean, the simple black case was as foreign as the black monolith in *2001 A Space Odyssey*. It gleamed in the slanting evening light – no dents, no scratches, no sign it had been thrown overboard and spent hours in the water. The antenna still protruded from the top of the box.

It was about a metre in all dimensions. There was a faint line about twenty centimetres down from the top with locks on each side. Hare unlashed the box, coiling the rope neatly and stowing it on deck. I put my hands underneath and tried to lift it. All I could manage was to get it a few centimetres off the deck. 'Jesus Christ,' I said, 'how much does this thing weigh?'

Nigel scratched his beard and replied, 'Don't know, but it's bloody heavy. We couldn't have got it on deck if a wave hadn't helped us lift it over the rail.'

'Bloody right,' said Hare, 'it was all we could do to push it into this position and lash it down.' He laughed grimly. 'It's so fucking heavy that Nigel didn't stint with the ropes.'

I examined the locks closely. They were black metal with a key opening. Nigel was also looking at the locks. 'I've got a universal key down below,' he said. 'Back in a minute.'

He disappeared and Gordon and I looked at each other, with no idea what Nigel had in mind. He reappeared in a short time with a screwdriver and a large hammer.

Nigel grinned as he inserted the blade of the screwdriver in one of the key slots and gave it a heavy blow with the hammer. 'The main defence of a lock is the unwillingness of the thief to make a mess or take too much time,' he explained. He tried to turn the screwdriver; it didn't move so he hit it again. 'We don't care what the locks look like, and have days before we get to port, so these babies are toast.'

Hare watched as bits of metal flew from the lock and observed wryly, 'I don't think this is going to take days.'

Nigel said nothing as he twisted the screwdriver and the remnants of the lock turned easily. In a short time, the other locks were broken and the box was ready to be opened.

We'd discussed what was in it off and on during the day. 'Drugs,' suggested Gordon. 'What else would be worth this much effort?'

'But why smuggle drugs *out* of New Zealand?' I asked. 'Surely they'd be smuggling them into the country.'

'Unless it's some sort of trans-shipment scheme,' said Hare. 'You know, backdoor into Australia or something.'

'Seems bloody complicated to me,' said Nigel. 'There must be an easier way to get drugs into Sydney.'

We talked over everything we could think of – guns, money, jewels, pounamu (New Zealand jade) – but nothing seemed to make sense. Gordon finally killed the discussion when he said it was probably All Black memorabilia.

'I think *you* should open it, Adam,' said Nigel. 'You've spent the longest time with it.'

I thought back to my night huddled on top of this box, big on the deck but tiny in the ocean, and couldn't believe I had survived, that I was here on the *Storm Petrel* and about to open it. Without a word I put my hands on the cold plastic and lifted.

The top came off easily. A box of electronics was attached to the underside of the lid, obviously the controls of the tracking system. I grabbed the wire attaching it to the antenna and unscrewed the connection. 'No one will be tracking this box anymore,' I said. I placed the lid behind me on the deck and looked inside. The box was lined in black plastic sheeting, sealed with some sort of thermal system to make it waterproof. Nigel took the knife from his belt, inserted the point through the plastic, and cut a long slit across the box.

Night was coming and the light was failing and we couldn't make out what was beneath the plastic. I took Nigel's knife and cut the plastic so I could fold it back. Inside the plastic sheeting was white Styrofoam packing like they put in TV and stereo boxes. There was a finger-sized hole in the top. I stuck a finger in and pulled. The foam came away and underneath, nestled in more foam, were blocks of money. Blocks of New Zealand one hundred dollar bills, to be exact. Each of the blocks of bills was wrapped in another layer of plastic, clear this time. I guessed that altogether the blocks measured about half a metre on a side and, judging by the top piece of foam, probably about the same thickness.

'Fuck me,' said Gordon. 'Money. A shitload of money.'

Hare whistled softly and said, 'Damn. No wonder they wanted to sink us and get this box back.'

Nobody said anything more for a while. I cut through the plastic on one of the blocks and picked up a bundle of the bills. They weren't worn, but they weren't unused, either. I did a quick count – there were one hundred in each banded stack, and I guessed one hundred stacks in each plastic-wrapped block. 'I think each block is a million dollars,' I said.

'Damn,' said Gordon, judging the remaining contents of the box, 'must be ten million dollars here.'

Nigel raised his eyes and swept the horizon. 'It's almost dark. We don't have time to count this now. We need to pack it up and lash it down. After all we've been through I don't think we want it to get wet or washed over the side.'

'You're right,' I agreed. 'We know what's in the box now. We just need to figure out where it came from and where it was going.'

CHAPTER 25

David Callaghan was at home having breakfast with his wife when his cell phone rang. He pulled it from his pocket and frowned when he saw the caller ID. 'Sorry, dear. I have to take this. Work.'

His wife nodded tolerantly as he rose from the table and stepped into the kitchen.

'Brandon,' Callaghan said into his phone, 'it's breakfast time and calls from the ship cost a fortune. What's so fucking important?' He listened to the hiss of the line for a few seconds before Captain Kennicott's voice came through.

'Sorry sir, but something's come up I think you should know about. We've had a bit of a storm. One of our observers is missing.'

'Missing? Are you sure?'

'Yes, sir. One of the crew says he saw him go over the side. Says he jumped.'

'Jumped? In the Southern Ocean? Was he on drugs?' There was silence on the line and then Callaghan said, 'Dammit. I don't suppose I need to guess who this observer was, do I?'

'No, sir, I doubt it.'

'Fuck. Anything else?'

'Well, we deployed those boxes where we were supposed to. We tracked their beacons as long as we could. Everything went to plan, except for one.'

Callaghan listened to the hiss on the line again. The satellite connection was encrypted, but any mention of the boxes made him nervous. Finally, he said, 'Brandon? Are you there? What's this about one of the boxes?'

'Yes, sir, I'm here. One of the boxes … it stayed with the others for most of the night. But then it started acting funny.'

'Funny? What do you mean funny?'

'It kept going north, downwind like the others, but it sped up. It's moving at about 6 knots.'

'Six knots?' Callaghan could think of only one way to explain that behaviour. 'What about the other boxes?' He needed to know that the other vessel had recovered the boxes.

'We can tell from the trackers that the other boxes are safely on board. We see the vessel that collected them on the radar screen, and from their heading and speed it looks as though they're chasing the other box.'

'Okay, thanks, skipper. Fortunately, once the boxes are over the side, they're not our responsibility.'

'Um, what about the observer? Do you want us to notify Maritime Safety?'

Callaghan's mind raced, weighing his options. 'No, another man overboard would be too hard to explain. We don't want any more attention. Who else knows about this? Just the men we trust?'

'Yeah, so far it's only the guys who were deploying the boxes.'

'Good. Keep it that way. Tell them to keep their mouths shut. We'll take it from here. You look after your ship and have a safe voyage home.'

He leaned against the kitchen bench and thought hard. *Stone overboard and one of the boxes missing. Probably on another boat.* That was the only explanation for its increased speed. His mind worked on the probabilities, the possibilities, and reached a conclusion. He picked up his phone and dialled.

'Alexander? We have a problem. Someone may have picked up one of our buoys by mistake. And our problem employee has disappeared ... No, I don't know whether they're related, but we can't afford to take a chance ... Yes, that's right. It's still very fluid down there, but I think we can contain it ... You think the woman may be involved? ... Well, that's true. Stone's proved hard to control. Perhaps you're right, maybe we need some insurance ... Use your judgement but don't make a mess ... I'll let you know if we need her ... Yeah, you too.'

Callaghan put the phone back in his pocket and returned to the dining room. 'Sorry dear, a problem on one of our ships.'

His wife looked up with a small frown on her face. 'Nothing serious, I hope?'

Callaghan shook his head and picked up his fork. 'No, nothing to worry about. It's sorted now.'

———

It took Alexander Ivanov less than an hour to dispatch two of his employees to respond to David Callaghan's call. They packed the few things they needed and were on a flight by lunchtime. When they landed they hired a car and spent the afternoon reconnoitring the neighbourhood and working on a course of action.

Other than waiting for dark, they didn't bother with subtlety. The two men parked their car on the street and walked up the path to the front porch. The porch light was off and the street lights were widely spaced. Large pools of darkness from the trees around this and the neighbouring houses covered the lawn and the porch. Light seeped around a curtained front window but did nothing to illuminate the darkness around the house.

The two men stepped onto the porch, moving softly, one standing in front of the door and one to the side. The first man raised a hand and the two exchanged a glance before he pushed gently on the door. It didn't open. He looked at the simple lock and the light timber of the door frame, then nodded to his partner and braced his feet, his rubber soles giving a firm grip on the concrete surface of the porch. He drew back slightly and then rammed his whole body forward, into the door, ripping the lock from the door frame. There was surprisingly little noise as he arrested the door's motion before it crashed into the wall. With one stride he was inside the house, closely followed by his partner.

Emma heard a noise, looked up from her book and called out, 'Who's there?' She listened intently but heard nothing else. Her heart rate increased as her imagination filled her mind with all the things she'd heard on the news – home invasion, beatings, killings, rape. She put her bookmark in the book and set it on the table beside her as she stood up from her chair.

She looked around for a weapon and then decided that was ridiculous – told herself to stop being a girl and go have a look. She went and opened the door to the front hall. When the door opened the light illuminated the two men. Emma tried to slam the door, but she was too slow. The man in front stuck out a hand and stopped the door, then shoved it hard into her. She stumbled back into the lounge, losing her footing and falling to the floor. The two men were on her in an instant. She had time for one scream before a hand covered her mouth. The big man held her while the other pulled a small plastic bag from his pocket. He opened it and withdrew a sweet-smelling cotton pad. His partner removed his hand as he clamped the pad over Emma's nose and mouth and waited. In a very short time, her eyes closed and she stopped struggling.

———

Emma woke in her bed, her hands and feet tied tightly and a gag in her mouth. She could see daylight outside her window and, from the angle of the sun, she knew it was morning. She hadn't been awake long before the big man came into her bedroom. He saw she was awake, walked over to her bed and picked her up. He carried her to the kitchen where his partner untied her hands. Then, as the big man held her tightly from behind, the smaller one held her left arm and hand, her fingers splayed on the kitchen bench. With his free hand, he held up the large kitchen knife he'd removed from the block on the bench.

'Now, we want you to make a phone call, tell your employer you're going to be away for a couple of days. We're going to remove your gag. Are you going to behave?'

Emma looked into the empty blue eyes and shuddered. She closed her eyes and slowly nodded her head.

'Good girl. Now, just to be clear, you're going to say you're not feeling well. It's not serious and you'll be back in a day or two. If you do that, if you act natural and they believe you, then you'll be fine. But,' he paused for effect, 'if you get clever and do something stupid like ask for help, then you won't be so fine. This looks like a very sharp knife. I believe it could cut right through one of your fingers.' He looked at her calmly and said, 'We were told to keep you safe in case your boyfriend appears again. Insurance if we need to keep him in line. But safe doesn't mean there can't be a few bits missing.'

Emma started crying. Her eyes remained closed and no sound escaped through her gag, but her body shook and tears flowed down her cheeks. She'd been scared before – she'd been almost hit by a large pine tree that hadn't fallen where it was supposed to, saved from a long fall while rock climbing by the last piece of gear holding her to the rock face – but she'd never felt anything like this. The other occasions had been accidents; this was an encounter with evil.

Her captors waited silently until she stopped crying. Her fear was no less; she'd just run out of tears. Finally, she opened her eyes, looked at the knife poised over her fingers, and nodded.

'Good girl,' said the smaller man. He reached over and worked the gag from her mouth. Emma gasped for air, the relief of being able to breathe freely almost overwhelming.

The smaller man picked up the phone and put the receiver on the bench. 'What's the number?'

Emma hesitated for a second and then gave it to him. The man punched the numbers into the handset, put the phone on speaker and then held it up to Emma's mouth. They all heard it ring three times before it was answered. 'Macintyre Forestry,' said a pleasant voice, 'how may I help you?'

Emma glanced at her captor and licked her lips. 'Hi, uh, Rochelle. It's Emma here.'

'Oh, hi Emma, how are you?'

Emma swallowed and said, 'Uh, I'm fine. No, actually I'm not so good. I think I'm coming down with something. Bit of a sore throat. Probably nothing, but I'm going to take it easy for a day or two, just in case.'

'I'm sorry to hear that, Emma. I hope you're okay. I'll let the others know. Call if there's anything you need.'

'Thanks, Rochelle. I'll see you soon.'

They heard the line disconnect and her captor put the phone back in its cradle.

———

A night and most of a day had passed. Emma was sitting in a kitchen chair, hands and feet bound. They'd offered her food, but her stomach was in knots and she'd declined. She'd had a little water but struggled to keep even that down.

There was always at least one of them with her. At night they'd tied her up and laid her on the sofa. She'd slept eventually, exhaustion ultimately overcoming her fear and discomfort. They told her to relax, they weren't going to hurt her, they were only holding her as insurance.

'Insurance for what?' she'd asked and received a shrug in answer. Emma wasn't dumb, she knew that hurting her was exactly what they were here for. No one kidnaps someone unless they're prepared to hurt or kill them. She remembered all too clearly the threat to cut off her fingers if she didn't cooperate.

The clock on the wall said it was just after 4 p.m. 'Where's your buddy?' Emma asked the bigger man.

He muttered in reply, 'He had to go do something else.' Emma guessed this man was in his early thirties, big and reasonably fit, maybe still played club rugby on the first fifteen. His face was a little knocked around but he wasn't bad looking – for a total criminal asshole.

'I need to go to the toilet.' Emma squirmed slightly in her chair to reinforce the point.

They'd taken her to the toilet twice before. Both times the smaller man, the one who'd threatened to cut off her finger, had stood in the doorway and watched her. This guy seemed less comfortable around women, or at least not as interested in watching her pee.

He considered her request. 'Sorry, you'll have to hold it until he gets back.'

'Look, I have to go. Bad. What are you worried about? Muscles like that, you can't handle a woman?'

'It's the rules. Two of us have to be here any time we untie you.'

Emma chewed her lip. 'This is so embarrassing, but I think it's my time of the month. I need to get a tampon or there's going to be a mess.'

The big man was noticeably discomfited by this news. The rules were the rules, but what was he going to do with a woman who had blood all over her?

'Okay. But I've got to keep an eye on you.'

Emma shrugged. 'Whatever. But could you hurry? I think it's getting desperate.'

He untied her and followed her to the bathroom. He stood in the doorway while she opened the mirrored drug cabinet and found the packet of tampons. She opened it and retrieved one and stepped over to the toilet. She held the tampon up and looked at the man. 'Really? You're going to watch me insert this? Can't I have a little privacy?' The man didn't say anything, so Emma said, 'Your buddy gets off on watching me, but I thought you were better than that. Was I wrong?'

He looked around the room. There was a window with frosted glass, but it was too small for Emma to escape through. 'I'll be just outside.'

Emma swung the door shut as far as she dared, about halfway. She heard her captor take up position outside the door, out of her sight. 'I won't be long,' she called out, loudly enough for him to hear her.

She quietly went back to the drug cabinet and quickly searched through the usual clutter of aspirin, plasters, razor, suntan lotion, antibiotic cream, hand cream, face cream. In the back, behind the suntan lotion, was a fat plastic tube with a blue cap at one end and a tapered orange cap at the other. She'd reacted badly once when she'd been stung by bees at a forestry site and ever since then she'd kept an EpiPen in her car and at home. In an emergency, it could deliver a dose of adrenalin to prevent anaphylactic shock. She grabbed the device and stuck it in the right back pocket of her jeans.

She carefully closed the cabinet and flushed the toilet. 'Okay. All done.'

She walked back into the hallway. Her captor was standing against the wall, between the bathroom and the lounge. She heard him follow her as she went back down the hallway.

Emma walked through the lounge and into the kitchen. She stood by her chair and turned to face the man as he entered the kitchen. He'd placed the cords they used to bind her on the kitchen bench. As he stepped past her, she reached into her back pocket and pulled out the plastic tube. It took only a second to thumb off the blue cap. For a moment he was facing away from her, reaching for the cords. With no hesitation she slammed the orange end into his butt, driving the concealed needle straight through his jeans. She felt him flinch and held the tube against him as long as she could.

'What the fuck!' he screamed and jumped back. The EpiPen was ripped from her hand and from his ass and fell to the floor.

'You bitch!' he yelled. 'What have you done?' His eyes were alternately filled with fright and rage, looking from her to the pen and back. With a yell he leapt towards her, hands outstretched.

Emma jumped to the side and avoided his first rush. 'Wait!' she shouted. 'I wouldn't do that if I were you.'

His system was overloaded with anger and confusion and he didn't know what to think, so he stopped, gasping, and looked at her.

'I injected you with adrenalin. It's safe for most people. You're not allergic to it, are you?'

'You bitch!' he yelled again and lunged for her.

Emma ducked beneath his hands and avoided his charge again. 'Adrenalin raises your blood pressure and can cause a heart attack.

Running around is only going to bring on the effects sooner. You might be okay, but I'd get to a hospital right away if I were you.'

'Fuuuuuuck!' he screamed and ran at her. He was beyond rational thought and she easily tripped him, sending him crashing to the floor. She wanted to kick him, stamp on his face, but knew escape was more important. She ran to the door and opened it. The outdoors had never smelled as good. She turned back to her captor and said, 'Really, ring 111. Get an ambulance. Stay still. Don't move. You might live.'

She swung back to the door and took a step onto the porch but came to an abrupt halt when she collided with something. Something big. And solid. And in a suit. She looked up into the unsmiling face of Detective Killand.

'Detective!' she exclaimed. 'What are you doing here? How did you find me? You scared the shit out of me.' She reached out and gripped his arms tightly. 'Thank God you're here. I was kidnapped ... I just escaped ... There's a guy inside ...' She stopped when the detective gently removed her hands and put his arm around her.

'Hush,' he said, 'I know. It's going to be all right. You'll be safe now.'

Emma froze. Her immediate relief at being rescued by the police was replaced by a growing unease. She and Adam didn't entirely trust Killand. And he was based in Dunedin, so what was he doing at her house in Hawkes Bay? The arm that had felt comforting suddenly felt confining.

Killand released her and stood back, looking closely into her face. Emma tried to smile but could only manage an uncertain nervous tic. Her confused emotions sapped her energy, and she felt as though the tide had receded and left her lying inert on the soft sand.

Killand said, 'Your safety is our only concern. That's why I'm sure you won't mind being more firmly restrained this time.' He stepped back and gestured with his left hand. 'Take her.'

Emma's eyes had clouded with puzzlement when he spoke, and they filled with terror when the smaller of her captors appeared from out of sight along the porch and grabbed her. 'No!' she yelled before a hard hand closed over her mouth. She started to struggle but it was futile. Strong arms held her tightly, unable to move.

Killand nodded towards the door. 'Take her back inside. Use the cable ties this time, and gag her. Then take a look at your partner and see if he needs medical attention.'

The man didn't speak; he just carried Emma inside and shut the door with his foot. Killand took out his phone and dialled a number. It rang twice before it was answered. 'Just as well I came to check on things. The shipment wasn't adequately secured.' He listened for a moment and then said, 'No, no. Everything's fine now. Some of the fastenings became loose but they've been replaced. The package will be ready whenever we need it.' He listened again and then turned off his phone without a reply.

CHAPTER 26

The wind had come around to the northwest and it took us more than four days to sail to Dunedin. I was exhausted. My time in the ocean and the stress of the chase caught up with me. I collapsed on my bunk and fell into a restless sleep. When I awoke I felt better, but the fate of the factory ship and her crew was still vivid in my mind and I felt no closer to understanding why Theo had been killed.

We were fortunate and the weather was fine for most of the return voyage. I spent long hours in the cockpit with Nigel at the helm and Gordon sitting across from me. It occurred to me that the *Storm Petrel* was well named: she floated effortlessly across the waves, leaving almost no wake.

'Okay, Adam, tell us about the money.' It was late afternoon on the third day, the sun still bright on the water, the sail drawing full on a starboard reach. Gordon was tucked in a corner of the cockpit with a beanie and jacket against the chill of the breeze. Nigel had the helm, moving easily with the motion of the boat, eyes everywhere, responding to every shift in the wind and waves. Hare was below, sleeping while he was off watch. Nigel spared a glance at me when he asked the question, and then returned to concentrating on sailing the boat.

The night after we'd opened the box, Gordon and I had talked about what it meant in the privacy of our bunks. It was a short distance between what Connor had discovered and the money in the box. 'They're creative,' Gordon had said, referring to Blue Ocean. 'Creative but consistent.'

'Yeah,' I'd agreed, 'it's got to be money laundering. It's the only thing that makes sense.'

'Callaghan must have some very rich friends. Very bad rich friends.'

'Now some very bad but not-so-rich friends. Probably soon-to-be angry friends. Friends we want to keep away from.'

Most people think a sailing vessel is quiet, and it is – compared to an engine-driven ship. But there's always noise: the rush of water along the sides, the creak and slap of the rigging, the occasional clank of something loose down below, and the soft rush-crash of whitecaps breaking on the tops of waves. I listened to the sound of the *Storm Petrel* and thought about how to respond to Nigel. Finally, I said, 'Seeing that money was as much a surprise to me as to you.'

After another pause for thought I said, 'We talked about this when we were speculating about what was in the boxes, remember? If the boxes held cash, then what was it for? Payment to somebody? Payment for what? Is it real or counterfeit? We think from other things we've discovered that it's part of a money laundering scheme. But if that's the case, then whose money is it? Where's it going?' I shook my head. 'We know Blue Ocean is doing something illegal, something involving lots of cash, but we don't know what it is. Not for sure.'

Nigel didn't look happy. 'That's all you can tell us? Nothing about what's really going on?'

'We found some computer files that suggest this,' I gestured vaguely towards the box on deck, 'is the tip of the iceberg. But all we have is suspicions.'

Gordon said, 'And a box with a shitload of money.'

We were all quiet, and then Nigel said, 'So this has all been for nothing? You're no further ahead than you were before you sailed on the *Polar Princess*?'

'No,' I said, thinking about those long hours clutching to the box, certain I was going to die. 'It hasn't been for nothing. We have more pieces of the puzzle, but we still can't see the whole picture.'

————

When we were within cell phone coverage I borrowed Gordon's phone and tried to call Emma. There was no reply. I left a message on her answerphone telling her I'd call again soon. Then I called the airline to book a ticket to Auckland. Nigel said we'd probably berth late in the morning, so I booked a flight departing at 4 p.m.

As we sailed home, we listened to the news on the radio, but there was no mention of a shipwreck on the Bounty Islands. Nor was there any mention of someone lost overboard from a fishing vessel. This was a puzzle. Was Callaghan hoping there would be no body washing up on the Bounty Islands this time? How could Blue Ocean explain my boarding of the *Polar Princess*, but not getting off? These questions added to my worries and I didn't sleep well the last night on the boat.

A northwesterly slowed our return trip, but it brought warm sunny weather to the city and it was good to proceed up the long approach to Dunedin harbour under a clear sky. It was after 11 a.m. when we made fast to the wharf and offloaded our gear.

I was anxious to get to Auckland and then fly on to see Emma, but we had two hours before I had to leave for the airport. Gordon had booked a flight to Wellington at about the same time so we'd go to the airport together. I'd called Emma repeatedly without success. She might have been away in a remote forest out of cell phone coverage, but I was getting more concerned.

We stood in the sunshine on the wharf. I looked at Nigel, Hare and Gordon, their faces lined with fatigue and covered with two weeks of beard growth. 'I can never thank you guys enough,' I said. 'If it wasn't for you then, well ...'

Gordon reached out and shook my hand. 'I didn't have this kind of trip in mind when I volunteered to help – storms, rescues, shipwrecks, boxes of money. Wellington's going to seem tame.' He turned to Nigel and said, 'We wouldn't have made it without you. I thought we were dog tucker for a while. I was there and I still can't believe you pulled it off.'

Nigel murmured, 'It was a bit more adventurous than my usual voyages, I'll admit.' It was hard to believe, but there was a twinkle in his eye as he said it.

'Damn,' I said, 'I think you enjoyed it.'

Nigel shrugged. 'We got home safe. In the end that's all that counts.' He held out his calloused hand to me, 'I'm mighty glad we happened across you, Adam. Your trip to the Southern Ocean was a bit more touch and go than ours. I think we're all glad it's finally over.'

'Yeah, thanks.' I shook hands with all of them. 'I owe all of you. Big time. Anything you need, just ask.'

'Well, I don't know about the rest of you, but I need a beer,' said Hare.

We all laughed, and then I said, 'Just one more thing. I need a souvenir from our voyage.' It took me ten minutes to get what I wanted. When I had it I left the boat and joined the others on the wharf. I had no clothes except those on my back, but my duffel was nearly full.

As we walked towards the pub, Nigel's words echoed in my mind and triggered a thought. Was it really over? Callaghan knew someone had his ten million dollars. I was afraid he was the type who wouldn't stop until he recovered it. I couldn't hide forever. Once he knew I was alive then he'd figure I had the money. As long as I was alive and they didn't have the money, it wasn't over.

We had several beers and lunch at a pub near the port. Eventually, it was time for Gordon and me to head for the airport and for Nigel and Hare to return to the *Storm Petrel*. We'd agreed they'd take the box of money to the shed Nigel used for storing his sailing gear. He'd booked a small truck with a Hiab crane for the transfer.

At the airport, I said farewell to Gordon again and watched him board his plane. I checked my duffel at the airline desk and waited in the departure lounge for my flight. We left on time and had an uneventful trip to Auckland. I spent the time thinking about Emma.

PART III

NEW ZEALAND AND THE SOUTHERN OCEAN

CHAPTER 27

I couldn't go home. It was still a wreck from the fire, so I had the taxi take me to a local motel. I checked in, dumped my bag and lay on the bed, truly relaxing for the first time since I'd sailed from Dunedin. I hadn't realised how stressed I'd been until I was back on solid ground and away from danger.

I woke from my doze at about 11 p.m. It was late, but I decided to call Emma one more time before going to bed. I dialled her number and listened to it ring. This time it was answered. 'Mr Stone.' A vaguely familiar voice, definitely not Emma's.

'Who is this? How did you get Emma's phone? How did you know it was me?'

The husky voice said, 'I'm an associate of David Callaghan. We met briefly in his office.'

I thought back to my visits to David's office and suddenly remembered the figure on the Dunedin wharf. 'You're the Russian agent from Vladivostok.'

'Indeed. As to how I knew the call was from you, you left several messages on her phone. And who else would call at this hour?' He paused before continuing. 'There were some unusual events down south, and you are a remarkably resourceful fellow. I hear you had an … interesting voyage.'

'*Interesting*. Yes, that's probably the best word for it. The boys on the ship were such fun. A laugh a minute. And then the opportunity to see the Bounty Islands. Well, what can I say? We had a great time playing tag with another ship down there. And you wouldn't believe the flotsam we picked up. Really, you think the ocean's a vast empty place, but in fact, it's full of such remarkable things.'

'Jetsam. If it's thrown overboard, then it's jetsam.'

'Hmm, who'd believe English was your second language?'

Alexander was silent for a moment, then he said, 'I think it's time to get down to business. You have something I want. I have something you want. We need to make an exchange.'

'Really? You have something I want? I don't think so. I have a big black box. A box filled with things you want. But there is absolutely nothing you could have that I want.'

'Is that so? I thought you were fond of Ms DeSilva.'

The words drove an icicle through my heart. When he'd answered Emma's phone I'd been afraid of this, but even so I wasn't ready to face the reality of it. I couldn't speak. 'Mr Stone? Are you there? You've tried to call and have been unable to get through. Unfortunately, Emma's been entertaining several of my men and hasn't been able to come to the phone.'

Fear and rage burned through me and I shouted, 'You bastard! If you've harmed her—'

Alexander interrupted, 'Now, now. There is absolutely no need to worry. She is in perfect condition. Not a hair out of place. My men have been very careful to take good care of her.'

I brought my feelings under control enough to say, 'Okay. What do you want?'

'We want the box with our money. Bring it to the freight terminal at Auckland airport and we will release her.'

'And if I don't?'

There was a long silence. Then Alexander said, 'Bring the money, Adam.'

'Let me talk to her.'

'I'm sorry, that's impossible. She's not here.'

'Where is she?'

'You know I can't tell you that.'

'But she'll be there? At the exchange? At the airport?'

'No. It's not convenient for her to be there. When we have the money we will release her. We can show you a video to prove it's happened.'

My mind raced frantically. Every scenario I could think of ended with Emma dead and the box of money gone. Worrying about Emma reminded me of the clarity of her thinking. I asked myself, what would she do? And the answer was clear – she'd do what she always did. Take the initiative. Keep them off balance. Don't let them set the terms for the exchange. I would have to change the rules, force them to adapt. And perhaps make a mistake.

I tried to control the strain in my voice when I replied, 'It may not be convenient for me to have the money there. Let me think about it. I'll call you back.'

I hung up the phone and tossed it on the bedside table. My hands were shaking. Fuck! I was gambling with Emma's life. But what else could I do? My response had been instinctive, not rational. These men had killed my brother and tried to kill Emma and me. I knew they wouldn't hesitate to kill Emma if they thought it necessary. But deep in my unconscious, I knew they were greedy men; everything they did was driven by money. I was gambling that if they weighed the death of Emma against the loss of ten million dollars, then they would decide they wanted the money.

My thoughts were a jumble, but I was certain of one thing – I wasn't handing over anything until I knew that Emma was alive. I wasn't handing over anything unless Emma was there and they released her to me.

As I sat on the bed my ideas slowly began to coalesce. There were no details, and there were large gaps, but right then that didn't matter. It would have to be enough. The fear and rage I'd felt when Alexander told me they had Emma was gone, replaced by a cold determination that odds didn't matter anymore. We would prevail because failure wasn't an option.

———

Before I left the motel, I made a couple of phone calls. I'd been looking out of the motel room's window at the bright green lawn outside. It was a perfect summer day, with the sun beating down from a clear sky and a gentle breeze to moderate the heat. The grass had just been cut and it looked as good as it was ever going to look. I could see birds flitting between the shrubs on the road boundary and heard the sound of a lawnmower somewhere in the distance.

The first call was to Gordon in his office in Wellington. The receiver was slippery in my hand, the sweat from tension and fear rather than the heat. 'Gordon, it's Adam.'

'Adam! I wasn't expecting to hear from you so soon. Have you heard from Emma? How is she?'

'That's why I'm calling. They have her, Gordon. They have her and they won't give her back until they get the money.'

'Shit! How'd … No, that doesn't matter. What can I do?'

Once again, I silently thanked Emma for bringing Gordon onto the team. There were no questions, no excuses, just an offer to help. 'I'm still working on it, but I need you in Auckland. Tomorrow if you can make it.'

'I'm on it. I'll text you my flight details when I know them. Where are you? Where do you want to meet?'

I gave him the address of my motel and thanked him.

My next call was to Nigel and was similar to the first one. 'Nigel, Adam here.'

'Hey, Adam. How's it going? Need something from the box?'

'It's Emma, Nigel. They have her. I spoke with one of the bastards from Blue Ocean. He said they'll give her back when they get their money.'

'Bugger. I assume you're calling because you need help. What can I do?'

I gave him the outline of my plan and told him what I might need of him. The only thing he said was, 'I'll be ready.'

The third call was to Connor. I got straight to the point, 'Connor, they have Emma.'

He was silent for a moment and then let out a low groan. 'Oh, no. Shit! How is she? Is she alive? I told you guys to be careful.'

'I don't know. They wouldn't let me talk to her. I have to assume she's alive.' I took a deep breath and steadied myself. 'A lot has happened since we talked, and you need to know about it.' I went on to describe briefly my trip to the Southern Ocean.

'Damn,' said Connor. 'Are you insane? How could you possibly think going to sea on the *Polar Princess* was a good idea?'

'Too late to worry about that now. I have their money and they have Emma. I'm sure they'll kill her if I don't give them the money.'

'I'm sorry Adam. What are you going to do?'

I told him what I had in mind, and there was a long silence on the phone. 'Can you do it?' I prompted. 'Is it possible?'

I heard Connor sigh, then say, 'Yeah, it's *possible*. But can I do it? I don't know. I'd need some special gear and software. I think I could find ...' His voice trailed off, then resumed, 'This is serious shit, Adam. I'm a backroom guy. I do the background stuff. I don't do the action man thing. This would make me part of it. Make me a target.'

'She needs you, Connor. I need you. I can't be in two places at once, and you're the only one who can help.'

There was another long silence, then Connor said, 'Okay, I'll try. But look, I may not be able to get ready in time. I'll need to get the stuff, set it up and get in position. There'll be no time for a test run. I've never used this gear before and can't guarantee it'll work first time.'

'Thanks, Connor. Don't worry. Do your best. It'll work. It has to.'

My final call was to Blue Ocean Seafoods. I told Ms Adams, David's PA, that I had something to give him. She went away, and when she returned she said, 'Would tomorrow afternoon be alright? About 3?'

I said that would be fine and hung up.

CHAPTER 28

The office was becoming familiar: the solid desk, the nautilus shell, the wall of windows. But the man behind the desk wasn't the same. There were lines that hadn't been there before. The confident air was slipping. Callaghan didn't get up. 'Adam. I wish I could say I was happy to see you but I'm not. You seem to bring me nothing but trouble.'

'Trouble?' I put the package I'd brought with me on his desk. It had been X-rayed at the entrance while a guard in the foyer had efficiently searched me for weapons, wires, something he didn't like. He didn't find anything.

Ms Adams was waiting for me when I exited the elevator. 'He's expecting you,' she said and led me through the door by the receptionist and along the spartan corridor. Her manner was frostier than on my previous visits. I was sorry about that; I quite liked Ms Adams.

She opened the door without knocking and held it for me. I heard it close softly behind me as I stepped into the office. Everything was as I remembered, including the spectacular view of the harbour through the floor-to-ceiling windows.

Callaghan ignored the package and asked, 'Did you enjoy your voyage on the *Polar Princess*? Did you find the closure you were seeking?'

I smiled and replied, 'It was a remarkable trip. I had no idea life on your ships was so exciting.'

'Well, everyone has their own experiences. We here at Blue Ocean are certainly grateful for your services.'

'Thank you. And my report was acceptable?'

'Absolutely. A model of the work we'd like to receive from our observers. Full of astute observations and recommendations.'

'Really, *my* report? It was that good?'

'I assure you, I don't think I've seen a better one.'

'That's interesting, seeing as I didn't write one.'

'My dear fellow, I read it just yesterday. Here, I'll show you.' He pressed a button on his desk phone, 'Carol? Could you please bring me a copy of Mr Stone's report? Thank you.'

'Come on, David. You know I didn't write a report. I didn't even return to port on the *Polar Princess*.'

There was a knock on the door and Carol walked in and dropped a bound document on Callaghan's desk. She gave me an unreadable look as she left.

Callaghan handed it across the desk to me. I looked at the cover, 'Science Representative's Report, Polar Princess, Ross Sea, 20 November to 27 January'. My name was at the bottom of the cover. I tossed the report on his desk without opening it. 'No wonder it's the type of report you want to receive. You wrote it.'

Callaghan shook his head. 'I'm sorry, Adam. You were on the voyage. You wrote the report. I don't know why you're trying to say otherwise.'

'I'm saying otherwise because I was thrown off your ship and nearly drowned. Fortunately, I was picked up by another boat and they brought me back to New Zealand. I didn't write that report. I didn't return to port with the *Polar Princess*.'

'Adam, I assure you everyone who boarded the *Polar Princess* in November got off her in January. Believe me, our operations are watched like a hawk. Cameras record everything, every movement. Do you seriously think the police would not be here instead of you if you hadn't returned with the ship?'

'Look, David, I don't know what—'

He raised a finger to interrupt me. 'Wait a minute, I have the video here somewhere.' He tapped his keyboard for a minute or so. 'Yes, here it is. The video of you returning to Dunedin.' He swivelled his screen around towards me and pressed a key.

I saw a grainy black-and-white video. It showed a wharf and parts of three fishing vessels tied up alongside. One of them was the *Polar Princess*. There was activity at her stern, unloading boxes of frozen toothfish.

'Let me skip forward. This isn't very interesting.' He played with his keys and the images flashed past, then slowed and stopped. 'Yes, this is it.'

I watched the screen. A figure came down the gangway and turned towards the camera. It was wearing a hoodie so the face was largely obscured. It was wearing my clothes. The figure disappeared out of sight beneath the camera. 'There you are, Adam. That's you, leaving the *Polar Princess*. Everyone accounted for.'

I'd wondered how they'd explained my absence. The answer was simple; they hadn't had to. They'd smuggled someone on board, easy to do with people and boxes leaving and boarding the ship during unloading. They'd dressed him in my clothes and he'd walked ashore. He didn't actually look much like me, but with a hoodie and the poor quality video it would be hard to prove it wasn't.

Callaghan noticed me squinting slightly against the slanting afternoon sun. 'Here, let me draw the curtains. You don't need to have the sun in your eyes.'

'No, it's fine. Please, I enjoy the view of the water. It's relaxing.' I shifted my gaze from the window to him. 'Okay, David, let's stop the horseshit. I got your message. You have something I want, I have something you want. All we have to do is agree on the terms for delivery. '

Callaghan eyed the package on his desk. It was about twenty-five centimetres on each side, wrapped in plain brown paper and sealed with brown tape. He grunted, 'Then what's this?' He gestured at the package and sat further back in his chair.

'As a sign of good faith I've brought you one million dollars. You understand I couldn't bring the whole box. It weighs 100 kilos.'

He sat silently, his eyes flicking between me and the package. At last, he said, 'I have no idea what you're talking about.'

I gave a small laugh. 'It's okay, David. You don't have to worry. Your guard took my phone and searched me. I'm not wearing a microphone. You can speak freely here. Everything's off the record.'

He still didn't say anything.

'What? Did you think that when your buddy Alexander called demanding an exchange, I wouldn't come straight here? Do you think I'd follow some ridiculous instructions to deliver the ransom without seeing Emma? Do I strike you as the sort of guy who'd do that, David?'

'Ransom?' He shook his head. 'I'm sorry Adam, but I don't have any idea what you're talking about.'

I reached for the package and tapped it with a finger. 'Shall I open it? Show you it's real? The money? Part of the money you lost?'

He raised a hand. 'You're confusing me, Adam. Are you saying someone demanded a million dollars in ransom?'

'Not just one million, David. You're not listening. This is just a good-faith payment. If you deliver what I want, then I'll give you what you want. All of it. The full ransom. A large black plastic box containing the other nine million dollars.'

He shifted in his chair and I could see his eyes change. 'Ten million dollars. I don't know where or how you may have obtained ten million dollars, but I'm certain it's got nothing to do with me.'

I let my hand drift across the package, feeling the hard weight of the cash inside. 'Okay, David, let me tell you a story.' His eyes were on me but he appeared totally relaxed. Maybe I could change that. 'Once upon a time, there was a fishing company. It was a profitable fishing company. It delivered value to its shareholders and claimed to catch its fish sustainably, though what that means is questionable when most of the fish were caught by bottom trawling that destroys seafloor habitats.'

I looked at Callaghan and continued. 'Then a new CEO took over. A CEO who wanted to make his mark. He'd fought his way to the top, and it didn't take long for him to spot an opportunity to increase the value of the business. Not the company, mind you, but definitely the business. He saw that boats were leaving New Zealand empty and coming back full. This was obviously inefficient. But what could they sail with that they could profitably get rid of before returning to port? Nothing of value needs to be regularly disposed of, so dumping at sea wasn't the answer. And trans-shipment of legitimate exports makes no sense as it would be easier and cheaper just to use a commercial shipping line. But ... trans-shipment of illegal exports might make sense. Smuggling them out of New Zealand, loading them on another ship, and then smuggling them into another country. But what could it be? Drugs are the obvious possibility, but New Zealand is an importer of drugs. And there's no firearms industry here, so smuggling guns was out.'

I ran my hand over the package and sat down in the chair across the desk from him. 'We'll never know what triggered the *eureka* moment. Did the CEO have the idea and search for someone to make it happen? Or did he meet someone with the need who asked if the CEO could help? However it transpired, the CEO eventually asked himself: what do all illegal activities have in common? It doesn't matter if it's selling cocaine in Chicago or machine guns in Mali: they need to get their illegal cash back into legitimate circulation. The drugs industry in New Zealand is a minnow by world standards, but its needs are the same. So the CEO or someone else had the bright idea of taking some of that illegal cash on one of your ships and tossing it overboard, to be picked up by another vessel and taken overseas where the financial laws are more lax, where there are more opportunities to deal with it. Somewhere like, say, Russia?'

'Really, Adam, I have work—'

I held up a palm to silence him. 'I have no direct knowledge of this, David, but I have a hunch that if you were to travel to the Bounty

Islands then you might find a Russian factory ship there, stuck on a reef. And if you looked on board that ship then you might find five large black plastic boxes, each containing ten million dollars. Boxes I saw thrown overboard from the *Polar Princess*. Unless, of course, they've been removed along with the crew.'

Callaghan was silent. I wasn't sure if it was the loss of sixty million dollars or the fact that his scheme was no longer a secret that concerned him more.

'It was those boxes that got Theo killed, wasn't it?' I asked. 'He was somewhere he wasn't supposed to be and saw them going over the side. I doubt he knew what was in them, but he was smart enough to know it was something illegal. You killed him to shut him up, to make sure he didn't report what he'd seen at the end of the voyage.'

I waited and watched his face. I wanted him emotional, but not angry. 'Come on, David. It's almost over. I've come a long way to get here. It's just you and me. There are no witnesses, no recordings. You won. You have Emma and you're going to get the money. You've outsmarted us at every turn. Just, I want to know, tell me what happened.' I could see Callaghan thinking hard. I hoped he'd decide to do something stupid.

After a long silence, he looked at me and said, 'As usual, you're partly correct. Your brother was in the wrong place at the wrong time. But there was no intention to kill him.' Callaghan turned to stare out his windows. Puffy clouds floated past on the breeze, stark contrast to the dark story he was about to tell.

His voice was soft when he spoke again. 'It was night. Pitch black. Rain. Hard rain. The summer nights at that latitude are short, but the storm blotted out all light. Your brother went to the mess about midnight for coffee and a sandwich. The other observer, Phil Coetzee, was there and appears to be the last person to see him alive.

'There was a big southerly swell, six, maybe eight metres, and the captain had told everyone to stay below. The ship was moving so much that it was difficult to walk, far too dangerous to work on deck. Everything was shut down, everyone except those on watch in the bridge and engine room was supposed to be in their cabin. Why did

Theo go on deck?' He shook his head. 'Maybe he looked through a porthole, saw something outside. Whatever the reason, he went to the recovery room. He couldn't see much, but he was able to see people pushing the boxes over the side. Coetzee had followed him. He was in on the scheme; he knew what was in the boxes. He panicked. He picked up a gaff used to haul the fish over the side and hit your brother on the head. Only he hit him too hard and killed him. Before they could secure the body, a wave took it over the side. The rest you know.'

He paused and looked at me. 'We could have handled it. We have the cover story, scientific buoys, for just this sort of event.'

I was silent for a long time before I said, 'You're saying that Theo was killed by mistake? That all of this,' I gestured futilely, 'this death, this violence, this lying, was because of a mistake?'

Callaghan didn't say anything. I made an effort to control my emotions. I reminded myself that Theo was dead but Emma was still alive and now, more than ever, I needed to save her.

I took a deep breath and tried to calm myself. 'Okay. Okay. Here's the deal. I have one of your boxes, with ten million dollars of illegitimate money. One million of that is here on your desk. Yesterday, I received a phone call from your Russian buddy telling me to take the box of money to Auckland airport. He implied that if I did not do so, then Emma would be killed.'

Thinking about Theo and Emma, I felt the rage sweep through me again. I slammed my hand down on his desk and shouted, 'Emma! I know you have her. *You* ordered her to be kidnapped. *You* know where she's being held. *You* know how to get her released.' I regained my composure with difficulty and sat back in my seat. I said more quietly, 'So that's what I want. I want you to tell whoever has her that she has to be at the *Polar Princess* in Dunedin tomorrow night. I'll have the rest of the money. If Emma's there, then we'll make the exchange. If she's not then you'll never see your money again.'

Callaghan's head rolled back against his chair and he laughed. It was a good laugh and lasted a long time. He finally calmed down and shook his head. He reached forward and pulled the package towards him. He lifted it and felt its weight, holding it for a second before putting it back on his desk. 'Oh, Adam, you think you've got it all figured out. You think you're so clever. Why shouldn't we kill Emma and forget about the money? Why shouldn't I just kidnap you, too, and get my associates to find out where this box of money is?'

'Because I'm not alone. Other people know I'm here. Other people know you have Emma. They know about the box, about the ten million dollars that was thrown off one of your ships in the Southern Ocean. The ten million dollars that was meant to be collected by the *Sergey Belov*. If Emma disappears, if I disappear, then they will go to the police and the media with the money and the story.' I reached across the desk and pulled the package of money back towards me. 'However, if you take the money and Emma and I go free, then we have no hard evidence, nothing more than circumstantial evidence to take to the police. And so far circumstantial evidence has gotten us nowhere. So, David, what do you say?'

Callaghan was quiet for a long time. His eyes didn't leave my face. A single tic affected one eye, otherwise, he showed no outward sign of stress. Finally, he shifted in his chair and said, 'You are a very persistent fellow. I'm afraid my associates and I underestimated you. I will pass on your message. Ms DeSilva will be in Dunedin tomorrow night. As will I. But listen carefully – if there is any sign of the police, any sign of your clever tricks, then we will kill her. And you. Your bodies will be found with drugs on them and your deaths will be attributed to a drug deal gone wrong. You will be gone, Ms DeSilva will be gone, the money will be gone. If you cooperate and deliver the money, then both of you will be free to go. As you say, there will be no proof of any illegal activity, no connection to me or Blue Ocean.' He stood up and pulled the package towards him. 'I accept your good faith offer. Now, unless there's something else? No? Then I'll see you tomorrow night.'

I turned and left without a word. I knew the bastard was at least partly right. I had coincidences and suspicious activities and some illegally obtained information from Connor, but that was it. No proof that Callaghan killed Theo, no proof he was laundering money with his fish boxes, no proof he was laundering money with the *Polar Princess*, no proof he'd tried to kill me. I hoped Connor would come through and give me something more tangible. Callaghan might say otherwise, but I knew he wouldn't let us walk away tomorrow night. My plan was looking more desperate by the minute.

CHAPTER 29

I was exhausted when I got back to the motel room. I wanted a drink, but there were things I needed to do, and Emma's life might depend on me doing them. I paced the room, going over every word I'd had with Callaghan, considering nuances of meaning, of intent, of treachery I might have missed. I went over my plan again and again, looking for weaknesses, but there were so many I gave up. There were too many things that could go wrong, any one of which could destroy everything.

I'd been in the room for about an hour when there was a knock on the door. I looked through the peephole and unlocked and opened the door when I saw who was there. 'Connor!' I said with relief. 'Damn, I was worried. Did everything go as we planned? Did the equipment work?'

Connor had a grin from ear to ear. 'Adam, it was fucking amazing. Crystal clear. Every word.' He held up a thumb drive. 'You should listen to it – it'll blow your socks off.'

So I did, and it did. When it was finished I pulled the thumb drive from my computer and held it in my hand. I looked at Connor and said, 'Thanks, Connor. You don't know how much this means.'

'Oh, I think I do,' he said, still smiling. He threw his pack over his shoulder and added, 'And you will too. All that gear, and my time … the bill's going to be eye-watering, absolutely eye-watering.'

Shortly after Connor left, there was another knock on my door. I greeted Gordon warmly when he entered. I offered him a beer, which he accepted, and we sat at the table in the corner of the room. I outlined the situation and explained his role. I could hear the tension in Gordon's voice when he replied. 'Dammit, Adam. They have Emma! Are you sure this is going to work? It's her life we're talking about.'

'I know, Gordon, believe me, I know. But I wouldn't trust those Blue Ocean guys to shit in a paper bag. I trust you and Connor and Nigel, and that's it. But there's only so much we can do. We need someone official to back us up. That's where you come in.'

I heard Gordon take a deep breath and release it. 'Okay. This is worse than that crazy trip to the Bounties. You know that, don't you?'

'Yeah, maybe, but this time they're not calling the shots. We're going to be prepared.' I held up the thumb drive with Connor's analysis of Blue Ocean's Russian business on it. 'This is the stuff we told you about in your office, the stuff Connor discovered about Blue Ocean's finances, the two hundred million dollars they're moving every year.' Then I held up the other thumb drive, the one Connor had just given me. 'And this, my friend, this may save our asses. It's a recording of an interesting conversation I had at Blue Ocean earlier today. The files on the first drive should get the attention of the police. The recording on the second one should get some action.'

I plugged the drive into my computer and played the recording for Gordon. A grim smile appeared on his face as he heard Callaghan's story. I confess I was feeling slightly more optimistic when I listened again to the file on the thumb drive.

Gordon took the drives and put them in his pocket. 'Got it. I'll call the police first thing tomorrow. I'm a reporter, I can be very persuasive.'

He stood up and moved to the door. We shook hands again and I said, 'Gordon, thanks, we're counting on you.'

'Whatever happens, Adam, I'll be there tomorrow night.'

After Gordon left I felt totally drained. It had been a long, hard day, and I'd taken some big gambles. I went to bed, tossed and turned, sure I would never go to sleep. I was dead to the world in ten minutes.

CHAPTER 30

It was after midnight and the wharf was dark except for a few halogen lights high on poles near the water. The lights were widely spaced and their bright glow emphasised the hard shadows and did little to dispel the gloom in the wide gaps between them. Nigel drove the truck slowly along the cracked concrete, headlights off, easing past a container stored outside one of the warehouses. I sat beside him in the truck cab. My head swivelled constantly, looking for anything amiss. 'It's not too late,' I said softly.

'Fuck off,' said Nigel. 'It was too late when we picked up the box.'

I had flown to Dunedin that morning with no idea how I was going to get the box of money to the agreed rendezvous. I'd called Nigel to get directions to the shed where it was stored, and he told me he was coming along for the delivery. I'd reluctantly agreed. I didn't want to get anyone else involved in what could be a very dicey situation, but I desperately needed help to move the box. I remembered how coolly Nigel had handled the pursuit at the Bounties, and I reassured myself that if anyone was qualified for this job then it was him.

As we loaded the box on the truck I filled Nigel in on our money laundering theory, Emma's kidnap, Connor's recording and Gordon's visit to the police that morning. Gordon had called me just as I was boarding the flight to Dunedin. 'All set, Adam.'

'No problems? No questions?'

'Plenty of questions. The situation is quote, "highly unorthodox", unquote, but she agreed with your plan. She understands the danger to Emma and won't interfere unless you signal her. She's going through the information on the thumb drives you gave me. If she can confirm it, then she'll be ready to move in a couple of days.'

I'd thought about that for a moment. Without a police presence at the handover we would be terribly exposed, but I couldn't risk Emma's death if they were discovered. I had to trust that Gordon, Nigel and I would be able to get Emma back on our own. 'You're a champion, Gordon. See you tonight?'

'I'm on my way to the airport. See you.'

By the time I'd finished telling all this to Nigel, the loading of the box was almost complete. Nigel worked the Hiab crane controls and settled the heavy box on the truck bed. 'Let me get this straight,' he said. 'You've orchestrated quite an evening. We're taking a shitload of money to this meeting. How do you know Emma's going to be there?'

I shrugged. 'I don't.'

'You're trusting these guys to have her there? And to release her when you give them the money?'

'Trust but verify. Gordon and you will be there to cover my back.'

———

Nigel brought the truck to a stop outside a warehouse. We'd gained access to the wharf without difficulty. Nigel told the guard he was taking some supplies to his boat. The guard hadn't said anything, just opened the gate for us. Vessel movements were often dictated by tides, so coming and going in the middle of the night wasn't unusual.

A fishing vessel was tied up at the wharf alongside the warehouse, hawsers looped over bollards fore and aft. The tide was in and a gangway sloped steeply up from the wharf to the deck of the ship. There were no lights on board, not even over the gangway. I was surprised for a moment that no one was standing watch, but I reminded myself that this was New Zealand, not New Guinea, and the threat of crime on the wharf was probably not great. In the dim illumination from the wharf's overhead lights, I could just make out the name of the ship painted on its bow: *Polar Princess*.

I'd been nervous since I left Blue Ocean Seafoods the previous day, but my heartbeat went up another notch as I sat and looked at the ship. I had a box with nine million dollars in it on the back of the truck; Blue Ocean had Emma. If things didn't go right, then I'd lose them both. I reached for the door handle. 'Fuck it. Let's take a look.'

We left the truck and looked carefully around the wharf. There was no sign of life, nothing out of the ordinary. The silence was broken only by the faint slap of waves against the wharf piles, and the soft onshore breeze brought the scent of the ocean to us.

Before we could move, a dark shape stepped out of the gloom alongside the *Polar Princess*. The size and easy movement were familiar. 'Judd,' I said, 'so nice to see you again.'

'Stone,' he replied. His eyes glittered dully and a thin smile twisted his lips, pale in the darkness of his beard. 'You must be the luckiest man alive.'

'Down boy. We're here to talk. Your persuasive talents aren't required.'

As Judd started walking towards us another form appeared at the top of the gangway. I looked up and said, 'David, how good of you to make it.' I gestured towards Judd. 'I can't say I'm delighted to see the bos'n.'

'Judd is very useful. So much going on, I thought it advisable to be prepared.' Callaghan gestured towards Nigel and asked, 'And who's your friend?'

'It's a heavy box. It took two of us to lift it.'

No one moved for a long moment. Then Callaghan said softly, 'Show me the money.' His eyes almost glowed with intensity in the harsh halogen lighting.

'Uh-uh. I want to know Emma's alive first. I see her; you get to look in the box. When she's safe with me, you get to take the box.'

Callaghan glanced at the burly mate. 'Judd could just take it from you.'

Nigel pulled a large wrench from a pocket in his overalls. 'He could try.'

Callaghan stared at us, his blue eyes cold in the darkness. I wondered if he or one of the crew had a gun. 'Very well.' He snapped his fingers and said, 'Bring her.'

There were faint noises from out of sight on deck and then Emma appeared alongside Callaghan at the head of the gangway. Her hair was tangled, her clothes were rumpled and there were smudges on her face, but my heart leapt when I saw her. She was gagged and her hands were tied behind her back, but she was definitely alive. She stood tall and looked straight at me and I thought I saw relief (love? I hoped for love, but would take relief) in her eyes. Peters, the mate, stood at her shoulder and kept a close eye on me.

'There. Are you satisfied? Now show me the money,' Callaghan demanded.

I took my eyes off Emma and looked at Callaghan. Then I turned to Nigel who was standing by the box and said, 'Open it.'

The latches were broken so all he had to do was lift the lid. He pivoted and leaned it against the back of the box. Inside, the black plastic lining obscured the contents. Nigel paused and looked at me.

'Show me the money!' Callaghan repeated impatiently.

We'd taken out the top layer of foam packing so when I nodded and Nigel pulled back the plastic sheet the blocks of one hundred dollar notes appeared, each wrapped in clear plastic. 'The gap is from the money I took to your office,' I said, though Callaghan was so focused on the box it was hard to tell if he heard me.

Nigel picked up one of the plastic-wrapped bundles and held it up in the light. 'There are nine of these in the box. We counted the money in the one Adam gave you, it had a million dollars. This is the other nine million.'

Callaghan gestured towards the box. 'Judd, check it out.'

Judd walked past me, giving me the hard eye as he did so. Nigel moved to give Judd access to the box. Judd stood by it and looked at me again, then at Nigel, and grunted. He picked up the block of money Nigel had handled. His knife appeared as if from nowhere and he gently slit the plastic. He pulled out a few bills, examining them closely. He put the bundle aside and retrieved another from the box. He repeated the process of opening it with his knife and examining the bills inside. After what seemed an age but was probably no more than a couple of minutes he grunted again and said, 'Looks okay.'

Callaghan's eyes gleamed in the dim light. 'Right, let's get a sling on that box and get it on board.'

I held up a hand and wiggled a finger. 'Uh-uh. What did I say? We've seen Emma, you've seen the money. Now you get the money when I get Emma.'

The light in Callaghan's eyes changed from greed to rage in an instant. I could see him almost trembling as the anger coursed through his body. Finally, he could contain it no longer and he shouted, 'Give me my money!'

Before anyone could move a small red dot appeared in the centre of Callaghan's chest and a voice drifted out of the darkness, 'Actually, it's *our* money.'

Callaghan's head jerked up and he involuntarily raised his hands to try and brush away the red spot. I looked at Nigel. He moved his head a fraction sideways and we both sidled a step away from the ship and the box. I didn't know what was going on, but the appearance of a laser sight didn't bode well for everyone just shaking hands and walking away.

'Really, David,' the voice continued, 'you've been a very bad boy. Thanks to your incompetence, we've lost a very large amount of money. Your investors aren't amused. They've asked me to tidy things up.'

I'd only heard it twice, but I immediately recognised the voice of Alexander Ivanov. And I saw we were in deep shit. If Stepan Sokolov and whoever else was behind the scam wanted Alexander to tidy up, then our future could be short.

I saw a look of fear flick across Callaghan's face, but he had long ago learned how to control fear. His fear must have made him reckless, though, because he said with some heat, 'Alexander, is that you? Listen, you fuck, you're the one who's incompetent. You tried to kill Stone, twice, and failed! If you'd listened to me this whole mess wouldn't have happened.'

The red dot didn't move. Alexander's voice was as soft as a serpent's hiss. 'David, do you need to be reminded who is the master? And who is the servant?'

I saw Callaghan lick his lips, fear once again appearing on his face. 'Alexander, listen, you're making a mistake. We've got the ten million dollars back. It's right here. These two and the woman are the only outsiders who know anything. Kill them and everything will be okay.'

I didn't like the direction the conversation was taking. I did not doubt that Alexander was prepared to kill anyone who was a problem. And despite what he had said, I suspected that in his eyes we were still a bigger problem than Callaghan. I cleared my throat and stepped forward a pace, looking in the direction of his voice. 'Alexander. How nice to see you again. You are a man of many talents. Fish importer by day, assassin by night?'

From the darkness, Alexander seemed to ignore me and said, 'Don't worry, David. You fucked up, but we know we can count on you, just as we always have.' The red dot shifted from Callaghan's chest to mine. I suddenly desperately needed a toilet. 'Mr Stone, what can I say? We Russians learn to be multi-talented. What about you? What are you doing here on the wharf with a box containing nine million dollars? Are you also multi-talented? Fish observer by day and, what, thief by night?'

Before I could respond a high-powered torch beam lanced through the night, revealing Alexander standing about ten metres to my left. His salt and pepper hair gleamed like silver in the light's intense beam, but his grey eyes were invisible in the shadows beneath his dark brows. The person holding the torch was a similar distance to my right. I turned from Alexander to see who else was making a surprise appearance. The light was shining directly into my eyes so I held my hand up, trying unsuccessfully to see who was behind it. Then I heard the sound of footsteps on the concrete wharf and a dark figure appeared. The light shifted from my eyes and I could see who held the torch – Detective Killand. And beside him was Gordon. This was starting to remind me of that circus act where clowns keep coming out of a tiny car. I wondered if there were any more clowns still to appear.

Killand held the torch in his left hand. Gordon shifted and I saw the detective had a pistol in his right hand, pointed at Gordon's back. Gordon looked terrified. Between Alexander and Killand, I figured there were two guns too many at the party. Killand and Gordon walked forward and stood by the box.

'Gentlemen,' the detective said conversationally, 'am I interrupting something?' He slowly looked at each of us and finally addressed Callaghan, 'I found this one lurking in the shadows. I thought he should have a closer view of the proceedings. We wouldn't want him to miss anything.'

Callaghan didn't seem surprised by the detective's appearance. 'Ah, indeed.' Looking at Gordon he said, 'You must be Mr Crawford, the friend Adam was telling me about. The friend who knows all about our little venture. Is that so?'

Gordon had to swallow before he could speak. 'I don't know what you're talking about.'

'It's okay, Gordon,' I said, 'it's time to cut the bullshit.' I looked at Killand and said, 'Detective, how good to see you. I wasn't sure where your loyalties lay. It's good to have that cleared up.'

'Fuck off. You didn't have a clue.'

'I wasn't sure, but I had plenty of clues. You tried to hinder us from the start. At every step, you tried to discourage our investigation. You and Callaghan were the only two people who knew Emma and I were in Auckland the day we were run off the road. Not enough to prove you were bent, but more than enough to make us suspicious. And take precautions.'

I turned and looked up at Callaghan. 'When we spoke in your office yesterday, you said I had nothing, no proof of any illegal activity. And you were right. I knew you were responsible for Theo's

death, but I couldn't prove it.' I moved closer to the gangway and took
my phone out of my pocket. I shook my head and chuckled, 'You
know, kids these days, they're amazing. Really! They start learning
computer programming in elementary school. By the time they're in
high school, they're writing code like professionals. And the Internet!
The Internet is just awesome. You can find just about anything you
want if you look hard enough. Some of the things you can find are just
unbelievable.' I continued to walk towards Callaghan, staying focused
on his eyes. So far there was nothing to see – no interest, no fear,
nothing.

'You may have seen movies where spies rig up this fancy gear with
lasers and computers and shit and listen in on conversations inside a
building? They analyse the vibrations on the glass windows. Can you
believe it? I mean, how can that even be possible? But it is. And it
turns out a bunch of French teenagers wrote software to do just that
and turned it in for an assignment in their computer science class. Even
better, they put the code on the Internet so everyone can use it. Today
you don't have to be James Bond to listen to conversations in a closed
room. Anyone can do it. Well, almost anyone.'

I was at the bottom of the gangway, looking straight up at
Callaghan. I thought I saw a spark of something in his eyes and I
continued, 'If you're freaking smart then you can cobble together a
system from off-the-shelf components and, after about a week of
pulling your hair out, you can get the software to talk to it and make a
recording. If you're smart and motivated, very motivated, then you can
do all that in a couple of hours.'

I held up my phone. 'David? Did you know that was possible? I
really enjoyed the view out of your windows the other day. My
freaking smart colleague found a spot across the Viaduct Harbour with
a view of your office. And after telling about a dozen pensioners he
wasn't working for Jimmy Spittal's America's Cup team, he recorded
everything we said. Do you remember our conversation, David? I've
extracted a few bits to refresh your memory in case you've forgotten.'

I pulled up the audio app on my phone and pressed play. The

recording wasn't very loud, but the night was quiet and I knew Callaghan could hear it.

Coetzee had followed him. He was in on the scheme; he knew what was in the boxes. He panicked. He picked up a gaff used to haul the fish over the side and hit your brother on the head. Only he hit him too hard and killed him ... Ms DeSilva will be in Dunedin tomorrow night. As will I. But listen carefully – if there is any sign of the police, any sign of your clever tricks, then we will kill her. And you. Your bodies will be found with drugs on them and your deaths will be attributed to a drug deal gone wrong. You will be gone, Ms DeSilva will be gone, the money will be gone.

I said, 'You know another thing about the Internet, David? They've got this thing called the Cloud. I guess it's not actually a thing, it's more of a network, but anyway it exists. And the great thing about the Cloud is once something's there then it's bloody hard to get rid of it. Copies of this recording are on the Cloud. I don't understand it, either, but there are so many copies they can't be found and deleted.'

I turned off the app and asked, 'So, David, what do you think? Sounds to me like evidence of murder and intent to commit murder. Should we go to the police?' I looked at Detective Killand. 'Oops. They're already here. Aren't you, Detective?'

Killand almost snarled, 'You think you're pretty smart, don't you? But you haven't thought it through, Stone. If your evidence against us is that bad then we've got nothing to lose, have we?' He raised his pistol and put it to Gordon's head. 'Things won't get worse if we kill you all.'

I turned and looked at Alexander. 'Yes, you can shoot us. But that won't put the genie back in the bottle. I don't know what the penalty is for financial crimes, but I'm pretty sure it's a lot less than for murder.'

The red dot from Alexander's rifle was still on my chest. My heart was beating like a pneumatic drill but I felt strangely calm, almost as though I was standing outside the scene watching it unfold. Alexander had the rifle and I was pretty sure he was the person in charge. He would decide if we lived or died. The red dot didn't move.

Finally, Alexander lowered his rifle and said, 'You've left us no choice, Mr Stone. Because of your insufferable persistence, it appears we must wind up our affairs. It was good while it lasted, but like all good things, our operations here in New Zealand have come to an end. A good businessman knows when to cut his losses. However, *all* is not lost. We have learned a great deal about how to manipulate financial systems. We will return to Vladivostok, regroup, and resume somewhere else.'

He walked and stood beside me. His grey eyes showed no emotion when he said, 'We've thought very hard about what to do with you. Believe me, we would dearly like to kill you as payment for the trouble you've caused.' He gestured towards Emma, Nigel and Gordon and added, 'And your friends who have assisted you. Fortunately for you, it is still to our advantage to minimise the knowledge of who we are and what we've done. To give us time to disappear. As much as I'd like to let the detective have his way, dead bodies on the Dunedin wharf is not the optimum outcome for us. And as your brother showed, even disposing of your bodies at sea would have its risks. We prefer to let you go, but only if you do as we say.'

He moved to the foot of the gangway and put his hand on its railing. 'Ms DeSilva will accompany us on the *Polar Princess* to Vladivostok. If you and your merry men, *all* of your merry men, join us for the voyage, then when we arrive, you will be set free to do as you wish. If you come with us, then once you get off the ship, you will be able to say whatever you like about what happened. Whether you are believed or not is of no consequence to us. By the time you return to New Zealand all evidence of our companies, our business activities, anything to do with us will be gone. We will have disappeared. Any efforts to pursue us may make you feel better but they will be futile. He climbed the gangway to the deck of the *Polar Princess* and stood beside Emma.

'If, however, you do not join us, then Ms DeSilva will be killed. Your recording is quite convincing. You can play it to the Dunedin police department and get them to send a dozen cars to this ship. Send the SWAT team. Hell, send the SAS. It doesn't matter. If you do anything stupid, anything *creative*, then I will shoot her.' He reached up and ran his hand over Emma's hair. She tried to shy away but was hemmed in between him and Peters. He looked at me and added, 'I'm not unreasonable. I'll give you fifteen minutes to decide. Get on board with our box in fifteen minutes. Or don't. The choice is yours.'

CHAPTER 31

The time was almost up. We'd huddled behind the truck and talked about our options, or lack of them. In the background, we saw bodies moving on the *Polar Princess* as they prepared for sea.

Finally, I said, 'My position is the same as it was when we started. I can't let them kill Emma. You guys can suit yourselves, but I'm going on the ship.'

Gordon said, 'Adam, you idiot, don't you see? They'll kill Emma anyway – and us, too, if we're on board. Callaghan may not have the guts for it, but Alexander sure does, and I think Killand would enjoy it, too.'

'You know what they said,' I answered. 'It's all of us or none of us. If anyone stays behind, they'll kill Emma.'

Gordon put his head in his hands. 'We're so fucked.'

Nigel hadn't said a lot during the discussion. He raised his head now and looked at each of us. 'If I'm not on board, then Emma's going to die. As long as I'm alive, as long as Emma's alive, then there's still a chance we'll stop these fuckers. It's a risk, it's a big risk, but I'm with Adam. I'm going on the ship.'

There was a long silence. I looked at each of my mates in turn, seeing their anxiety and indecision. White knuckles and wrinkled brows reflected their tension.

'Well fuck,' said Gordon at last, 'I can't very well let my cousin be killed, can I?'

I didn't really think if we got on the *Polar Princess* we'd get to Vladivostok. Gordon was right. Alexander and Killand were ruthless and would have no compunction about killing us. But I also agreed with Nigel. If we were on board and alive, then we had a chance. I had no idea how we would overcome armed men. They would have to make a mistake, and we would have to be ready to act on it.

They searched us when we boarded the *Polar Princess*, taking our cell phones and everything else in our pockets. Alexander and Callaghan stood on the wharf at the foot of the gangway as Peters led us aboard. I looked back at the wharf and saw our truck parked there. It hadn't taken long to move the box from the truck to the deck of the ship. I was last in line, waiting for the others to move up the gangway, and heard Alexander say, 'You have much to do, David. It will be a few days before anyone suspects anything. That should be plenty of time for you to tidy our affairs here. If you're on a plane by Thursday, then you'll be fine.' He held out a hand and the two men shook hands warmly.

Callaghan said, 'Good luck, Alexander. And safe voyage.'

Alexander smiled broadly. 'See you in Vladivostok.' He followed me up onto the deck of the ship, leaving Callaghan on the wharf. When we entered the hatch that led to our cabins, Alexander turned and climbed a ladder to the bridge.

Feeling like a lamb being led to slaughter, I followed Peters inside the ship. The observer, Phil Coetzee, was standing just inside the hatch. 'Phil, you decided to stay on board?' I asked.

'Wouldn't miss it for the world,' he said. 'So much fun last time.'

I pushed past him and Tamati appeared from the darkness of the deck. I thought I saw a look of amazement or disbelief flash across his face when he saw me, but he quickly regained his composure. Without a word, he followed me into the passageway. I slowed and, over my shoulder, asked him, 'Ishmael, what the hell are you doing? You're not part of this, are you?'

He shook his head and muttered, 'I thought you were dead.'

I turned and grabbed his arm. 'You don't have to do this ...'

He shook my hand off and stared hard at me, slowly shaking his head again. 'You shouldn't have come back, Adam.'

I was baffled. I thought Tamati was my friend. He'd helped me escape from the *Polar Princess*. Why was he still here? Why was he helping Alexander take us captive?

I didn't have time to pursue these thoughts. Gordon and I were put in the cabin I'd shared with Finn on my previous voyage. Nigel was in the cabin just aft of us. Before he left, Peters opened the door to the cabin across the passage from ours and I saw Emma. She was sitting on her bunk, still gagged and her hands tied. When she saw me tears started leaking down her cheeks and her shoulders shook. Judd, the bosun, sat on a chair just inside the door. He leered at me when he saw me but didn't say anything. He didn't have to.

We were locked in our cabins, though I don't know why they bothered. We had come aboard voluntarily. We were not going to jeopardise Emma's life with any foolish actions. Gordon and I didn't talk. In a short while, we heard and felt the increased beat of the diesels and sensed the slight movement as we slipped away from the wharf.

By mid-morning, we were released from our cabins. There was no place for us to go, no way we could contact anyone, and it would be a nuisance for them if they kept us locked up – someone would have to bring us food and escort us to the toilet. The first thing I did was cross the corridor and open Emma's door. Judd was gone and she was freed from her bonds. When she saw me, she stood up and ran to me. I took her in my arms, comforting her as best I could. 'Adam, you idiot,' she murmured into my shoulder. 'Why did you come? Why are you here?'

'Life on the family seed farm in Methven doesn't look so bad now, does it?' I asked, trying to lighten her mood, even for a moment. Her face was still pressed against me, but I thought I could see the faintest hint of a smile. 'Don't worry,' I added, 'it will be okay. It was the only way. We're going to go with them to Vladivostok. Then they'll let us go. It'll be fine. You'll see.'

Emma pulled her head back and looked into my face. 'You are such a fool. Do you really believe that? They will say anything, do anything.'

'Did they hurt you? Did they …?' I couldn't ask the question.

Emma shook her head. 'No, I'm okay. They haven't done anything to me. As long as you were out there, then I still had value to them. Now that you're here, I don't know.' She stared at me and said with a note of steel in her voice, 'We *will* get even, Adam. They killed Theo and they will pay. I don't know how, but they will pay.'

'Look, Emma, we're still alive. We're going to stay alive. Whatever it takes, we're going to stay alive.'

At dinner that night, Alexander was in a talkative mood. Looking towards Nigel he said, 'Mr Pierce? I don't think we've been properly introduced. I'm Alexander Ivanov, a business associate of David's. You're the captain of the boat that rescued Adam, is that right?'

Nigel glanced at me and took another bite of food. He took his time, chewing and swallowing before replying. 'I'm the captain of the *Storm Petrel*, yes.'

'You've been to the Bounty Islands many times?'

'A few.'

'And you are experienced with small boats in that environment?'

Nigel didn't answer, just shrugged. Then he said, 'That's where we're heading, isn't it? The Bounties? I could tell from the sun that we're heading southeast, hardly the direction for Vladivostok.'

'Very observant of you. Yes, we're heading back to the Bounties. There are some things there that we need to collect.'

'Some black boxes?' I asked. 'Five black boxes?'

'Indeed.' Alexander sat back in his chair and wiped his lips with a napkin. 'It seems you gentlemen will be useful on this voyage after all. Few of our crew are familiar with small boats. You will help us recover the boxes. Your lives depend on your success.'

We looked at each other but didn't say a word. I felt a sudden flush of excitement flow through me. Getting off the *Polar Princess* could offer the opportunity we needed. I held Nigel's eyes and lifted my chin slightly. He responded, signalling he had a similar thought. We would be ready. All we needed was for them to give us a chance.

The *Polar Princess* made good time on the voyage and we sighted the Bounties on the afternoon of the second day after leaving port. The sky was overcast and the wind was blowing force 6 with a three-metre southwesterly swell. Dozens of sea birds glided through the wave troughs and lifted smoothly over the foaming crests.

We approached from the northwest with the waves on our beam. The ship rolled uncomfortably and larger waves broke across the bow of the ship, smothering it in foam and spray. I stood on the bridge, feet braced against the roll, and peered forward in the gloomy afternoon light. Off the port bow, I could just make out the main group of the Bounty Islands. The granite stood out as light grey patches against the darker sea and sky. The sea was calmer than on our previous visit, and there was only a thin white line at the base of the islands where the waves were breaking.

Directly ahead, to the southeast, were the rocks and the wreck of the factory ship, the *Sergey Belov*. I strained my eyes but could see nothing in that direction. The bridge was crowded; everyone who wasn't on duty had come to look for the wreck.

We steamed closer and were within five nautical miles when Peters, the mate, called out, 'I see her!' A few moments later, I picked out the wreck as well. She was still upright but had settled with about a ten-degree list to starboard, her decks only a few metres above the sea. I took the binoculars from Peters and had a closer look. Several of the bridge windows were broken, probably a result of the violence of the impact on the reef. The bridge and accommodation block for'ard looked untouched, but there was a black smudge around the broken bridge windows. The funnel and large A-frame aft were intact but looked odd; it took me several seconds to realise both were twisted out of their normal positions. There were more black smudges in the after-part of the ship. The poor buggers on board hadn't just had to cope with going aground; they'd had to fight a fire as well. Waves occasionally broke over the decks, and white water revealed the location of the rocks that had sunk her.

There was no sign of life, or the boxes. Had any of the crew survived? Even though they'd tried to kill us, the thought of dying in this place put me in a sombre mood.

'Right,' said Captain Kennicott, 'we'll head around west of those rocks and take up position south of the wreck. We will launch our inflatable boat in the lee of our starboard side and you can approach the wreck from the southeast, boarding her midships. The list and the lee from her hull make that the most advantageous point for boarding.'

Nigel stepped forward to stand beside the captain and examined the wreck, the sea and the sky. He said, 'Small boat work is going to be dangerous in these conditions. If it blows any stronger, then it would be suicide to try to board her.'

Alexander clapped his hands and said, 'Good. Then let's get started.'

Captain Kennicott gave the orders and the *Polar Princess* altered course to the south. We followed Judd down from the bridge to the deck. A rigid inflatable boat similar to the one we'd used on the *Storm Petrel* was lashed there. In short order, we freed it and began preparing for the first trip to the wreck.

It took an hour for the *Polar Princess* to reach station south of the wreck, sufficiently far away to avoid any chance of also ending up on the rocks. The *Polar Princess* headed into the southwesterly swell with just enough way to maintain position. When the time came to launch the inflatable boat, the *Polar Princess* would swing broadside on to the swell to provide the protection of its lee.

When we were in position, Alexander came down to the deck and said, 'Nigel, you and Adam will make the first trip. Judd will go with you to make sure you don't get up to any more of your tricks. Remember, Emma's here and her fate is in your hands. Just get the boxes and we can be on our way to Vladivostok.'

Emma had come out onto the starboard wing of the bridge and stood looking down at us. She seemed pale, but it may just have been the light. Her eyes found mine, and although there was no joy in them, she lifted her hand slightly. I raised my hand and let it fall, trying to put her out of my mind and focusing on what had to be done.

Judd had rigged a simple lifting harness for the inflatable boat. As Nigel and I got into the boat, our motions were impeded by our storm gear and I thought briefly of how awkward I'd felt in my immersion suit the last time I'd left the *Polar Princess*. Judd took position in the stern, near the outboard motor. He pushed the button to start the motor and listened to it idling for a few seconds. He lifted his arm and twirled it, giving the symbol to lift, and the inflatable lurched off the deck. The *Polar Princess* was broadside to the swell and was rolling quite a bit. The crane operator needed all his skill to lift us off the deck and over the rail without sending us swinging wildly into part of the ship. I was gripping the safety line along the port tube with one hand and my life vest with the other, and I could feel the tension in Nigel's body beside me. Judd looked impervious, his body swaying as we swung over the side and hung poised over the grey water. He waited patiently, judging the waves and the motion of the *Polar Princess*, and then gave the signal to lower us.

Even in the lee of the *Polar Princess*, the waves seemed threatening in our small craft. We hit the water hard and pitched forward on a wave, jerked to a halt by the lifting cable. We scrambled to release the clips of the lifting harness and watched the cable swing free. Judd engaged the clutch on the motor and we surged forward and away from the hull of the *Polar Princess*.

I only appreciated the effect of the lee of the ship when we left its protection. The motion of the inflatable changed immediately when we felt the full power of the swell. I was unpleasantly reminded of my night spent clutching the black box. I fought down those fears, knowing I was in an almost unsinkable boat; that it was daylight; that the sea conditions were not as bad; that I wasn't alone. Even though I knew he would not hesitate to kill me, Judd's seamanship was reassuring.

We headed almost due north with the swell on our stern quarter. The inflatable laboured obliquely up the back of a swell and then, with a roar of the propeller, we pitched over the crest and coursed down the face of the wave. We made good progress even though Judd kept the power well below the motor's maximum.

We'd left the *Polar Princess* about a nautical mile south of the wreck. From the top of the swells, I could look forward and see the upperworks of the *Sergey Belov* and look aft to see the *Polar Princess* holding position, steaming into the swells. It was getting late, and I could feel the afternoon light fading towards evening. My anxiety level rose another notch – I didn't want to have to look for the *Polar Princess* in the dark.

We'd discussed the recovery of the boxes before we left the *Polar Princess*. The inflatable had a very shallow draft, so there was little chance that we'd hit a rock, but we kept a sharp watch nevertheless. We would manoeuvre to a position downwind of the wreck and then approach in its lee. That side of the wreck hadn't been visible from the *Polar Princess,* so we couldn't accurately judge what we would find. We would have to assess the conditions and decide how to board the wreck once we were alongside.

We couldn't see the boxes, but it was unlikely they'd been taken below in the wild sea conditions the night they'd been recovered. They were most likely on deck, somewhere invisible from the *Polar Princess*. If they weren't, then they had probably been washed overboard. But we would have to be sure. If they weren't on deck, then someone would have to search the interior of the wreck to look for them. I hoped it wouldn't be me.

At last, Judd judged we had gone far enough north and swung us around to the west, towards the wreck. His eyes were darkness inside darkness, brown orbs lost in his black beard and the late afternoon shadows. I looked at the wreck more closely as we approached. It was hard to believe this was the vessel that had looked so threatening when chasing us through the storm. The menacing bows and towering upperworks now looked sad, the paint faded and streaked with rust. The effects of the fire were clearer, blistered and smoke-blackened paint revealed in more detail as we got closer. When we were a few hundred metres from the wreck we could see the boxes, lashed behind the bridge structure. A big smile lit Judd's face and he reached for the radio clipped to his jacket. 'Rover to base, rover to base, we see the targets, over.'

I faintly heard Alexander reply, 'Base to rover, excellent. Report progress when recovery complete. Out.'

Judd clipped the radio to his jacket and concentrated on manoeuvring us closer to the wreck. Water boiled on either side of us, revealing rocks within a few metres of the surface. Even in the lee of the wreck the swell was significant, at least a metre, and confused, an unpredictable tossing of the waters rather than the steady passage of waves on the open ocean.

As Judd glided us towards the wreck Nigel stood in the bow of our craft, painter in hand, ready to board. In a remarkable display of seamanship, we kissed the hull of the wreck at the lowest point of its deck, just aft of the bridge structure. Nigel grabbed the rail and swung aboard. He held us close to the side with the painter and shouted, 'Got 'er!'

I scrambled forward, put my foot on our craft's pontoon and, when a wave lifted us level with the sloping deck, grabbed the rail and jumped, joining Nigel on board. With a grace belying his size Judd followed me, coming aboard as effortlessly as getting out of a car. He had a long line looped over his shoulder, the line we'd use to tow the boxes back to the *Polar Princess*. Nigel secured the painter to the railing and let out sufficient slack to allow the inflatable to move freely on the waves.

Judd wasted no time. The five boxes were right before us, lashed to cleats on the deck. No instructions were necessary. The three of us moved to the nearest box and in no time had untied its lashings. We tried to lift it. Judd raised his end but Nigel and I were able to lift it for only a few seconds before dropping it back to the deck. It was obvious we would be lucky to move the box to the edge of the deck, and there was no way we would be able to lift it over the rail.

Judd got on the radio and reported. He finished by saying, 'I'm going below to see if I can find some tools to remove the railing. It will save time if we don't have to come back to the ship for them. Out.' He clipped the radio to his jacket and looked at the sky. The light had faded even more; there wasn't much of the day left.

'You buggers stay here,' he said. 'Don't fucking move. You heard what I said. I'm going below to look for some tools so we can get rid of the railing. I won't be long.' Without a backward glance, he pulled a waterproof torch from one of his jacket pockets, strode to the nearest hatch, opened it and disappeared inside. We heard a loud curse and then nothing.

For a moment neither Nigel nor I said anything. It felt surreal, standing on the slanted deck of a wreck in the middle of the Southern Ocean, the sky dark in the east and the grey waters around us cold and unforgiving. Finally, Nigel said, 'Well, we're off the *Polar Princess.* Do you have any ideas about what to do next?'

I wished I did. I knew this was an opportunity and I wished I could see what it held. But I didn't. Judd was with us but Alexander, Coetzee and the crew were still on the *Polar Princess* with Emma. We had no weapon. Judd could have a dozen weapons on him, it was impossible to tell what was beneath his storm gear. In the end, all I could say was, 'No.'

Judd was gone for about ten minutes. He appeared in the hatch, holding in his right hand a large angle grinder. As he moved to the railing he said, 'Fucking stinks of ammonia below. Must have ruptured the refrigeration tanks when she hit. The ammonia and fire would have killed everyone or driven them off the ship.' He looked at the wild ocean between the hulk and the nearest island, barely visible to the east. 'And no one would have survived a swim through that. Not even you, Stone.' He grunted and lifted the angle grinder. 'We're lucky. I found this in a locker above the water line. It runs, but I don't know how long the battery will last.' He braced himself and, without hesitation, started cutting. A shower of red sparks flew from the grinder as the cutting blade sliced into the mild steel of the railing. The first cut was completed in a matter of minutes.

As Judd bent to cut the lower bar of the railing, a wave came over the side and wet him to his knees. He didn't seem to notice as he resumed his attack on the railing. He worked his way steadily through the bars until all that was left was a single stanchion holding the cut rails. He bent over but had to wait while another wave washed over his feet before he applied the angle grinder to the steel. He was almost through the stanchion when the grinder stopped.

'Fuck!' Judd repeatedly pulled the trigger but there was no response from the grinder. Nigel and I watched as he threw the tool as far as he could into the ocean before turning to us. 'Come on, you bastards, we've got to finish the job.'

We sidled across the deck and joined Judd by the stanchion. 'You,' he pointed at Nigel, 'grab the top railing over there.' He pointed aft. 'When I give the word, you're going to pull like buggery. And you, Stone, grab it over there.' He pointed for'ard. 'You're going to push. We're going to twist this bastard off.' His massive hands gripped the top of the stanchion. 'Right. One, two, go!'

Out of the corner of my eye, I could see Nigel straining against the railing and Judd throwing his entire weight against the stanchion, wrenching it back and forth. I concentrated on my feet, trying to maintain traction while I pushed against the railing. I was very conscious that if the stanchion broke, my effort could catapult me into the ocean.

For an agonising moment, nothing happened. I felt my feet start to slip on the wet deck when, without warning, the stanchion bent and twisted. The railing slipped away from the ship, out of my grasp, but Nigel and Judd kept pulling and heaving until the overstressed metal failed with a loud snap. Without ceremony, Judd took the stanchion and the attached sections of rails and tossed the lot into the ocean. The stump of the stanchion protruded about twenty centimetres from the deck, part of it smoothly cut and the rest a bright, jagged edge.

By this time it was nearly dark. There had been no sunset; the sky was completely covered in low clouds. We could see the boxes, but even the stern of the wreck was lost in shadows.

'What are you waiting for?' growled Judd. Apparently, we weren't going to wait until tomorrow to start the recovery of the boxes. He secured the tow line to the box we'd freed from the deck cleats and tied the other end to the railing still on the wreck. We worked together and laboriously the three of us slid the box to the edge of the deck, in the gap where we'd removed the railing.

'You pussies should be able to launch it from here,' Judd said. He used the painter to pull the inflatable close to the hull and stepped on board. Nigel released the painter and we watched the small vessel drift a few metres away, rising and falling in the waves that materialised out of the gloom. Judd tied the tow line off to a cleat on the inflatable and moved the small boat further from the wreck. 'Right then, get that box in the water.'

Nigel and I stood behind the box and, on the count of three, pushed as hard as we could. Nothing happened until the tow line came tight, and then with the help of the inflatable the box started to move. In seconds it slipped smoothly over the side. Like the box I'd been so intimately familiar with that crazy night I'd spent in the Southern Ocean, it rode in the water with about half of its height exposed. I felt no pleasure watching Judd carefully manoeuvre the box away from the wreck and then nose the inflatable back in to pick us up.

Getting off the wreck was easier without the railing. As the inflatable rose on a wave I stepped onto the hull tube and down into it. I took a seat amidship as Judd manoeuvred to pick up Nigel. A wave lifted the small craft away from the wreck just as Nigel began to step on board. He adjusted his step but his foot slipped and he almost fell. Somehow, with remarkable agility, he recovered and jumped aboard. Judd didn't wait for him to take his seat; he gunned the motor and began the slow trip back to the *Polar Princess*.

It was nearly full dark. The foam on the waves gleamed in the dim light as they loomed out of the darkness and flowed past us. We corkscrewed through the waves, crossing them on our starboard bow as we steered south towards the *Polar Princess*. Our small craft had a compass near the wheel, and I could see Judd glancing down frequently to correct our course. The heavy box on the end of the tow line made the trip more uncomfortable, jerking us almost to a halt when the line came taut and then letting us surge ahead as it went slack.

I felt a knot of anxiety ease when at last we saw the deck lights of the *Polar Princess*. The ship glowed like a Christmas tree, all of its lights on to guide us home. Judd brought us up to the side of the ship and passed the tow line to one of the deckhands. It took only a few minutes to attach it to the crane's lifting wire and lift the box on board. I sat in the inflatable and looked at the black box dripping on the deck in the harsh overhead lights. It was hard to imagine how much sorrow these boxes had brought us.

Once the box was secure the line was lowered again and we attached the clips of the lifting harness. Judd and the crane operator carefully judged the waves, and one minute we were bobbing in the water and the next we were being lifted smoothly on board.

CHAPTER 32

The next morning it was cold when we assembled on deck. The weather was much the same, though the state of the sea had worsened slightly. There was no break in the cloud cover, and the gloom made it feel colder than it was.

Alexander stood with his hands deep in his jacket pockets. 'Right. Same as yesterday. You got the first box, we know what we're doing now. Don't do anything stupid and we'll be out of here soon.'

Emma came out on the deck to watch us off. She was dressed warmly in clothing they'd found for her on the boat: long trousers, jersey, jacket and hat. While they were preparing to lift the inflatable she came close to me and whispered, 'Be careful, Adam. One hand for the ship, one eye on your back. Come back to me.'

I smiled, though I don't think I'd ever felt less like smiling. 'Don't worry; we'll be fine.'

We launched the inflatable and followed our previous course back to the wreck. The wind had increased and was approaching force 7. I estimated that the swells out of the lee of the *Polar Princess* were almost four metres high and the wind was blowing the top off the breaking waves. The little craft rode the swells like a jockey on a racehorse. I huddled low to avoid the wind and flying spray as much as possible, and I saw that Nigel kept a sharp eye on the conditions. Judd stood at the helm, seemingly impervious to the elements. Sea water dripped from his eyebrows and beard and plastered his curly hair to his head, but his body moved smoothly with the motion of the vessel and his hands were firm on the wheel.

As before, the wreck offered some shelter from the swell and, although conditions were better than the open ocean, they were worse than the previous afternoon. Nevertheless, with considerable care, Nigel and I were able to board the wreck and secure the tow line to the next box. In the debriefing the night before, Nigel had suggested we try using the tow line to help pull the boxes the entire distance across the deck. With the tow line secured Judd took up tension and, at Nigel's signal, applied power and began to pull on the box. Nigel and I crouched behind it and pushed as hard as we could. Somewhat to my surprise, the idea worked and the box slowly slid across the deck and into the water. Judd kept a close eye on the box as he increased power to the outboard and turned into the southerly swell.

We'd also discussed whether Nigel and I needed to shuttle back and forth with the boxes. I'd argued that getting on and off the inflatable was a risk, and Nigel pointed out that Judd could handle the transfer of the boxes perfectly well without us. I could tell Alexander didn't like it, probably just because he didn't trust any ideas coming from us. In the end, he agreed that we would stay on the wreck. After all, there was no place we could go while Judd was ferrying the boxes back to the *Polar Princess*.

We found shelter the best we could until Judd returned. It seemed an age before he reappeared, manoeuvring the inflatable alongside the wreck and tossing us the tow line.

We tied the tow line around the next box. We used the same technique as before, and it started to move but got caught on a small ridge in the deck. It looked as though something had once been welded there and when it was removed the weld hadn't been completely ground off. Our usual system couldn't get the box over this obstacle. In a brief shouted discussion Judd agreed to board the wreck and help move the box past the weld. I could see Judd's anger as he swung the inflatable in a sharp turn and powered to the side of the wreck. He scrambled forward, tossed Nigel the painter, and waited in the bow to be pulled closer to the wreck. It was almost midday and the wind had shifted to the south. With the wind and waves from that quarter the wreck provided less shelter and getting on and off the listing deck was becoming harder.

It happened in a second. The inflatable was alongside the wreck, a wave lifting it to the level of the deck, Judd poised on the bow, ready to step aboard to help us lift the box over the ridge. Maybe his anger made him hasty, maybe the wave dropped unexpectedly – whatever the reason, when Judd moved he misjudged the distance. His right foot slipped off the edge of the deck and, unable to recover, he fell forward, face first onto the broken stub of the stanchion.

He was a big man and it was a heavy fall. The jagged steel ripped through his left eye and into his brain. He was dead before his left foot slipped off the inflatable and into the water. For a moment, his body hung by that awful pivot, swaying lifeless in the waves, his arms and legs swinging limply with the motion.

We were on him in a flash, grabbing him under his arms and heaving him onto the deck. The rush of adrenalin from the horror of what we'd seen made lifting his 110 kilo body seem easy. I'll never forget the terrible sight of his destroyed face lying there on the deck.

'Fuck,' said Nigel. 'What are we going to do now?'

My mind was spinning, but I knew this was it – this was the only opportunity we were going to get. I wasn't sure how we were going to take advantage of it, but I knew we had to do something. I grabbed one of Judd's arms and said, 'Nigel, help me get him out of sight. This is the opportunity we've been waiting for.'

Nigel grabbed the other arm and we started dragging the body towards the hatch in the side of the bridge structure. 'Man, he's heavy,' he said. He glanced at me and asked, 'What do you have in mind, Adam? This may be a stroke of luck, but I'm damned if I can see how to take advantage of it.'

'I'm not sure I do either, but we've got to do something.'

With the change in wind direction, the clouds had dropped and visibility was no more than a few hundred metres. We worked in a cold drizzle and finally got Judd's body up the sloping deck to the hatch. Together we half lifted, half dragged his body through the hatch and into the shelter of the superstructure. The sudden silence was almost physical. Cold, dreary light splashed across the floor from the hatch opening, but elsewhere the small room was filled with shadows, and the passageway leading into the ship disappeared in darkness. The stink of ammonia and smoke was strong. My eyes and nose burned and I had a short coughing fit. Judd had survived his trip below, so I knew the fumes weren't life-threatening.

I went back and stood in the hatch, looking at the three remaining boxes and the grey, turbulent sea, trying to come up with an idea. Nigel stood silently at my shoulder, waiting for me to speak. Gradually thoughts came together, too loose, too unpredictable to call a plan, but perhaps a script – one that might give us another opportunity.

I started talking slowly, unsure of my thoughts, unsure of how to express the vague ideas I was having. But as I spoke my thoughts got clearer and I gained confidence. When I was finished Nigel thought for a moment. 'Divide and conquer, that's the idea? Separate them, get them off guard, and neutralise them. Is that it?'

'Yeah, pretty much. We can only plan so much; the crucial events rely on luck and determination. If we act fast then we have a chance.'

Nigel slipped by me and stood looking at the box hung up on the deck. 'We're not going to shift this sucker on our own. What's our next move?'

I looked at the remaining boxes. 'Come on, let's see if we can move this other box.' We crouched behind it and, on the count of three, pushed as hard as we could. The box grudgingly moved a few centimetres and stopped.

Nigel stood and looked pensively at the box. Suddenly he snapped his fingers and turned back towards the hatch. 'Hang on, I have an idea,' he said as he disappeared inside the wreck. He reappeared in about five minutes with a big grin and a 2-litre bottle of cooking oil. He opened the container and poured the oil liberally in front of and on the upslope side of the box. I could see some of the oil disappear beneath it.

'Let's try again,' he said. 'A little lubrication may be just what we need.' We crouched behind the box and once again pushed as hard as we could. This time the box slid almost half a metre down the deck.

'You beauty!' I said. 'You're a genius. Now I'm afraid we might not be able to control it once it starts sliding. We'd better tie it off so we won't lose it if it goes over the side.'

We tied the tow line to the box and, using the oil, it took only a few minutes before the box was poised on the edge of the deck.

'Okay, Nigel,' I said, 'you take the box back on your own. Tell them Judd's gone below to see if there's anything else that should be salvaged from the wreck. Say he wants someone to come back to keep an eye on us in case he needs to spend more time below decks.' I thought for a second and added, 'See if you can get one of the guys with a gun, Alexander or Killand. We want to neutralise one of them if we can.'

'Yeah, that makes sense. What do I say if they ask why Judd didn't report on the radio?'

'Tell them part of the truth. The water's getting rougher, he stumbled getting onto the wreck and dropped the radio into the ocean.'

'Okay. Let's get going. They'll be wondering why it's taking so long.'

I brought the inflatable alongside the wreck again. Nigel judged the waves perfectly and stepped aboard. He moved to the console, started the motor and gently manoeuvred the little vessel away until the tow line was taut. He held up his hand and, when he dropped it, he increased power to the motor and I shoved the box. It slid silently off the deck and bobbed behind the inflatable. With another wave of his hand, Nigel turned and concentrated on navigating back to the *Polar Princess*.

I stood for a while on the deck, watching him grow smaller in the rolling sea. In seconds he disappeared into the mist. I wanted this to succeed, I wanted it very badly, but my stomach clenched with nerves as I thought about how many things could go wrong and the consequences of failure. I hadn't asked Emma or Gordon for permission to put their lives in immediate danger. I was pretty sure they would agree, as none of us thought we had anything to lose. But that was scant reassurance when I knew how easily we could all be dead before the day was over.

While I waited for Nigel to return I decided to explore the wreck to see if I could find anything that might be useful. I entered the hatch and stood over Judd's body. He lay on his back, feet just inside the hatch. His face was a mess, but there was remarkably little blood. His remaining eye was closed and his lips were a thin, white slash in his beard. I knelt beside him and made a quick search of his body. I unzipped his parka, peeled it away from his torso and unfastened his waterproof trousers. I felt his clothing but found nothing other than his torch in his pockets.

On his right side, almost underneath him, I found a sheath and a fishing knife. I removed the knife and looked at it. It had a thin serrated blade about twenty centimetres long, similar to knives I'd used for gutting fish on fishing boats. I unbuckled his belt and worked it through the belt loops, free from his body. The belt was far too big for me, so I took the sheath and knife off it and put them on my belt. The knife made me feel better. It was a formidable weapon – unless I was faced with a gun.

The reality of the situation suddenly hit me and I almost had to sit down. Was I seriously considering killing someone with a knife? I'd used a knife on thousands of fish, but using one on a human was something different. I pulled the knife from the sheath and looked at it, turning it in my hands. Could I actually stab someone to death? Feel their blood wash over my fingers?

I didn't know the answer. Perhaps it wouldn't come to that. Overcoming these criminals who held our lives in their hands didn't require killing them. Did it?

I put the knife back in the sheath and braced myself to go into the wreck. I needed to see what else I might find. Judd had gone inside to get the angle grinder and Nigel had gone to get the oil. Neither had said anything about what they'd seen, but I couldn't help thinking about the sailors and fishermen who'd been on the *Sergey Belov* when she was wrecked.

No one had met us when we'd boarded the ship, so there was clearly no one alive on board. Judd had probably been right – the ammonia and fire must have killed anyone who survived the collision.

I switched on the torch and moved slowly down the passage. My nose and eyes were still irritated by the strong smells, but I ignored the discomfort and went on. After a few metres, I came to the main stairway that linked the bridge with the rest of the ship. I sniffed – I could smell something other than the ammonia and smoke, but it was too indistinct to identify. I thought about going up the stairway, but that part of the ship probably contained only cabins and the bridge, unlikely to have anything useful.

I descended the stairs. On the next deck, I immediately saw the galley. Even though everything's fastened down tight while at sea, the collision with the rock had popped open doors and drawers and strewn their contents everywhere. It was easy to see where Nigel had found the oil, but there was nothing else there of interest to me. The unknown smell was stronger, and I was afraid I knew what it was.

I looked down the stairwell and black, oily water gleamed in the torchlight not far below the deck I was standing on. I wouldn't be searching any deeper in the wreck. Judd had found a tool locker on this level and there might be something else useful there. I wanted to hurry, to get back out to the fresh air as quickly as I could, but I felt an almost painful compulsion to carry on.

I went to the first door along the passage, which opened into the mess. There were two bodies there. They'd been dead for several weeks and were almost unrecognisable: bloated, sunken eyes, leaking fluids. The sight itself was bad, but it was the smell that was overwhelming. I vomited immediately, retching uncontrollably, my stomach spasming violently until I staggered backwards and shut the door. I suddenly had no desire to search for the equipment locker Judd had found, or to visit other parts of the ship. Clutching my aching midsection I climbed the steps and retreated through the hatch to the fresh air. I sank to the deck and sat with my back against the steel of the bridge superstructure.

They say smell is the stimulation of neurons in our nose by tiny particles released by the things around us. Anyone who has smelled something truly awful knows that is only part of the story. Sitting on the deck, buffeted by the wind and spray, if there were any particles from the bodies below then they were measured in parts per trillion. Yet I couldn't escape the smell. In my mind, it was as strong as the moment I opened the mess door.

The bodies had been a blow. The sight and smell of their decomposition were seared into my brain and left me in shock. I sat motionless for a long time, incapable of coherent thought, and was still not mentally prepared when I heard the faint sound of a motor. I looked up and scanned the waves south and east of the wreck. I finally spotted the inflatable through a break in the mist, surfing down the face of a swell. There were two people on board – Nigel was at the helm and another person was in the bow. The other person was wearing storm gear and I couldn't make out who it was. I stood and moved to the railing and watched Nigel angle across the swells towards the wreck.

They were no more than fifty metres away when the man in the bow looked up and I saw it was Detective Killand. A chill went through me and I unconsciously touched the knife at my waist, hidden by my parka. Whatever happened next was going to be tricky. I hoped Killand wasn't armed and we could keep him from getting suspicious long enough for us to subdue him.

Nigel brought the inflatable close to the wreck and Killand tossed the painter to me. I made it fast to the railing and pulled the boat alongside the deck of the *Sergey Belov*. The small boat was moving violently in the waves and I could see Killand wasn't comfortable. 'Where's Judd?' he called.

'He went below,' I said. 'He said he was checking for anything else we should salvage.'

'He hasn't finished?'

I held up my hands in a gesture of bewilderment. 'You know Judd. He wasn't keen to share his plans with us. He just told me to wait here and help get the next box off the wreck.'

Killand looked unhappy while he thought about this. 'Goddamn it. What's the problem? Are you going to push the next box overboard?'

I shook my head. 'No. One of them's hung up. It's going to take all of us to move it. Nigel and I tried, but it's caught on an old weld on the deck. We need your help to get it to the edge of the deck.'

'What about the other one?'

I looked over my shoulder and shrugged. 'We might be able to move it, but the one by the weld is in the way. We've got to get that one sometime. If we get it now then it clears the path for the last one.'

Killand thought about this and finally scowled and stood up gingerly in the inflatable. He watched the deck closely and did a fair job of scrambling onto the wreck. His feet were soaked by a wave breaking over the side but otherwise, he was fine. Nigel quickly moved forward and joined us.

Killand put his hands on his hips and looked around at the sloping deck, the rusting steelwork, the grey sky and white-capped sea. The rain had plastered his hair to his head. His dark blue eyes showed no sign of fear, even though I was sure he'd never been in a situation like this before. I couldn't see a bulge in his parka pockets, so figured that even if he had a gun he wouldn't be able to get to it quickly. His scowl deepened, if possible, and he growled, 'I don't like it. Why isn't Judd here?'

I shrugged. 'Like I said, he went into the ship. He didn't say where he was going or how long it was going to take.'

Killand looked up at the bridge structure looming above us and swore again. 'I'm going to find him. And you're going to help me. I want you both where I can see you.'

I glanced at Nigel. 'Are you sure that's a good idea? Judd said he wanted us to get these boxes back to the *Polar Princess*. I went below while I was waiting for you, just a few metres. There are bodies there and it's not pretty.'

Killand almost sneered, 'Bodies? Haven't you seen dead bodies before? If Judd can stay below with them, then so can we.' He gestured towards the hatch. 'Now quit stalling and get moving.'

'Okay.' I gestured slightly with my head.

Nigel caught the signal and said, 'I'll go first.'

He stepped inside. Killand waited for me to follow Nigel into the ship. Judd's body lay to the right of the hatch. Once inside, I saw Nigel had moved to the left. I stepped beside him, just inside the hatch, and reached under my parka to draw Judd's knife. I held it by my side and waited for Killand to enter.

The hatch darkened and the next moment Killand was inside. He froze for a second when he saw the body. It took a moment for his eyes to adjust to the darkness and to recognise it was Judd. By then I'd stepped behind him, between him and the hatch.

He was quick. With a growl he turned and struck out at me, catching me with a glancing blow to my shoulder. I shoved his arm, keeping his spin going until he was facing Nigel. Killand quickly stepped to the right, over Judd's body, and stood in the half-darkness, his hands up in a defensive posture and his head swivelling between us. 'You bastards,' he gasped, 'I should have known you were up to something. I didn't think you had it in you to kill Judd.'

Nigel took a small step forward. 'We didn't kill him. He fell on the stub of the stanchion.'

'Well, I don't give a fuck. When we get back to the *Polar Princess* you guys are fucked, your bitch is fucked, your reporter friend is fucked.'

I held up the knife and said, 'That could be a problem.'

Killand laughed grimly. 'A knife? Really? Have you ever killed anyone with a knife? Do you know what it's like to kill someone?' He shook his head. 'I don't think so. I don't think you have it in you to use it.' It was as though he'd read my thoughts, knew the doubts I'd had only a short time before. I still didn't know the answer.

There was a strange smile on his face as he took a step towards me, and in that moment I wondered if he was entirely sane. He gestured towards my hand and said, 'I can tell you've never been in a knife fight. You can't make a proper strike if you hold the knife like that.'

As he finished the sentence he launched himself at me, arms outstretched to grab me. He was right; I'd never been in a knife fight. And he was right; I probably couldn't have made a proper strike with it. But I didn't have to. I instinctively raised the knife as he charged and he impaled himself on it. I felt the jar as he hit it and the scraping judder as it sliced through his storm gear and clothes and slid between his ribs. As I watched he stopped, his arms fell, and before the light went from his dark blue eyes I saw not anger, not sorrow, but surprise. Even a man like Killand would have regrets – an absent father, an indifferent lover – but he'd probably never had regrets about a fight. He'd probably never lost a fight before, and I was damned sure no one had slid a twenty-centimetre fishing knife between his ribs before.

CHAPTER 33

Suddenly there was a dead weight on my arm and I released the knife, letting it and Killand fall to the floor. There had been almost no physical exertion, but I was gasping from the emotional strain. My hand started trembling and then my whole body was shaking.

Nigel hadn't had time to react before it was all over. He looked again and again at me and at Killand. 'Holy shit,' he whispered. He came across the room and wrapped his arms around me. 'It's okay, Adam, it's okay. Everything's going to be okay.'

He continued to hold me until my shaking stopped. At last, I reached up and released myself from his arms and stepped away from Killand's body. I stood looking down at him for a long time. There wasn't much blood visible; most of it was probably inside his parka. I turned to look at Nigel, 'Sorry. Guess that didn't go quite the way we hoped.'

Nigel shrugged. 'That's the problem when you play it by ear.' He looked down at Killand's body and admitted, 'I had no hopes. And I'm not sorry this bastard's dead.' He looked at me and added, 'You shouldn't be, either.'

I took a ragged breath. 'No, I'm not sorry. But having two dead bodies isn't going to help. One person missing can be explained, at least for a while. Two missing people are going to be a problem.'

Nigel thought about that. 'It just means we'll have to be quick. When we return to the ship we'll have one of the boxes. They'll want that box and will let us on board even if they're suspicious. We'll just have to go with it and let things happen.'

I was still in shock – from Judd's grisly death, the horrible dead bodies of the fishermen, and now knifing Killand in cold blood – and wasn't capable of deep thought. The bits of my brain that heard Nigel agreed with him. We were committed, and it was useless to waste time on theorising. Sometimes success comes from just refusing to stop.

I had one more task before we returned to the grey light on deck. I reached down and pulled the knife free from Killand's body. I then frisked him but found no other weapon. He had a radio in his parka pocket. I looked at it, but couldn't see how we could use it to our advantage. I could report back to the ship, make up a story to explain Judd's and Killand's absence. But I suspected this would only alert Alexander before we returned, giving him more time to be suspicious. I dropped the radio and we went through the hatch, stood on the sloping deck and viewed the last two boxes.

Nigel walked around the box that wasn't hung up on a weld. It was further from the side of the wreck, and as I'd told Killand it was partially blocked by the other box. He said, 'Let's try to move it sideways, across the slope of the deck. I think if we shift it far enough then we'll be beyond the other box and it should move okay.'

He spread oil around the box. We braced ourselves and pushed. There was a moment of resistance and then it slid slowly across the deck. From there getting it to the side was a repeat of what we'd done with the other boxes. It was bloody hard work and I thought my lungs were going to explode, but at last, we had the box poised on the edge of the deck. Nigel boarded the inflatable and started the motor while I untied the painter, got aboard and shoved us clear of the wreck. Perhaps we finally deserved a break. The tow line came taut and the box slipped off the deck without a fuss. Nigel turned the craft and started the trip to the *Polar Princess*.

As we fought our way into the swell I looked back at the wreck of the *Sergey Belov* and thought of all the dead on board. So many lives ended for a few dollars – well, quite a few dollars. I wasn't particularly sorry they were dead – they'd tried to kill us after all – but I got no joy, no sense of revenge from their death. Like Theo's death, it all seemed such a bloody waste.

I watched the faded white superstructure disappear into the murk as we made our way south. The rain and wind-blown spume reduced visibility and the wreck disappeared long before we neared the *Polar Princess*.

It was a slow trip back to the ship. Visibility had dropped even further and Nigel had to use the compass to navigate a course. The ocean was rough and waves broke over the inflatable. I was wet underneath my storm gear from flying spray that found every gap. I was growing anxious when at last we spotted the lights on the *Polar Princess*, haloed by the rain. Nigel slowed even more and brought us into the lee of the ship. He manoeuvred so that the box drifted up to the *Polar Princess's* hull, where Tamati caught it with a gaff. We slipped the tow line and it was the work of a minute for him to fix it to the lifting wire and for the winch operator to lift the box onto the deck. Nigel held off about fifty metres from the ship as the box was made fast. I could just see the row of gleaming black cases nestled under a deck overhang.

Alexander was standing near the rail, Emma beside him. Both had storm gear on, with their hoods up. Phil Coetzee stood behind them with his hands thrust in his parka pockets.

Nigel gunned the outboard and moved our inflatable closer to the ship. Emma's face looked particularly wan in the grey light. Alexander looked angry and started barking questions as soon as we were close to the ship. 'Where's Judd? Where's Killand?'

I gestured vaguely. 'On the wreck. Judd says he needs a piece of equipment. He wrote it down for me.' I tapped one of my parka pockets.

'Equipment? What equipment? What for? What the fuck's going on, Stone?'

'Like I told you, they're still on the wreck, on the *Sergey Belov*. Judd found something he wants to bring back to the *Polar Princess*. Killand got excited about it, too, and insisted on staying on the wreck with him.'

The edge of Alexander's anger wavered and I saw a flash of confusion. 'What sort of thing? Other than the boxes there's nothing on that ship we want. What did they find?'

I shrugged, 'Judd didn't tell us shit. He seemed very pleased with himself, though. Whatever it is must be important. Killand acted like he didn't want to leave Judd alone with it.'

Alexander suddenly grew calm. He gave his little smile that had absolutely no mirth in it. 'I think that's bullshit. I don't know what's going on, but I know Judd and I know Killand. One of them would have radioed to tell us what they were doing.'

Nigel said, 'I told you, Judd lost his radio when he boarded the wreck.'

'Yeah,' said Alexander, 'and Santa Claus took Killand's?'

Nigel replied, 'As soon as Killand got on board Judd took him below. Killand didn't say anything about a radio. Are you sure he had one?'

Alexander stopped smiling and stood silently at the rail, clearly trying to understand what was going on, trying to stay three moves ahead. We bounced up and down on the waves in our inflatable, the only sounds the roar of the wind in the *Polar Princess*'s rigging and the crash of breaking waves.

Nigel and I said nothing and kept our eyes on Alexander, waiting for him to make a decision. He could send us back for the last box, and if we then returned without Judd and Killand he would know something was wrong and we'd be in deep shit. Or he could take a chance that we were telling the truth and let us come on board, in which case we might have a chance to overpower him. Not a good chance, but better than none.

With an angry jerk of his head, he turned and shouted, 'Peters! Get that boat on board.'

Our ploy had worked, but I felt a sick dread looking at Emma. We'd come too far to stop now, but I had no idea how we were going to overcome Alexander and the rest of the crew. All I knew was that if we failed, then we were dead.

'Ready?' Nigel asked as he started slowly nosing towards the *Polar Princess*.

'No,' I replied, though I knew he couldn't hear me over the noise of the wind and the motor.

Getting the inflatable back on board was tricky in any conditions but we were patient, judging the waves, and hooked the lifting harness to the inflatable without incident. We were soon swaying at the end of the wire, the little craft spinning as it was hauled on board.

Tamati guided the inflatable to its cradle. We landed with a thump and I felt the more solid motion of the *Polar Princess* beneath me. As I stepped onto the deck, Tamati moved close to me. He lifted his chin, asking in a tiny gesture the questions Alexander had been shouting, asking what the fuck was going on.

I had to make a decision. If Tamati was against us, then the less I told him the better. Actually, anything I told him could be fatal. On the other hand, if he was with us, then he might be useful – no, he might be vital. He was a friend; he'd helped me escape once before. I knew he had no love for Judd, or for anyone else in authority. This makes it sound as though I weighed my decision, but really, there was no conscious thought behind my response. Without a pause, I shook my head slightly.

His face didn't change, but I swear I saw a flash in his dark brown eyes. His nod was imperceptible. He stood back as Nigel and I stepped clear of the inflatable. Alexander strode towards us and in a moment was in my face, repeating the questions he'd asked before we'd been lifted on board.

Before I could answer, he stepped back and a pistol suddenly appeared in his hand. He held it by his side and the stakes instantly escalated. We hadn't seen guns on the voyage to the islands, but we knew they had them.

Alexander took a deep breath and visibly composed himself. 'Now, you gentlemen are going to start telling the truth, or I'm going to start hurting people. Beginning with Emma.'

I half-turned and saw him move until he was standing right beside Emma. Not good. The moment of truth had come and I didn't have a clue what to do. I had the knife but was too far from Alexander to use it. I had no doubt he would use his pistol. Now or later, it was obvious none of us were going to reach Vladivostok. I glanced at Nigel and his blank expression told me he had no more ideas than I did.

My indecision didn't last long. Tamati moved with the care and precision he always did. I doubt his blow was more than half-power, but he caught Peters with his right fist on the side of his head and the punch knocked him down and out. Peters' body rolled limply back and forth on the deck as the ship rode through the swells, his pale face a contrast to his bright storm gear that gleamed wetly in the misty rain. For a moment, no one moved.

Then, without warning, Nigel sprang towards Phil. The deck was slippery and rolling, but somehow he kept his footing and reached Phil in two strides. Nigel dropped his shoulder and took Phil in the solar plexus, wrapping his arms around him. Before Phil could react, Nigel lifted him with more power than I thought his wiry body possessed, twisted him and dropped him on his head. It was a perfect spear tackle, outlawed in rugby for a decade. I could see why it had been banned – Phil collapsed on the deck and didn't move.

The die was cast. Two down, one to go. Without further thought, I yelled and pulled the knife and spun towards Alexander. I didn't care about the gun; I didn't care about anything except Emma. I would risk a bullet, risk death to save her. Except, of course, I was too late – far too late. Alexander grabbed Emma, swung her in front of him and put his pistol to her head. 'Stop!' he yelled, then more quietly, 'Just take it easy. Put the knife down.'

I stopped and looked helplessly at Emma. Her eyes were wide, but strangely, I thought I saw anger rather than fear. I slowly put down the knife and then just stood there, at a loss about what to do next.

Alexander looked at me without emotion. 'Our friends Judd and Killand. They're dead, aren't they?'

I didn't know how to respond, but it seemed that it was past the time for lies to be of any use. I didn't say anything, just nodded.

Alexander sighed. 'Oh well, a pity I suppose, but they were expendable. And I never liked the detective anyway. I mean, if you can't trust the police, then what's happening to society?'

I took a step towards Alexander, eyeing the gun warily and asked, 'Okay, what happens now? You can't hold her forever.'

'You're right, I can't. But I don't have to. In about one minute, you will either be dead or we will agree I can put the gun down. Now, you have two options. You can go on being stubborn and playing games and I will have no choice but to kill you, kill all of you. That would make things much simpler, but it would leave me with a problem.'

He shifted his weight slightly and pushed the gun harder against Emma's head. 'The problem is, there's one more box. And that box contains ten million dollars. And, although it pains me greatly, I have decided that the pleasure of killing the four of you is not worth two-and-a-half million dollars each. Your other option is to go back to the wreck and get the last box. If you get it then I'll let you live. You have my word. If you get the box, then you'll be free to go once we get to Vladivostok. If you refuse, then I'll kill you all right now.'

I stood, looking at Emma, at her eyes, her hair plastered to her head, at Alexander's hard face staring over her shoulder. She was almost as tall as him and he had to lift his arm high to hold the pistol against her head. I turned and looked at Nigel, Gordon, and Tamati. I felt that I'd let them all down. My desperate plan to make things right had turned to shit. All I had done was drag my friends into the gravest danger. I knew we couldn't trust Alexander. We'd never reach Vladivostok, no matter what he promised. But if we got the last box, then we'd buy time, time that might give us another opportunity to turn the tables on him.

By this time, the captain had brought the *Polar Princess* around to head into the swell. My body shifted automatically with the pitch and roll of the ship. The deck was wet and slick. Even in the best of conditions, I didn't think I could reach Alexander before he shot Emma, and me as well. In these conditions, it was impossible. I stood immobile, not saying anything, unconsciously delaying the decision to give up as long as I could.

Behind me, I heard Nigel say, 'It's okay, Adam. We tried. We got a couple of the bastards.'

That comment was still sinking in when I saw Emma's mouth form the words 'I love you' just before she disappeared over the side.

Thinking about it later, it seemed as though Emma moved with no hurry, putting her foot against one of the small vents that protruded from the deck to allow air to circulate to the lower parts of the ship. There was no haste but, once her foot was in place, she shoved up and back with great force. Alexander's lower back was tight against the rail as Emma shoved. The two of them rotated over the rail and dropped from sight into the water. I remember seeing Alexander's gun hand swinging wildly as he tried to maintain his balance but, with Emma so close and the pair of them moving so swiftly, he had no chance.

No one moved for a moment, unable to believe what we'd seen. I was the closest and reached the rail first, searching the ocean for any sign of Emma. The cold grey water swept unrelentingly past the ship, breakers surging against the side and foam whipping away astern. There was nothing, nothing, nothing … and then Tamati shouted out, 'There!' and pointed astern.

Two heads appeared about ten metres astern, drifting quickly away from us. I wasn't conscious of what I'd done, but while I was frantically searching for them I'd unzipped my parka and loosened my storm trousers. It was the work of a moment to pull off my rubber boots and storm gear and dive over the side.

I had a terrible sense of *déjà vu*; once before I'd gone over the side of the *Polar Princess*. By a miracle, I'd survived, but that time I'd had an immersion suit. This time I might as well have been naked, but this time I wasn't fighting for my life; I was fighting for Emma's.

Once again I felt myself falling towards the icy waters of the Southern Ocean. I hit the water and the shock almost killed me. I wanted to gasp from the cold, but I fought the reflex and thrashed my way to the surface. The greatest risk of drowning in cold water is from the initial shock and loss of breathing control. Inhaling even a small amount of water can be fatal.

Once on the surface, I gasped for air and looked around and spotted the *Polar Princess*. Nigel was running towards the stern, pointing back and away from the ship, presumably at Emma's head. I put my head down and swam as hard as I could in that direction.

Fortunately, I was swimming with the swell so the breaking waves flowed past my face rather than into it. I had been in the water for no more than a minute and could already feel the cold eating into me. Those damned Safety at Sea videos came back to haunt me. I knew I had about fifteen minutes before my core temperature got so cold I lost the ability to swim.

I couldn't see. As the swells rolled beneath me I rose up their front, lifted my head as high as I could at the crest to look around, and then slid down their backs into the troughs. Everything was grey – the sky, the ocean, the spume, the rain. I didn't have time to worry about anything but finding Emma. All I needed was a glimpse of something that wasn't grey and I would have a goal.

I glanced to my right and saw I was nearly even with the stern of the ship. Nigel was pointing almost in my direction. I thought Emma must be near, but try as I might, I couldn't see her. I stopped swimming and trod water, forcing myself to look carefully in every direction. I was about to give up and start swimming again when I saw a flash of yellow at the top of a wave about ten metres to my left, away from the ship. Without thought, I turned and swam in that direction.

Within a few strokes, I could see it was the hood of a parka. It was facing away from me, but as it slid down the back of a swell it rotated slightly and I saw a pale face inside. My heart was in my mouth as I closed the final few metres and reached out to touch it. Was it Emma? Was she alive?

I grabbed the parka hood and spun the body around. The face staring back at me was Alexander's, not Emma's. As I watched, the eyes opened and registered first surprise, and then panic. He raised his arms and tried to grab me. I pushed him away and heard him cry out, 'Help me! Help me!'

I ignored him, steadied myself the best I could and looked around again. After a few seconds, I spotted another blob of yellow a short distance further from the ship. I felt a hand clutch at my shoulder as I struck out in that direction. Fortunately, Alexander's grip was feeble, because I didn't have the strength for a fight. I felt the hand slide off my shoulder and I continued my desperate swim towards Emma.

I didn't know how long I'd been in the water, but I knew I was reaching the end. I could no longer feel my hands and feet. I swam with lifeless arms and legs; they could have been made of wood. My elbows no longer bent and I thrashed my arms like oars. I was telling my legs to kick, but I couldn't tell if they were responding or not. My world was closing down and I was only remotely conscious of the waves and spray. I knew my body sometimes moved forward and sometimes stood still, but I was no longer aware of why.

At last, I was able to reach out and touch the other parka. I'd seen Emma's face for the last few strokes, and that was all that kept me going. Her eyes were closed and I couldn't tell if she was breathing, but it didn't matter. With the last of my physical and mental strength, I put my arm around Emma and levered her body up into the classic lifesaving position. I started to sidestroke with her, unaware of the waves, the wind, or which direction the ship lay. All I knew was I had to keep our heads above water.

I woke when I started shivering in the bottom of the inflatable. I opened my eyes and the first thing I saw was Tamati, his brown eyes and wild black hair blowing like a pennant in the wind. 'I feel like shit, Ishmael,' I said through chattering teeth.

'You look like fucking Jonah after he came out of the whale,' said Tamati.

I didn't have the strength to roll over, but I could move my head. I looked to my right and saw a body wrapped in storm gear lying beside me. I was suddenly filled with an enormous sense of grief and loss and started crying silently, the tears flowing hot down my cheeks. Tamati must have noticed me crying and said, 'She's okay, Adam. She looks fucking worse than you do, but she's going to be okay.'

I heard his words, but they didn't sink in. I lay crying in the bottom of the inflatable as he and Nigel manoeuvred it back to the side of the *Polar Princess*. I was too far gone to notice when it was brought back on board and I must have passed out when they lifted me onto the deck.

CHAPTER 34

I woke and found myself lying on a bunk, snug in several blankets. The light was on and I could feel the *Polar Princess* heave beneath me as it rose and fell, twisting a path through the swells. I lay still and canvassed my parts, testing for aches and pains – or worse, lack of feeling. I was surprised to conclude that I seemed to be in one piece, though I was aware of a sense of overwhelming fatigue. After a seemingly endless time, I worked my hands free of the blankets and struggled to sit up. My head swam momentarily but quickly cleared.

I slowly looked around the room. I was surprised to discover I was in my cabin. Alone. I'd just stood up when the cabin door opened and Nigel entered. He was carrying a cup of coffee and his face broke into a broad smile when he saw me. 'Adam! You're up! Ready for some coffee?'

I was still woozy and my stomach ached from the sea water I'd swallowed. I shook my head and asked, 'Where are we? Where's Emma?'

'Sit down. Unless you need to pee, then there's no reason to be walking around the ship.' He guided me back to my bunk and helped me sit on the edge. 'We're headed back to Dunedin. Emma's across the passageway. She's okay.'

A wave of relief washed over me and I wanted to cry again. But everything was happening very slowly and I had time to regain control of my emotions before the tears started.

Nigel pulled up the desk chair and sat near me. He said with mock solemnity, 'For fuck's sake, Adam, you've got to stop jumping overboard. We can only save you so many times.'

I tried to smile, I wanted to smile, but I'm not sure I did. 'Thanks, Nigel, I'll try to remember that – if I ever go to sea again.'

Nigel stood and patted me on the shoulder. 'Get some rest. We've got a couple of days before we get to Dunedin. Plenty of time to get things sorted out.'

All of a sudden, rest seemed like a good idea. I lay on the bunk and didn't hear him close the door when he left.

I don't know how long I slept, but I woke to see Emma sitting in the chair Nigel had used before I drifted off. Her hair was uncombed and she was wearing castoffs too big for her, but she looked showered and fresh and very much alive. 'Hey,' she said softly.

'Hey,' I returned.

'Thanks.'

I didn't say anything, just looked at her. The last time I'd seen her, she'd been in the ocean and I hadn't been sure if she was alive. I thought about Theo's photo of her, the one of her laughing. I suddenly knew that's what I wanted most of all, to see her laugh like that again.

She reached out and ran her hand over my face. She tugged softly at the tangles in my beard and drew her fingers lightly up behind my ear.

'I love you.' I said it without thinking. It just came out, reflexively, like breathing.

'I know,' she said, and smiled.

———

Tamati later told me that when he and Nigel saw me start to swim towards Alexander's parka, they had launched the inflatable and come as quickly as they could. By the time they found me, I was swimming feebly with Emma in tow. They had pulled us out of the water and returned directly to the ship. Once on board, they had taken us from the zodiac to our cabins. They stripped off our wet clothes, scavenged any dry clothes they could find and, after dressing us, put us in bunks under layers of blankets.

Once he knew we were safe, Tamati talked to the crew and engineering officers about what had happened. He summarised the whole story, concentrating on the roles Alexander, Callaghan, Judd and the others had in the criminal activities, including Theo's death. He wasn't sure how many of them might also have been involved, but at that moment he didn't care: he just needed to get the ship headed back to Dunedin. Captain Kennicott saw the writing on the wall and relinquished command of the ship to the chief engineer. Tamati knew that Peters, Phil, Finn and Levi had been complicit in the illegal activities, and they were locked in their cabins. The return voyage was a gloomy trip for the remaining seamen.

Not long before we reached port I was sitting in the mess with Tamati and asked why Judd hadn't killed him and thrown him over the side for helping me when I'd escaped the *Polar Princess*. He leaned back in his chair and rubbed his hand across his chin. 'Shit, Adam, you remember that night. In all the rain and wind and poor light, what do you think they saw? I told them I followed you on deck and tried to stop you. I caught up with you at the rail. We struggled, I tried to hold you but you slipped out of my grasp and jumped.' He wiggled his hands. 'Judd was pissed as hell but what could he do? He yelled a lot and hit me a couple of times, but he couldn't be sure whether I was lying or not. And he didn't want to kill me if he didn't have to. The bodies were piling up.' Incredibly a look of humour came to his eyes. 'I stuck to my story – and lived so I could save your ass again.'

'Damn, not many people would have done what you did, Ishmael.'

He shrugged. 'Nothing special about what I did, just stubborn. I wasn't the one who went swimming in the Southern Ocean.'

When I asked him why he was still on the ship for the last voyage, he said the crew had been told they were heading off on another fishing trip. 'Sorry, bro,' he said, 'I thought you were dead, and I didn't know what to do. If I'd spoken out it would have been my word against the captain, and I knew how that would turn out. They offered so much money to stay on board I couldn't say no. The family needs the money. I had no idea the bastards had more shit planned.'

'I'm glad you were there. Otherwise, I might be still swimming.'

CHAPTER 35

David Callaghan rubbed a hand across his face, trying to scrub the fatigue from his bones. He'd been working almost non-stop for thirty-six hours and was exhausted. He leaned back from his computer screen and sighed. The paper shredder was at his left elbow and there was a stack of documents on his desk. Half a dozen files were open on his computer. It had been a bitch, but he thought he'd finally just about finished the job. Alexander had said he would have a few days, but Callaghan thought the Russian might have been optimistic. He didn't want to take chances. He wanted to be on an aeroplane and out of New Zealand as soon as he could.

He reached for the coffee cup on his desk – he'd practically lived on caffeine for the last twelve hours – and grimaced when he took a sip. It was cold, but he drank it anyway. The hard work was done but he needed the caffeine to stay sharp. He'd removed all traces of their money laundering scheme, so all that was left to do was to finish filling the resulting gaps in the records with innocuous data.

It had taken him hours to scour the records in Auckland and Vladivostok and find every reference, direct or indirect, to their illegal activities. Once he had the list, he started the painstaking process of deletion and replacement. Halfway through, he briefly wished he was faster with computers, but with so much at stake, he knew accuracy was more important than speed.

When the maintenance man brought the shredder to his office Carol Adams, his PA, had offered to help. The last thing he wanted was for someone to know what he was doing. He put her off, saying he was reading the files and deciding which to keep and which to shred as he went. She'd given him a long look but had left his office without comment. At that moment, he didn't care what Carol or anyone else thought; he wasn't going to hang around long enough for it to make any difference.

The *Polar Princess* sailed for the Bounty Islands and Vladivostok on Monday afternoon. He'd watched her disappear down the harbour and had then flown back to Auckland. He was in his office by ten p.m. Carol had kept him going, leaving him takeaways for dinner and bringing bagels and sandwiches throughout Tuesday. He'd worked through Tuesday night, pausing for a two-hour nap when he couldn't concentrate any longer.

He looked at his watch – it was 2 p.m. on Wednesday. He was pleased. He was ahead of schedule. Another couple of hours and he'd be on his way to the airport. His flight to Singapore and on to Vladivostok was booked. He could already feel his business class seat and taste the first glass of champagne.

His self-congratulations were interrupted by a knock on the door. Carol stuck her head in his office and said, 'Sorry to disturb you, sir. There's someone here to see you.'

Callaghan looked annoyed. 'Not now, Carol. Tell them to come back tomorrow.'

'I'm sorry, sir. I don't think they'll wait. It's the police. With a warrant.'

Callaghan almost panicked. *Fuck*, he thought. *Police? Why are the police here? What could they know? What could they prove?* He forced himself to relax and stay outwardly calm. He looked at his computer screen and the documents on his desk. His brain was in overdrive. How much time did he need? He looked up at Carol and said, 'Give me ten minutes.' She nodded and closed the door. He began shoving paper into the shredder and typing rapidly, deleting everything that had to be deleted.

The last sheet of paper went through the shredder and the last file vanished from his hard drive. He slumped back in his chair, no longer able to ignore the exhaustion of his efforts. He had closed his eyes for only a few seconds when Carol knocked again. She opened the door and held it while a Maori police officer entered. Carol looked carefully at Callaghan and then closed the door behind her as she left.

Callaghan studied the officer but wasn't sure what to think. She was young, but she looked formidable, her solid build amplified by her stab vest. She rested her hands on her duty belt and said nothing as she studied the room before returning her gaze to Callaghan. Her brown eyes gave nothing away and Callaghan felt the first cold tingle of fear.

'Officer...?' he asked.

'Sergeant Wero. Auckland Central. You're Mr David Callaghan?'

'I am, how can I help you?'

'Mr Callaghan, you are being arrested for fraud, money laundering and accessory to murder. You have the right to remain silent. You do not have to make a statement. Anything you say will be recorded and may be given in evidence in court. You have the right—'

'Hey! Hey! Wait a minute!' he interrupted. 'What do you mean I'm under arrest? I've done nothing wrong. I'm a respectable businessman.' Callaghan's stomach was tied up in knots and he wanted to vomit, but he hadn't become CEO of a major company without learning to handle stress. He sat up straight and put his fists on the desk in front of him.

'Be that as it may, sir, you are under arrest. Please let me finish your rights caution. You have the right to speak with a lawyer before deciding whether to answer any questions. If you cannot afford a lawyer then the police will provide a list of lawyers you can speak to free of charge.'

'Jesus! You've got to be joking. This is a big mistake. Search me. Search my office. There's nothing to find.'

'Don't worry, sir. We will search everything. Eventually. Right now, I have to ask you to come with me.' She pulled her handcuffs from her duty belt and stepped forward to stand beside his desk. 'Please stand up, turn around and put your hands behind you, sir.'

Callaghan was speechless. He thought his computer and files might be confiscated and searched, but he'd never dreamed he'd be arrested. How was it possible? They had no evidence. The sergeant stood implacably, waiting for him to move. His mind reeling, Callaghan finally stood and did as she instructed.

As she snapped the handcuffs around his wrists Sergeant Wero leaned forward and spoke softly into Callaghan's ear. 'Listen you sack of shit. We'll take your computer, but we don't need it. We already know about your Russian friends, the fish boxes, the boxes of cash, everything. You need to think very hard about what happens next. If you want to wear something other than prison overalls before you qualify for the pension, then I suggest you have a full and frank discussion with the prosecutor. She might be willing to listen.' The sergeant paused and leaned even closer before continuing, 'Then again, you might look cute with some prison tats.' She stepped back, tugged on the cuffs to make sure they were locked and said, 'Okay, let's go. Say goodbye to your old life forever.'

She kept a hand on his elbow and opened the door with the other before leading him out of the office and down the corridor.

———

The story was headline news for days: "Police Break Huge Money Laundering Scheme", "Fishing Company Exec Arrested, Police Inspector Implicated", "Shipwreck at the Bounty Islands". Gordon wrote some good stories, but not all of the ones he wanted to write. Emma and I insisted that we be kept out of the spotlight and that there would be no reference to Theo's death. The police managed to shut down any mention of the box with ten million dollars on the wreck of the *Sergey Belov*. Sergeant Wero kept us informed and said the Navy had sent a frigate to recover the box and the bodies of Inspector

Killand and Judd. We hadn't appreciated how lucky we were when we went back to the wreck – the Navy had to wait eight days for the weather to settle enough to allow them to board it. Nigel and Hare continued their charter work. Nigel confided that the shipwreck had become almost as big an attraction as the birds for his clients.

Connor's illegal hacking was never officially recognised. The material from it was on the thumb drive Gordon gave to Sergeant Wero, but she was smart enough to not mention it when it became obvious it wasn't needed for a trial. The police investigation found that Ivanov, Callaghan and Killand had run the money laundering operation pretty much on their own. With two of them dead, Callaghan was the only one awaiting trial. An inquest found that Judd's death was an accident and that Killand and Ivanov were killed in self-defence.

I drove to Hawkes Bay to see Emma. I wanted to use the driving time to reflect on all that had happened, and to think about the future. Had it been worth it? Did I feel better? Did I feel any sense of justice or retribution? All that was certain was it all seemed so unnecessary. Not just Theo's death, but the deaths of Judd, Killand, Ivanov and the sailors on the *Sergey Belov*. And the untold disruption of the lives of dozens of people, all because of the greed of a few men, men who sought vast personal gain by facilitating illegal activities. I've read enough history to know that greed and narcissism are nothing new, that they are part of the human condition, but that was cold comfort. I'd lived my whole life largely unaware of these realities. I mourned the loss of that naiveté, knowing I could never unlearn what I'd seen and been through. Twice surviving the icy waters of the Southern Ocean didn't bring me confidence and assurance or a sense of invulnerability. It brought me a sense of the fragility of life, how it can be changed or ended in a moment.

One thing I learned was that I wanted to spend the rest of my time with Emma. She had depths I wanted to explore, not on the edges of destruction and terror but in the loving comfort of simple shared experiences – a sunset, a glass of wine, a walk in the mountains, perhaps a family.

We hadn't spoken much, either on the *Polar Princess* or onshore before we returned to our homes. We were each too shattered to deal with anything more than eating, drinking and sleeping. I hugged her fiercely at the airport before she boarded her flight to Napier. We'd agreed we'd get together again "soon".

I waited five days before I called her. I suggested I come to Napier and we could talk. She seemed hesitant, almost listless, but agreed to my visit. Physically, I was almost back to normal. Mentally, I knew the most important thing for my continued recovery was to hear her voice.

The drive was long and I arrived in the late afternoon. I pulled into her driveway, walked across the lawn to her porch and knocked on her door. The damask roses were no longer blooming, but I could still remember their heavy scent. There was only a brief pause before Emma opened the door and was in my arms.

We kissed and hugged and didn't say anything, standing in the doorway, each rediscovering the feel of the other. Eventually, we parted and she pulled me inside, not letting go of my hand. She closed the door and led me to her bedroom. She undressed me slowly, feeling me for a long moment before stepping back and starting to unbutton her blouse. I gently pushed her fingers away and finished undressing her. When I was done we just stood looking at each other, no urgency, no haste, as though we had arrived at the calm eye of the hurricane.

When we were done, we lay together and finally started to speak. 'I love you, Adam,' she said. 'I can never forget what you did. How you saved my life. I can never repay you for that.'

I rolled onto my side and propped my head on my hand. I looked into her face and ran the tip of my finger along her lower lip, marvelling at its perfection. 'I love you, Emma. I love you more than I can say. Don't thank me. I'm the one who put you in peril. I'm the one who got you kidnapped and almost killed.'

'No, it was our plan. Both of us. We knew what we were getting into. Knew the risks. Well, sort of. I'm a big girl; I knew what I wanted to do.'

'Hey. I'm not going to fight you about it. But we have no debts, no obligations. All I care about is being with you.' I took a deep breath and said, 'I want to marry you.'

Emma said nothing for a long time. Her eyes left mine and she stared straight up at the ceiling. Finally, I saw a tear form in her left eye and slide slowly down her cheek.

'What's the matter?' I asked. 'I'm sorry, is it too soon?' I touched the moist trail, wishing it away. 'I'm such an idiot. I'm sorry.'

She shook her head and looked at me again. 'No. Don't be sorry. It's beautiful. I'm very happy. But I can't marry you.'

I felt my heart stop. The world stopped. It was as if I was suddenly crushed under an immense weight and couldn't breathe. 'Wh ... what do you mean?' I stammered. 'We love each other. You said so. After what we've been through, I know there's no one else I'll ever be happy with.'

Another tear formed and slid down her cheek. 'I'm sorry, Adam. I'm really, really sorry. I can't marry you because I love you too much.'

'Too much? Emma, that's crazy. What do you mean you love me too much?'

'I lost Theo and I almost lost you. Twice. I couldn't take that again. I couldn't marry you knowing I might lose you at any moment. Your life is the sea. But for me, now, after what we've been through, I couldn't bear it. Every time you sailed, I'd wonder if you were going to come home. I'd live every day dreading the phone call telling me your ship had sunk or something had happened to you.'

'But that's crazy, Emma. Fishing's no more dangerous than most other jobs. Hell, it's safer than forestry, your job. What happened to Theo and me was way outside the bounds of normal.' I paused then added, 'I'll give up fishing. I'll do something else, anything else, just to be with you.'

She rolled over until she was on top of me and kissed me deeply. She positioned herself and slowly lowered herself onto me. She moved slowly, caressing me with her entire body, probably the most sensual and loving thing anyone had ever done with me.

'We don't have to say goodbye,' she murmured. 'We can be lovers.

We can be friends. We can walk a path like comets circling the sun, meeting and passing and soaring through space. Maybe one day what happened won't matter. Maybe one day we can be something else. Maybe one day your dreams can become our dreams. But today this is what I am. Today this is what I can offer.'

I didn't have to think. I said, 'Yes.'

ACKNOWLEDGEMENTS

I wanted to write a story set on a fishing boat in the Ross Sea and on New Zealand's Subantarctic islands. The description of the characters' time at sea and on the Bounty Islands is based on my experiences on scientific research vessels and on trips to remote islands looking for the breeding site of the Chatham Island taiko.

Greg Johansson and Graham Parker generously shared their extensive knowledge of fishing vessels and the Bounty Islands. Greg was the Chief Operating Officer for Sanford Ltd and has years of experience fishing in the Ross Sea. Graham is a partner at Parker Conservation and has led many scientific expeditions to the Bounty Islands.

Dave Misselbrook contributed to the story line by sending me information about the disappearance of observers from fishing vessels. Annemette Sorensen, Ginny Misselbrook and Sara Uruski gave valuable feedback on early drafts of the story.

My editors, Martin Diggle and Kate O'Connor, worked with me on the revisions that made the story clearer and more readable. Victoria Twead of Ant Press has provided guidance for every phase of editing and publication.

The book wouldn't have been possible without the advice and support of my wife, June Cahill.

ABOUT THE AUTHOR

Ray Wood was a marine geologist for more than 30 years. He and his wife have retired to a small farm on the east coast of the North Island of New Zealand where he spends his time looking after cows and vintage tractors, trying to grow truffles, making artistic gates and writing. His next novel is about financial intrigue in the forestry industry. Chainsaws, carbon credits and criminals – what could go wrong?

Contacts and Links

Email: raywood413@gmail.com

ALSO BY THE AUTHOR

SHORT ODDS

Bridget Crawford is in a bind. The bank's threatened to foreclose on her farm, her ex-husband's returned to town, and someone's stolen her cattle.

Veterinarian Hugh Jacobs is also in a bind. Tui Dancer, a horse in his care, has suddenly lost his winning form, his affair with Bridget is under strain, and a gang of amateur horse thieves and Chinese triads are trying to steal Tui Dancer.

With the pace and energy of a Dick Francis novel, this story gallops to an exciting and unexpected conclusion.

Available from Amazon: https://bit.ly/Short-Odds